EVERYMAN,
I WILL GO WITH THEE,
AND BE THY GUIDE,
IN THY MOST NEED
TO GO BY THY SIDE

HONORÉ de BALZAC

Eugénie Grandet

Translated from the French by Ellen Marriage
with an Introduction by
Peter Washington

E V E R Y M A N ' S   L I B R A R Y

119

This book is one of 250 volumes in Everyman's Library
which have been distributed to 4500 state schools
throughout the United Kingdom.
The project has been supported by a grant of £4 million
from the Millennium Commission.

First included in Everyman's Library, 1907
Introduction and Bibliography © Everyman Publishers plc, 2000
Chronology © David Campbell Publishers Ltd., 1992
Typography by Peter B. Willberg

ISBN 1-85715-119-4

A CIP catalogue record for this book is available from the
British Library

Published by Everyman Publishers plc,
Gloucester Mansions, 140A Shaftesbury Avenue,
London WC2H 8HD

Distributed by Random House (UK) Ltd.,
20 Vauxhall Bridge Road, London SW1V 2SA

EUGÉNIE GRANDET

INTRODUCTION

Though *Eugénie Grandet* was Balzac's greatest critical success in his own lifetime, it is now one of the few novels from his vast output to survive in popular esteem, while the critics have moved on to more rarefied works. This change in fashion would have caused mixed feelings in the author, who dismissed *Eugénie* as 'a good little tale, easy to sell'. He believed that his 'serious' novels – mainly studies in occultism – were underrated, but the good little tale has outlived them, and it is easy to see why. A simple plot, vivid characters and superbly described provincial settings are rendered in brilliant, sinuous prose, peppered with a ceaseless flow of epigrams and exhilarating generalizations. The novel is uncluttered by the cod sociology and mysticism which mar so many of Balzac's stories. Presented with a clarity and distance suggestive of Flaubert, the characters have an animal vitality which Balzac seems to recognize by constant analogies with the natural world: Grandet is a Bengal tiger or a boa constrictor, his wife an insect, their servant a dog. Probably a portrait of the author's mistress, Marie du Fresnay, Eugénie is an especially attractive protagonist, with her conviction that she is 'too ugly' for love. There are no improbable heroes or languishing duchesses to try the reader's patience, none of the melodramatic secrets, bizarre theories or endlessly postponed denouements to which Balzac is addicted – just a small group of people engaged in a quiet life which seems both impossibly remote and yet absolutely real. Above all, the action of the novel develops with an inexorable logic which make readers say to themselves: Yes, that is exactly how it would have been. This is the force of traditional realism – not photographic accuracy or even general fidelity to circumstance but the illusion of irresistible truth.

These are old-fashioned virtues – and this is an old-fashioned way of describing fiction – with little appeal for post-Barthesian celebrants of Balzac as semiological wizard, but they will probably always remain the best reasons for such popularity as he still has. Balzac's contemporaries, who found his more esoteric novels hard to fathom while perversely deploring his obsession with the minutiae of ordinary life in others, were always urging him write a second *Eugénie Grandet*. They liked its simplicity, its charm, the quiet, formal perfection of the story. Such advice displays their own limitations, but their judgement that this was his most finished and accessible novel has stood the test of time. Some of Balzac's gifts find greater scope in other, bigger books – his unrivalled fertility of invention, for example, his passionate intellectual curiosity, and his practical knowledge of how diverse lives actually work; he is the man to go to if you want to know what makes a cooper different from a cobbler, or a tramp from a tinker – but his greatest talent as a novelist is the simplest and yet the most important: the ability to tell a gripping tale. *Eugénie Grandet* contains the usual budgets of information about manners and customs, but they are perfectly integrated into the narrative – indeed, they constitute essential parts of it. What holds us is the story. Balzac is a king among story-tellers and *Eugénie* is his crown.

All his novels, even the weakest, are imbued with the hypnotic narrative power he shared with his English contemporary, Dickens, but the sheer quantity of his output means that he sometimes faltered. Such faltering is not unique to Balzac. Given the size and style of nineteenth-century novels – described by Henry James as fluid puddings or loose baggy monsters – it was inevitably common. Tolstoy and Dickens, Eliot and Dostoevsky: they all nod at times. But each great novelist nods in his or her own way, and Balzac's way takes the form of logghorea: a sort of manic twittering as he scuttles off down a dark irrelevant alley in search of his current obsession while the story languishes. There are no such moments in *Eugénie Grandet*, so disciplined is the writing, so perfectly paced the narrative, and so beautifully proportioned to its subject. Such qualities owe something to the book's brevity, but not much: a misshapen short novel can feel longer than *War and Peace*. What matters is the matching of material and treatment, the supreme mark of any writer's artistry. As contemporary critics observed, there is an almost classical sense of form in this book which goes with its classical transparency of narrative. Balzac's romantic passion for mysteries gives way here to his evident pleasure in working out a story in the most public and economical manner. We guess what is going to happen at the outset, but instead of diminishing our interest, this knowledge intensifies it. Knowing *what* will befall makes us want to see *how* it does so.

The plot, based on an age-old formula which can be summed up in a few words, concerns a rich father who forbids his only daughter to marry a poor man. This formula is given a new twist by the fact that the lovers are first cousins whose fathers are brothers: hers a millionaire miser, his a bankrupt suicide. From such thin material Balzac creates a rich fictional texture in which layers of meaning are suggested by the simplest effects such as describing the way in which meals are served, clothes worn or looks exchanged. Very little happens in the novel outside the daily round of domestic and commercial life, and little of that concerns Eugénie directly. Though the story takes her name, Père Grandet is the active character, not his daughter. Given Balzac's often expressed view that women are born to suffer, this is hardly surprising. Until the arrival of her cousin Charles, Eugénie's existence is like one of the sparsely furnished rooms in her father's house, an empty space waiting for something to happen. For a while the space is filled by love. Then, in one of Balzac's most powerful strokes, the emptiness returns in a new form at the novel's close.

Eugénie's transformation – we shall return to it in a moment – doesn't happen in a vacuum. As always in Balzac, the milieu is crucial. Like the vines and poplars on which they depend, the Grandets are rooted in the soil of Touraine to such an extent that their house seems to grow out of the hillside: 'Rain and frost had gnawed numerous irregular holes in the surface ... Above the bas-relief there was a projecting ledge of masonry where some chance-sown plants had taken root...' The building is weather-worn outside and crumbling within. In their dun-coloured clothes its inhabitants live on the edge of life, skimped even for heat and light by Père Grandet's miserly ways. Every detail is noted, down to the servant's warts. Balzac is a writer whose delight in appearances encompasses every mode from the interior decorator's passion for glitzy surfaces to the philosopher's interest in the hidden depths behind them. He loves grand theories, but he also loves lists, inventories, catalogues. He has an extraordinary grasp on the materiality of the world, the sensuous quality of objects. All his books are filled with *things* and *Eugénie Grandet* is no exception. Barrels, staves, bottles, carts, cobbles, knives, dishes, furniture, buildings, clothes, meals, animals, coins, shops and their meagre contents, luggage, playing-cards, letters, candles (both tallow and wax) – everything is lovingly described, from the rotting staircase in the Grandet house to the luxurious fittings of Charles's travelling bag. Everything has its place in a complete vision of life at a particular time and place. The dramatic virtues of this method – its distance from mere description – become apparent at critical moments in the novel. When Eugénie falls in love with Charles, there is a passage Proust must have drawn on for his patch of yellow wall. She looks into the dank garden, shaded by the massive town-ramparts into which it is built, and sees how 'The sunlight crept along the wall till it reached a maidenhair fern; the changing hues of a pigeon's breast shone from the thick fronds and glossy stems, and all Eugénie's future grew bright with radiant hopes. Henceforward, the bit of wall, its pale flowers, its blue harebells and bleached grasses, was a pleasant sight for her; it called up associations which had all the charm of the memories of childhood.' Out of context, this description is charming but unremarkable; in context it hints at the opposite of what it seems to say.

The story is set in Saumur which, though a typical French provincial town, is nevertheless not quite like any other provincial town. 'Here ... the whole trade of the district depends upon an atmospherical depression.' Within the geography of the region it has its own character, just as local speech inflects the national language in a distinctive way. And within the town its various classes are carefully distinguished. The secondary characters of the upper bourgeoisie – the Cruchots and the Grassins – are a particular triumph of this novel, their battle for Eugénie's hand – or rather, her fortune – providing a context within which we can assess the excesses of the Grandet household. Compared with them, the otherwise baffling figure of Père Grandet becomes comprehensible. He represents the pathological development of normal middle-class behaviour in Saumur, where social life is a series of skirmishes and commercial life a permanent war. Everything comes down to a battle of wills in which Père Grandet always prevails. As Balzac remarked: 'The life of a miser is a constant exercise of human power.' Grandet's boldness makes the Cruchots and the Grassins look pretentious and grubby – a point Balzac makes very neatly in his description of the snuff on Monsieur Cruchot's soiled shirt frill. However base his motives, Grandet shares his creator's magnificent energy, ambition and determination to conquer.

The town, or one part of it, is described in some detail before the action begins. This is more than scene-setting. Like Dickens, Balzac had a powerful sense of place. The modern writer who most resembles him is Simenon, whose claustrophobic provincial houses and fashionable Paris apartments owe more than a little to the older master: we can see in his approach to locale a stripped-down version of the Balzacian economy. Like Simenon, Balzac narrows his focus from a town in a region to one house in a particular street – and, in this case, to one room in that house where most of the action (or should one call it the non-action?) takes place. Here, the furniture is bleached by the sun, the curtains dusty and faded. When Charles Grandet arrives from Paris, he expects to find a chateau; instead, he walks into a hen-roost.

If geography is crucial to the novel, so is history. The story is set in the period of the Bourbon Restoration, but Balzac is careful to give us an account of old Grandet's rise to fortune under the various regimes which followed the Revolution of 1789. The town is conservative: 'There was little sympathy felt for the Revolution in Saumur.' The historical perspective, like the geographical setting, operates in different ways, from the macro-level of national events to the micro-level of individual lives, and the account of Grandet's career is a skilful way of linking the two. The same method is applied less minutely to his Parisian brother and nephew, and the cumulative effect is to place Eugénie's quiet life at the crossroads of the great and complex events which affect her at many removes. If her father had not made astute political choices, she would not be an heiress. If her uncle had not fallen victim to the bust and boom economics of the 1820s, she might never have met and fallen in love with her cousin. If the French had not developed imperial pretensions in the West Indies, that cousin might have found fortune at home and remained faithful to her. But, as in Greek tragedy, these events happen out of sight, to be described by the author as chorus, leaving the stage free for actions directly involving Eugénie herself.

The action is set in train by Charles Grandet's arrival from Paris – a reversal of the usual Balzac pattern, in which an ambitious provincial heads for the capital in search of fame and fortune. Charles might be his creator's own sardonic comment on the dashing young heroes for whom he had such a weakness. He is everything that local men are not: elegant, refined, handsome, sensitive, aesthetic. To Eugénie, these qualities of breeding and sexual attractiveness irresistibly suggest their moral counterparts: goodness, love, honour. The illusion is confirmed by Charles's grief at his father's death, which implies a depth of feeling that surely guarantees his decency? In the marvellous birthday scene, his aristocratic clothes and manners show up the coarseness of Eugénie's other suitors; and Balzac, always responsive to male beauty, contrasts his feminine delicacy amusingly with the masculine coarseness of the female servant Nanon. But the physical contrast underlines the moral difference. Where the sturdy Nanon is loyal, honest and self-sacrificing, Charles is weak and selfish. His charm is the outward expression of narcissism, polished and corrupted by Parisian life. Charles's good feelings are real enough – he reveres his mother's memory and the news of his father's suicide prostrates him – but they are shallow. For all his fine sentiments, Charles is a creature of fashion; in fact, his sentiments are the most fashionable thing about him, couched in the trashy language of contemporary romantic fiction, as we see from the letter to his mistress. The juxtaposition with Eugénie's simple language could not be more revealing. In a wonderfully ironic piece of writing, Balzac shows us how Charles's good feelings are corrupted by vanity and false ideals. Within hours of hearing about his father's suicide, his grief has transmuted into self-pity. When he writes to friends about the possibility of retrieving his own fortunes by marriage with Eugénie, it is not his concern for the future we deplore, but the artlessly egotistical style of it. He is truly a 'creature' of fashion.

As a result, Charles Grandet is not a bad man but just as much a slave to gold as his uncle, though the slavery takes a more graceful form. The novel's deepest irony is that Eugénie herself, despite her indifference to money, eventually becomes, if not her fortune's slave, then certainly its servant, and Balzac shows us exactly how this comes about. Though she may be passive, Eugénie is no victim. That role is reserved for her mother, one of those tragic middle-aged Balzac women who surrender to the tyranny of their husbands, finding relief only in the very piety which enforces their submission by equating religious obedience with domestic slavery. But Madame Grandet's daughter is made of stronger stuff. Despite Balzac's theory of female submission to fate, his own more spirited heroines – like some of the women in his elaborately amorous private life – assert their individuality within the narrow constraints of their lives. Eugénie is one of them. She is, after all, her father's child and, in every sense, his heiress. Always alert to the transmission of family characteristics, not least to their reappearance in surprising forms over long periods of time (it was one of the themes he bequeathed to Proust), Balzac delights in following Eugénie's faint but growing resemblance to Père Grandet as the years pass. Disappointment in love is the overt cause of this evolution, but Balzac also hints at a kind of genetic destiny for his heroine. Like Dickens, he was especially intrigued by the father–daughter relationship, but he sees deeper than his English contemporary whose sight was obscured by a sentimental view of young girls. Balzac, fascinated by family likenesses, observes that, as girls become women, they harden, however slightly, into images of their tribe. Eugénie will never become the monster her father was, but she is a kind of monster, all the same, set apart from the world by fabulous wealth and heredity.

Like every child, Eugénie has a double inheritance, from mother and from father, and in this case the inheritance embodies her creator's belief in a doctrine of human nature according to which the outward man is subject to physical laws, while the inner being is controlled by quite distinct spiritual and psychological powers. In Eugénie's life her father represents the first domain, her mother the second. So she submits to Père Grandet's authority while reserving the right to bestow her affections as she chooses. He embodies the might – and the right – of the material world for his daughter, and indeed, for his neighbours in Saumur. The point is made frequently and explicitly. Grandet is presented as a force of nature, one of Balzac's uncanny virtuosi who have privileged access to the secrets of the universe – in his case, the knack of making a vast fortune by manipulating the markets in wine, gold and timber. But he remains a peasant, and his gifts are the gifts of earth. Again and again Balzac emphasizes the miser's corporeality, linking him with soil, casks, vines, trees, the cooper's craft and, above all, the gold in which he takes such sensuous delight. It has been rightly said that, like so many of Balzac's characters, Grandet is possessed by an idea, in his case the idea of wealth; but, unlike the rich bankers and lawyers who fawn upon him, he craves not the kudos that wealth can bring but the bodily contact with his riches, numbering his trees and counting his gold each day. He needs to satisfy his senses more than his imagination.

If Eugénie accepts her father's authority, love awakens her to the knowledge that he cannot control – or even understand – her emotional life, any more than he understands her mother's spiritual life. To him, they are just feminine quirks. Eugénie's discovery is all the more compelling because, until the arrival of Charles opens her eyes to other possibilities, she has been content with her meagre existence, so completely does she identify with it. Not for her the absorbing dreams of an Emma Bovary. But once aroused, the animal placidity which has caused her to live so completely at one with her milieu, gives her the strength to preserve her love while accepting her lot. Nevertheless, the separation of emotional and imaginative life from social and moral duty which this entails inevitably gives rise to a conflict which wreaks its damage at first not on Eugénie herself but on her mother.

Having subordinated her worldly existence absolutely to her husband and her otherworldly hopes absolutely to the church, Madame Grandet, with nowhere to hide from domestic conflict, even in the recesses of her heart, finds herself fatally torn between loyalty to her daughter and the obedience to her husband enjoined upon her by society and by God. Her agony when she is forced to tell a white lie shows how vulnerable she is to any kind of pressure. Unable to bear it, she falls ill, and though she dies from an organic disease, it is is clearly rooted in moral causes.

Eugénie survives the trouble which kills her mother because she is apparently able to separate her inner life from her filial duty, but in the end she too pays a price for the separation. As the story concludes we realize that heartbreak has condemned her to a kind of living death. In her, Grandet's carnal joy in wealth becomes a despairing devotion to her inheritance. When Charles returns from exile in the Indies with a fortune, he has become the son-in-law Grandet might have welcomed: canny, harsh, self-serving. But the old miser has died and Charles has other ideas. With money of his own, he wants a wife who can help him to climb back into Parisian society, not an unsophisticated provincial girl, however rich. Disappointed in love after waiting so many years for its fulfilment, Eugénie falls back on the only other life she knows: filial duty. Once her father dies, the focus of this duty is his fortune. 'The pale cold glint of gold was destined to suffuse that saintly life and lead a woman who was all feeling to look upon any show of affection with distrust.' As a result she becomes simultaneously the guardian and the prisoner of Grandet's hoard, like a dragon in a fairy tale.

The power of money is one of the great themes of mid-nineteenth-century fiction in ways late twentieth-century readers can easily relate to, given resemblances between the 1830s and the 1980s. It was Thiers, the guiding light of the Bourbon restoration, who encouraged his fellow countrymen to 'Enrichissez vous!' much as President Reagan and Mrs Thatcher exhorted their followers 150 years later. Balzac, who was, for all his aristocratic pretensions, at heart a bourgeois of the bourgeois, accepted this policy in practice, though deploring it theoretically from his standpoint as a conservative supporter of church and crown. He delighted in the flashier fruits of new wealth while energetically chronicling the corruptions to which its cult gave rise. With a passion for luxury which left him permanently in ruinous debt, he understood from experience the appetites money feeds and creates, but he also realized that the sheer quantity of money generated by revolutions in industry and commerce was a terrifying new power in human affairs, the power of capital, which swept all before it, destroying traditions, institutions and even whole communities as it went. Money had become a force in its own right penetrating every sphere of life: politics, manners, morals, relationships. Even individual self-consciousness could be formed by it.

Eugénie Grandet contrasts the new capitalism – operating only in Paris – with older attitudes to money which still prevail in the provinces. Financiers may be a rarity in Saumur, but everyone appreciates the value of their goods 'to a barrel-stave'. Dependent on the climate to ripen their grapes, they speak of 'golden weather' and 'in language which likewise is no mere figure of speech', they say 'It is raining gold louis.' They all know 'the exact value of sun or rain at the right moment'. This is Grandet. No modern capitalist, he nevertheless understands instinctively how to ride the business cycle. But for him, gold is an object of love and a source of self-esteem, before it is a means to power; it lacks the dynamic, invasive quality of capital as described by Balzac's contemporary, Karl Marx. He worships it as an idol of himself, not as an alien god. He even takes erotic pleasure in it. 'When Mme Grandet and Eugénie were fast asleep, the old cooper would come to be with his gold, and hug himself upon it, and toy with it, and fondle it ...' Though we are shown at the beginning of the novel how his avarice has affected him physically and emotionally – 'Certain small indefinable habits, furtive movements, slightly mysterious promptings of greed did not escape the keen observation of fellow-worshippers. There is something vulpine about the eyes of a man who lends money at an exorbitant rate of interest; they gradually and surely contract' – he is not in any sense neurotic. He believes himself to be in control of his fortune and his destiny.

Eugénie, by contrast, is profoundly troubled by her relationship to wealth once she discovers what it means. As an heiress, she is herself a traditional form of commodity, yet she is also a woman of her age with aspirations to individuality and self-expression. Traditionally, heiresses traded their gold for admission to the aristocracy and considered the deal well done. They still do; but in the nineteenth century women began to discover ideals of female emancipation and romantic love which conflicted with the demands of the marriage market. This new ideology also undermined the custom which had relieved the dynastic obligations of heiresses by allowing them to take lovers. The custom is still followed by Balzac's aristocratic women, like Charles's mistress, but it would never do for a high-minded, romantic girl like Eugénie who experiences a typical Balzacian discord between her dreams and the base realities of life. To the traditional predicament of an heiress, always liable to be forced into a loveless marriage, she adds the divided consciousness of a modern woman torn between duty and desire.

While Marx laboured in the British Museum, another German contemporary of Balzac translated the conflict between dreams and realities into a different medium, mythologizing gold as the nexus of love and power in a monumental sequence of operas, *The Ring of the Nibelungs*. Comparisons between Balzac and Wagner are unavoidable. Sharing a taste for the sort of life that goes with silk dressing-gowns, both had more than a touch of the charlatan about them, combined with a serious sense of purpose and indestructible self-confidence. While deeply mistrustful of the masses and attached to dubious notions of the Artist and His Role, they were acutely sensitive to new political and philosophical movements. Above all, they possessed the energy, vision and vulgarity necessary to create new forms of epic art in the nineteenth century. Both worked on the largest scale. Wagner's Ring cycle is nothing less than a history of the universe, while Balzac's *Human Comedy* sets out to be a complete account of the contemporary world in a panorama which embraces both natural and supernatural forces. They are perhaps the last great artists in their respective mediums to attempt such audacious completeness – and certainly the last to place humankind firmly at the apex of their vast cosmologies.

Like Wagner, Balzac only invented his great design once it was under way. Indeed, he only became the novelist we now know at the age of thirty when he published his first serious novel, *Les Chouans*, under his own name. Before that, he had earned a living supplying pseudonymous pot-boilers for a rapidly expanding market, while hoping to make his fortune as a printer. The printing business soon collapsed in financial chaos – the first of many such hopeless enterprises – and in 1829 Balzac began to concentrate on writing. The pressures on him were enormous. He was in direct competition with other, equally prolific novelists – notably Eugène Sue, and Dumas *père* (the collected works of Dumas alone occupy 286 volumes) – and the appetite for fiction was growing at a rate comparable to the appetite for television in the late twentieth century. In the mid-1830s the serial novel became fashionable in France and England, and Balzac responded to it (as Dickens did) with increasing productivity. He frequently claimed to be working sixteen or eighteen hours a day keeping his publishers happy – not an easy task, given his habit of promising books to different firms at the same time.

Under such burdens, it is all the more amazing that he had the artistic strength of purpose, the breadth of vision, and (not least) the time and stamina to do more than cater for the publishing conveyor belt. In addition to almost one hundred novels and stories completed by the time of his death in 1850, fifty-three further titles were planned or considered but never executed. On Balzac's own account, the design of the *Human Comedy* was conceived in the year of *Eugénie Grandet*. In fact, his plan evolved over time and several incarnations. In 1833 it was to be called *Studies in Nineteenth-Century Manners*. What prompted the idea is hard to say. Balzac had the French taste for *grands projets*. He shared the cult of Napoleon and the passion for massiveness and completeness which distinguished contemporaries from Proudhon to Berlioz. But he also seems to have thought of the scheme as a marketing ploy, telling his Polish mistress, Eveline Hanska, that 'I have the same scorn for money that you yourself possess. But money is indispensable and that is why I am going to work all out on the great and extraordinary enterprise that will burst onto the scene in January.' Writing to Eveline again in the following year, however, he had evolved a grander and more elaborate plan, dividing the novels into different categories with different philosophical justifications. The studies in manners were now to be part of a far more complex structure in which novels would be arranged under general headings: causes and effects, sentiments and ideas, individuals and groups. He had even worked out how many volumes each category would require. The thinking is muddled – how, exactly, does one separate causes from effects in story-telling? – but the confidence is magnificent. So certain was he of success that he commissioned other writers to produce prefaces to the series before the books had been written. The extraordinary thing is that, not only were many of these novels actually produced but a good number of them are masterpieces.

Readers of *Eugénie Grandet* are bound to wonder if it makes any difference whether we read this particular novel on its own or in context. Perhaps there is no answer to the question, yet the emergence of Balzac's grandiose plan at the very time he was writing the book compels us to ask it. The experience of reading a writer who owed much to Balzac is relevant here. Proust's *A la recherche du temps perdu* is a single narrative arc, which might seem to make knowledge of all the parts necessary to understanding the whole, but that is not the case. Acquaintance with the closing pages of this enormous work is certainly essential to grasping its author's grand design; but, as readers of *Swann's Way* will know, many parts of *A la recherche* (which, like the *Human Comedy*, remained unfinished) can stand alone. Reading the whole of Proust sequentially is certainly a very different experience from reading the parts independently, but both are possible, and some would argue that there is more life in the parts than the whole. Proust's Wagnerian attempt to trump Balzac by integrating all his characters into one narrative shows severe signs of strain in the later volumes, suggesting that the looser framework of the *Human Comedy* has its advantages. By appearing in his novels only as narrator, and not as subject, and by making his reflections on the meaning of Life and Art the background of his works and not their theme, Balzac also avoids the narcissism and portentousness which sometimes afflict Proust.

In consequence, *Eugénie Grandet* stands up as a near-perfect work of art – an achievement celebrated by the other great nineteenth-century novelist directly influenced by its author. In his magnificent essay, *The Lesson of the Master*, written at just the time Proust was embarking on *A la recherche*, Henry James, considering possible approaches to the criticism of fiction, rejects theory in favour of an appeal to 'some great practitioner, some concrete instance of the art, some ample cloak under which we may gratefully crawl'. The practitioner he has in mind is Balzac. James, like Proust, had the loftiest aesthetic aims. Both men were also keenly alert to the craft of fiction, studying the work of other writers much as an apprentice joiner might study the chairs and cabinets of master carpenters. For James, Balzac was the greatest of novelists because he was the writer who most completely united technical skill with artistic vision and a sense of what the novel was *for*. Behind his predecessor's lofty vapourings about the *Human Comedy*, James grasped the important point: Balzac had done what no other nineteenth-century novelist before him had done. He had given fiction a serious purpose, taking it beyond moralized entertainment and raising it to the traditional status of philosophy and history. And he had achieved this without in any way compromising its distinctive identity as fiction.

James returns to this theme several times in critical essays, but his most touching tribute to Balzac comes in more appropriate form as a story. Written just one year before his own first major novel, *The Portrait of a Lady*, which it forshadows in many respects, *Washington Square* is James's equivalent to the apprentice's masterpiece – the work with which a pupil pays tribute to his teacher and gives notice that he is now a complete and independent craftsman. His novella is a reworking of *Eugénie Grandet* in the setting of upper-middle-class New York, the world in which James himself grew up. The action is roughly contemporary with Balzac's novel, the plot formula is identical, and the books of similar length. A wealthy doctor prevents his only daughter and heiress from marrying the handsome suitor to whom she has given her heart, thereby turning her into an old maid. Reading these two stories side by side tells us more about both of them than any amount of criticism ever can. Consider, for example, the handling of the suitors, Morris and Charles, or the treatment of the subsidiary characters. Consider, above all, the endings of the two stories, where Balzac has the edge in force and James in artistry yet both are equal in controlled emotion. James brings a lighter touch to the subject, Balzac a broader vision. James emphasizes the comedy, Balzac the pathos. One sees how much the later writer learnt from his predecessor, and how much light he casts on that predecessor, yet one also sees how very different they are. Their virtues are complementary, their vices largely out of sight. Read *Washington Square*, and you turn to Balzac with a renewed sense of prose fiction's extraordinary ability to reinvent itself in each generation. Then read *Eugénie Grandet* and you cannot help agreeing with James's verdict: in fathering the modern novel Balzac was the greatest writer of his time.

Peter Washington

PETER WASHINGTON is General Editor of Everyman's Library and author of *Literary Theory and the End of English* and *Madame Blavatksy's Baboon*.

SELECT BIBLIOGRAPHY

———

BIOGRAPHY

There is an outstanding recent life of the novelist by Graham Robb (Picador, 1994) but the biographies by V. S. Pritchett (Knopf, 1973) and André Maurois (Bodley Head, 1965) are still well worth reading.

GENERAL CRITICISM

Much of the vast critical literature is listed in Robb's biography. In addition to the James essay already mentioned there is a fine piece by Proust about Balzac and Sainte-Beuve reprinted in *Against Sainte-Beuve*, translated by John Sturrock (Penguin, 1988). Among later writers, Roland Barthes (in *S/Z*, Cape, 1975) and Georg Lukács (in *Studies in European Realism*, Merlin Press, 1972) offer idiosyncratic and sharply contrasted approaches to Balzac. Christopher Prendergast (*Balzac: Fiction and melodrama*, Edward Arnold, 1978) and Peter Brooks (*The Melodramatic Imagination*, Yale University Press, 1976) both provide re-interpretations of the whole oeuvre. More traditional studies can be found in F. W. J. Hemmings, *An Interpretation of 'La Comédie humaine'* (Random House, 1971) and H. J. Hunt, *Balzac's 'Comédie humaine'* (Athlone Press, 1959).

CHRONOLOGY

DATE	AUTHOR'S LIFE	LITERARY CONTEXT
1799	Born in Tours, 20 May.	Death of Beaumarchais.
1800		Madame de Staël: *De la littérature.*
1801		
1802		Births of A. Dumas *père* and Victor Hugo. Chateaubriand: *Le Génie du christianisme.*
1803		Death of Laclos. Birth of Mérimée.
1804		Birth of George Sand and Sainte-Beuve.
1805		Chateaubriand: *René.*
1807	Enters the Collège des Oratoriens in Vendôme, where he remains a boarder for six years.	
1808		Birth of G. de Nerval.
1810		Birth of Musset. Madame de Staël: *De l'Allemagne.*
1811		Birth of Gautier.
1814	Joins his family in Paris.	Death of the Marquis de Sade.
1815		
1816	Registers with the Faculty of Law in Paris and takes post as a clerk in a solicitor's office.	Constant: *Adolphe.*
1817		Death of Madame de Staël.
1818	Goes to work for another solicitor.	
1819	Bachelor of Law. Forsakes a legal career for his literary ambitions. *Cromwell*, a tragedy, severely criticized by a family friend and left unpublished in his lifetime.	Chénier: *Oeuvres complètes.*
1820	Begins two ambitious literary works of a philosophical nature (*Falthurne* and *Sténie*) which remain unfinished.	Lamartine: *Méditations poétiques.*

DATE	AUTHOR'S LIFE	LITERARY CONTEXT
1821		Birth of Baudelaire and Flaubert.
1822	Publishes (in collaboration) two pot-boilers, *L'Héritière de Birague* and *Jean-Louis*, and (single-handed) *Clothilde de Lusignan* under the anagrammatic pseudonym Lord R'Hoone. Two further novels (*Le Centenaire* and *Le Vicaire des Ardennes*) under the pseudonym Horace de Saint-Aubin.	Victor Hugo: *Odes et Poésies diverses*. Stendhal: *De l'amour*.
1823	Horace de Saint-Aubin: *La Dernière Fée*.	Birth of Renan. Stendhal: *Racine et Shakespeare*.
1824	Horace de Saint-Aubin: *Annette et le criminel*.	
1825	Horace de Saint-Aubin: *Wann-Chlore* (the last of his youthful pot-boilers).	
1826	Establishes himself as a printer in Paris.	Vigny: *Cinq-Mars*.
1827		Victor Hugo: *Préface de Cromwell*.
1828	Abandons his new career amid heavy debts and returns to writing.	Birth of Taine and Verne.
1829	Honoré Balzac: *Le Dernier Chouan ou la Bretagne en 1800* (later *Les Chouans*), the first of his novels to be incorporated in *La Comédie humaine*. 'A Young Bachelor': *Physiologie du mariage*.	Mérimée: *Mateo Falcone*. Victor Hugo: *Les Orientales*, and *Le Dernier Jour d'un condamné*. Musset: *Contes d'Espagne et d'Italie*.
1830	Prolific activity as a journalist and begins to sign his work Honoré de Balzac. Eight short stories, six of which are 'scenes of private life' and two, 'philosophical tales'.	Death of Constant. Victor Hugo: *Hernani*. Stendhal: *Le Rouge et le Noir*.
1831	*Le Peau de chagrin*. Further short stories.	Victor Hugo: *Notre-Dame de Paris* and *Les Feuilles d'automne*. George Sand: *Indiana*.
1832	*Le Colonel Chabert*, *La Femme de trente ans*, *Le Curé de Tours*, and the largely autobiographical *Louis Lambert*. Other short stories, including the first of his *Contes drolatiques* in the manner of Rabelais.	

CHRONOLOGY

Villèle forms a government.

Charles X (1824–30).

Fall of Villèle.

Polignac becomes chief minister; takes repressive measures.

The capture of Algiers. The July Revolution. Accession of Louis-Philippe (1830–48).

DATE	AUTHOR'S LIFE	LITERARY CONTEXT
1833	The beginning of a long correspondence with a married Polishwoman living in the Ukraine, Madame Hanska ('L'Etrangère'). *Le Médecin de campagne, L'Illustre Gaudissart, Eugénie Grandet.*	
1834	*La Recherche de l'absolu. Histoire des Treize.*	Musset: *Lorenzaccio.* Sainte-Beuve: *Volupté.*
1835	His collected *Scènes de la vie privée* and *Etudes philosophiques,* with important prefaces written to the author's order by Félix Davin. *Le Père Goriot, Melmoth réconcilié, Séraphita.*	Vigny: *Servitude et grandeur militaires* and *Chatterton.* Gautier: *Mademoiselle de Maupin.*
1836	Travels to Turin. *Le Lys dans la vallée, Facino Cane.*	Musset: *Confession d'un enfant du siècle.*
1837	New visit to Italy. *La Vieille Fille, Illusions perdues* (first part), *César Birotteau.*	Mérimée: *La Vénus d'Ille.*
1838	Again travels to Italy (including Sardinia). *Les Employés, La Maison Nucingen, La Torpille* (part of *Splendeurs et misères des courtisanes*).	
1839	President of the Société des Gens de Lettres. Two plays, including *Vautrin.* Candidate for the French Academy, but steps down in favour of Victor Hugo, who is not elected. *Le Cabinet des antiques, Gobseck, Une Fille d'Eve, Massimila Doni, Béatrix* (first part), *Les Secrets de la princesse de Cadignan, Illusions perdues* (second part).	Stendhal: *La Chartreuse de Parme.*
1840	First performance of *Vautrin* (banned by the authorities two days later). Founds the short-lived *Revue parisienne* and writes for it an important essay on Stendhal's *La Chartreuse de Parme.* Moves to 47 rue Raynouard (now the home of a Balzac museum). *Pierrette, Pierre Grassou, Z. Marcas, Un Prince de la Bohême.*	Birth of Zola. Mérimée: *Colomba.*
1841	*Le Curé de village.* Contract for *La Comédie humaine.*	

CHRONOLOGY

Fieschi's assassination attempt on Louis-Philippe.

Uprising attempt of Louis-Napoleon Bonaparte in Strasbourg.

Revolt in Algiers begins. Louis Blanc: *L'Organisation du travail.*
Louis-Napoleon Bonaparte: *Les Idées napoléoniennes.*

Louis-Napoleon Bonaparte makes second failed coup.
Government of Thiers (March). Mehemet Ali crisis (October).
Government of Guizot (to 1848). Proudhon: *Qu'est-ce que la propriété?*

DATE	AUTHOR'S LIFE	LITERARY CONTEXT
1842	First performance of *Les Ressources de Quinola. L'Avant-Propos de la Comédie humaine, Mémoires de deux jeunes mariées, Albert Savarus, La Fausse Maîtresse, Autre étude de femme, Ursule Mirouët, Un Début dans la vie, La Rabouilleuse.*	Death of Stendhal. Birth of Mallarmé. Sue: *Les Mystères de Paris* (to 1843). George Sand: *Consuelo.*
1843	Visits St Petersburg to stay with Madame Hanska (widowed in 1841). Returns via Germany. First performance of *Paméla Giraud; Une Ténébreuse Affaire, La Muse du département, Honorine, Illusions perdues* (final part).	Victor Hugo: *Les Burgraves.*
1844	*Modeste Mignon, Les Paysans* (first part), *Béatrix* (second part).	Birth of A. France and Verlaine. A. Dumas *père*: *Les Trois Mousquétaires.*
1845	Travels with Madame Hanska. Candidate for the French Academy (unsuccessful). *Un Homme d'affaires, Les Comédiens sans le savoir.*	A. Dumas *père*: *Le Comte de Monte-Cristo.* Mérimée: *Carmen.*
1846	Madame Hanska's child still-born. *Petites misères de la vie conjugale, L'Envers de l'histoire contemporaine* (first episode), *La Cousine Bette.*	George Sand: *La Mare au diable.*
1847	Madame Hanska in Paris for three months. Balzac visits her in the Ukraine in the autumn. *Le Cousin Pons, La Dernière Incarnation de Vautrin* (final part of *Splendeurs et misères des courtisanes*).	Lamartine: *Histoire des Girondins.* Michelet: *Histoire de la Révolution.*
1848	Witnesses the February Revolution in Paris. First performance of *La Marâtre.* Goes to the Ukraine in September, where he remains until spring of 1850. *L'Envers de l'histoire contemporaine* (second episode).	Death of Chateaubriand. Birth of Huysmans. George Sand: *François le Champi* and *La Petite Fadette.*
1849	Fails twice more to secure election to the French Academy. Suffers several heart-attacks.	Sainte-Beuve: *Causeries du lundi.*
1850	In March marries Madame Hanska. They return to Paris in May. Balzac dies in August.	Birth of Maupassant.

HISTORICAL EVENTS

Guizot's railway law. Railway mania in France (to 1846).

France and Morocco at war.

Anglo-French expedition against Madagascar.

Economic crisis in France. Teste trial discredits government. Algerian revolt suppressed.

February Revolution. The fall of Louis-Philippe. June Days: workers' uprising in Paris suppressed. Second Republic (1848–51). Year of Revolutions in Europe.

Election of Legislative Assembly. French restore Pius IX; fall of Roman republic.

EUGÉNIE GRANDET

To Maria

Your portrait is the fairest ornament of this book, and here it is fitting that your name should be set, like the branch of box taken from some unknown garden to lie for a while in the holy water, and afterwards set by pious hands above the threshold, where the green spray, ever renewed, is a sacred talisman to ward off all evil from the house.

IN some country towns there are houses more depressing to the sight than the dimmest cloister, the most melancholy ruins, or the dreariest stretch of sandy waste. Perhaps such houses as these combine the characteristics of all the three, and to the dumb silence of the monastery they unite the gauntness and grimness of the ruin, and the arid desolation of the waste. So little sign is there of life or of movement about them, that a stranger might take them for uninhabited dwellings; but the sound of an unfamiliar footstep brings someone to the window, a passive face suddenly appears above the sill, and the traveller receives a listless and indifferent glance – it is almost as if a monk leaned out to look for a moment on the world.

There is one particular house front in Saumur which possesses all these melancholy characteristics; the house is still standing at the end of the steep street which leads to the castle, at the upper end of the town. The street is very quiet nowadays; it is hot in summer and cold in winter, and very dark in places; besides this, it is remarkably narrow and crooked, there is a peculiarly formal and sedate air about its houses, and it is curious how every sound reverberates through it – the cobble stones (always clean and dry) ring with every passing footfall.

This is the oldest part of the town, the ramparts rise immediately above it. The houses of the quarter have stood for three centuries; and albeit they are built of wood, they are strong and sound yet. Each house has a certain character of its own, so that for the artist and antiquary this is the most attractive part of the town of Saumur. Indeed, it would hardly be possible to go past the houses without a wondering glance at the grotesque figures carved on the projecting ends of the huge beams, set like a black bas-relief above the ground floor of almost every dwelling. Sometimes, where these beams have been protected from the weather by slates, a strip of dull blue runs across the crumbling walls, and crowning the whole is a high-pitched roof oddly curved and bent with age; the shingle boards that cover it are all warped and twisted by the alternate sun and rain of many a year. There are bits of delicate carving too, here and there, though you can scarcely make them out, on the worn and blackened window sills that seem scarcely strong enough to bear the weight of the red flower-pot in which some poor workwoman has set her tree carnation or her monthly rose.

Still further along the street there are more pretentious house doors studded with huge nails. On these our forefathers exercised their ingenuity, tracing hieroglyphs and mysterious signs which were once understood in every household, but all clues to their meaning are forgotten now – they will be understood no more of any mortal. In such wise would a Protestant make his profession of faith, there also would a Leaguer curse

Henry IV in graven symbols. A burgher would com-
memorate his civic dignities, the glory of his long-for-
gotten tenure of office as alderman or sheriff. On those
old houses, if we could but read it, the history of France
is chronicled.

Beside the rickety little tenement built of wood,
with masonry of the roughest, upon the wall of which
the craftsman has set the glorified image of his trade –
his plane – stands the mansion of some noble, with its
massive round-arched gateway; you can still see some
traces above it of the arms borne by the owner, though
they have been torn down in one of the many revolutions which have convulsed the country since 1789.

You will find no imposing shop windows in the
street; strictly speaking indeed, there are no shops at
all, for the rooms on the ground floor in which articles
are exposed for sale are neither more nor less than the
workshops of the times of our forefathers; lovers of the
Middle Ages will find here the primitive simplicity of
an older world. The low-ceiled rooms are dark, cavern-
ous, and guiltless alike of plate-glass windows or of
show cases; there is no attempt at decoration either
within or without, no effort is made to display the
wares. The door as a rule is heavily barred with iron and
divided into two parts; the upper half is thrown back
during the day, admitting fresh air and daylight into the
damp little cave; while the lower portion, to which a
bell is attached, is seldom still. The shop front consists
of a low wall of about elbow height, which fills half the
space between floor and ceiling; there is no window
sash, but heavy shutters fastened with iron bolts fit into
a groove in the top of the wall, and are set up at night
and taken down in the morning. The same wall serves
as a counter on which to set out goods for the cus-
tomer's inspection. There is no sort of charlatanism
about the proceeding. The samples submitted to the

public vary according to the nature of the trade. You behold a keg or two of salt or of salted fish, two or three bales of sail-cloth or coils of rope, some copper wire hanging from the rafters, a few cooper's hoops on the walls, or a length or two of cloth upon the shelves.

You go in. A neat and tidy damsel with a pair of bare red arms, the fresh good looks of youth, and a white handkerchief pinned about her throat, lays down her knitting and goes to summon a father or mother, who appears and sells goods to you as you desire, be it a matter of two sous or of twenty thousand francs; the manner of the transaction varying as the humour of the vendor is surly, obliging, or independent. You will see a dealer in barrel-staves sitting in his doorway, twirling his thumbs as he chats with a neighbour; judging from appearances, he might possess nothing in this world but the bottles on his few rickety shelves, and two or three bundles of laths; but his well-stocked timber yard on the quay supplies all the coopers in Anjou, he knows to a barrel-stave how many casks he can 'turn out', as he says, if the vines do well and the vintage is good; a few scorching days and his fortune is made, a rainy summer is a ruinous thing for him; in a single morning the price of puncheons will rise as high as eleven francs or drop to six.

Here, as in Touraine, the whole trade of the district depends upon an atmospherical depression. Landowners, vine-growers, timber merchants, coopers, innkeepers, and lightermen, one and all are on the watch for a ray of sunlight. Not a man of them but goes to bed in fear and trembling lest he should hear in the morning that there has been a frost in the night. If it is not rain that they dread it is wind or drought; they must have cloudy weather or heat, and the rainfall and the weather generally all arranged to suit their peculiar notions.

Between the clerk of the weather and the vine-growing interest there is a duel which never ceases. Faces visibly lengthen or shorten, grow bright or gloomy, with the ups and downs of the barometer. Sometimes you hear from one end to the other of the old High Street of Saumur the words, 'This is golden weather!' or again, in language which likewise is no mere figure of speech, 'It is raining gold louis!' and they all know the exact value of sun or rain at the right moment.

After twelve o'clock or so on a Saturday in the summer time, you will not do a pennyworth of business among the worthy townsmen of Saumur. Each has his little farm and his bit of vineyard, and goes to spend the 'week end' in the country. As everybody knows this beforehand, just as everybody knows everybody else's business, his goings and comings, his buyings and sellings, and profits to boot, the good folk are free to spend ten hours out of the twelve in making up pleasant little parties, in taking notes and making comments, and keeping a sharp look-out on their neighbours' affairs. The mistress of a house cannot buy a partridge but the neighbours will inquire of her husband whether the bird was done to a turn; no damsel can put her head out of the window without being observed by every group of unoccupied observers.

Impenetrable, dark, and silent as the houses may seem, they contain no mysteries hidden from public scrutiny, and in the same way everyone knows what is passing in everyone else's mind. To begin with, the good folk spend most of their lives out of doors, they sit on the steps of their houses, breakfast there and dine there, and adjust any little family differences in the doorway. Every passer-by is scanned with the most minute and diligent attention; hence, any stranger who may happen to arrive in such a country town has, in a manner, to run the gauntlet, and is severely quizzed from every doorstep. By dint of perseverance in the methods thus indicated a quantity of droll stories may be collected; and, indeed, the people of Angers, who are of an ingenious turn, and quick at repartee, have been nicknamed 'the tattlers' on these very grounds.

The largest houses of the old quarter in which the nobles once dwelt are all at the upper end of the street, and in one of these the events took place which are about to be narrated in the course of this story. As has been already said, it was a melancholy house, a venerable relic of a bygone age, built for the men and women of an older and simpler world, from which our modern France is further and further removed day by day. After you have followed for some distance the windings of the picturesque street, where memories of the past are called up by every detail at every turn, till at length you fall unconsciously to musing, you come upon a sufficiently gloomy recess in which a doorway is dimly visible, the door of M. Grandet's house. Of all the pride and glory of proprietorship conveyed to the provincial mind by those three words, it is impossible to give any idea, except by giving the biography of the owner – M. Grandet.

M. Grandet enjoyed a certain reputation in Saumur. Its causes and effects can scarcely be properly estimated by outsiders who have not lived in a country town for a longer or shorter time. There were still old people in existence who could remember former times, and called M. Grandet 'Goodman Grandet', but there were not many of them left, and they were rapidly disappearing year by year.

In 1789 Grandet was a master cooper, in a very good way of business, who could read and write and cast accounts. When the French Republic, having confiscated the lands of the Church in the district of Saumur, proceeded to sell them by auction, the cooper was forty years of age, and had just married the daughter of a wealthy timber merchant. As Grandet possessed at that moment his wife's dowry as well as some considerable amount of ready money of his own, totalling some two thousand louis d'or, he repaired to the bureau of the district; and making due allowance for two hundred double louis offered by his father-in-law to that man of stern morals, the Republican who conducted the sale, the cooper acquired some of the best vineland in the neighbourhood, an old abbey, and a few little farms, for a song, to all of which property, though it might be ill-gotten, the law gave him a clear title.

There was little sympathy felt with the Revolution in Saumur. Goodman Grandet was looked upon as a bold spirit, a Republican, a patriot, an 'advanced thinker', and what not; but all the 'thinking' the cooper ever did turned simply and solely on the subject of his vines. He was nominated as a member of the administration of the district of Saumur, and exercised a pacific influence both in politics and in commerce. Politically, he befriended the *ci-devants*, and did all that he could to prevent the sale of their property; commercially, he contracted to supply one or two thousand hogsheads of white wine to the Republican armies, taking his payment for the aforesaid hogsheads in the shape of certain broad acres of rich meadow land belonging to a convent, the property of the nuns having been reserved till the last.

In the days of the Consulate, Master Grandet became mayor; did prudently in his public capacity, and did very well for himself. Times changed, the Empire was established, and he became *Monsieur* Grandet. But M. Grandet had been looked upon as a red Republican, and Napoleon had no liking for Republicans, so the mayor was replaced by a large landowner, a man with a *de* before his name, and a prospect of one day becoming a baron of the Empire. M. Grandet turned his back upon municipal honours without a shadow of regret. He had looked well after the interests of the town during his term of office, excellent roads had been made, passing in every case by his own domains. His house and land had been assessed very moderately, the burden of the taxes did not fall too grievously upon him; since the assessment, moreover, he had given ceaseless attention and care to the cultivation of his vines, so that they had become the *tête du pays*, the technical term for those vineyards which produce wine of the finest quality. He had a fair claim to the Cross of the Legion of Honour, and he received it in 1806.

By this time M. Grandet was fifty-seven years old, and his wife about thirty-six. The one child of the marriage was a daughter, a little girl of ten years of age. Providence doubtless sought to console M. Grandet for his official downfall; for in this year he succeeded to three fortunes. The total value was matter for conjecture, no certain information being forthcoming. The first fell in on the death of Mme de la Gaudinière, Mme Grandet's mother; the deceased lady had been a de la Bertellière, and her father, old M. de la Bertellière, soon followed her; the third in order was Mme Gentillet, M. Grandet's grandmother on the mother's side. The avarice of these three old folk had been so intense that they had hidden away their money for years past so as to rejoice in its secret contemplation. Old M. de la Bertellière used to call an investment 'throwing money away'; the sight of his hoards of gold repaid him better than any rate of interest upon it. The town of Saumur, therefore, roughly calculated the value of the amount that the late de la Bertellière was likely to have saved out of his yearly takings; and M. Grandet received a new distinction which none of our manias for equality can efface – he paid more taxes than anyone else in the country around.

He now cultivated a hundred acres of vineyard; in a

good year they would yield seven or eight hundred puncheons. He had thirteen little farms, an old abbey (motives of economy had led him to wall up the windows, and so preserve the traceries and stained glass), and a hundred and twenty-seven acres of grazing land, in which three thousand poplars, planted in 1793, were growing taller and larger every year. Finally, he owned the house in which he lived.

In these visible ways his prosperity had increased. As to his capital, there were only two people in a position to make a guess at its probable amount. One of these was the notary, M. Cruchot, who transacted all the necessary business whenever M. Grandet made an investment; and the other was M. des Grassins, the wealthiest banker in the town, who did Grandet many good offices which were unknown to Saumur. Secrets of this nature, involving extensive business transactions, are usually well kept; but the discreet caution of MM. Cruchot and des Grassins did not prevent them from addressing M. Grandet in public with such profound deference that close observers might draw their own conclusions. Clearly the wealth of their late mayor must be prodigious indeed that he should receive such obsequious attention.

There was no one in Saumur who did not fully believe the report which told how, in a secret hiding-place, M. Grandet had a hoard of louis, and how every night he went to look at it and gave himself up to the inexpressible delight of gazing at the huge heap of gold. He was not the only money-lover in Saumur. Sympathetic observers looked at his eyes and felt that the story was true, for they seemed to have the yellow metallic glitter of the coin over which it was said they had brooded. Nor was this the only sign. Certain small indefinable habits, furtive movements, slightly mysterious promptings of greed did not escape the keen observation of fellow-worshippers. There is something vulpine about the eyes of a man who lends money at an exorbitant rate of interest; they gradually and surely contract like those of the gambler, the sensualist, or the courtier; and there is, so to speak, a sort of freemasonry among the passions, a written language of hieroglyphs and signs for those who can read them.

M. Grandet therefore inspired in all around him the respectful esteem which is but the due of a man who has never owed anyone a farthing in his life; a just and legitimate tribute to an astute old cooper and vine-grower who knew beforehand with the certainty of an astronomer when five hundred casks would serve for the vintage, and when to have a thousand in readiness; a man who had never lost on any speculation, who had always a stock of empty barrels whenever casks were so dear that they fetched more than the contents were worth; who could store his vintage in his own cellars, and afford to bide his time, so that his puncheons would bring him in a couple of hundred francs, while many a little proprietor who could not wait had to be content with half that amount. His famous vintage in the year 1811, discreetly held, and sold only as good opportunities offered, had been worth more than two hundred and forty thousand livres to him.

In matters financial M. Grandet might be described as combining the characteristics of the Bengal tiger and the boa constrictor. He could lie low and wait, crouching, watching for his prey, and make his spring unerringly at last; then the jaws of his purse would unclose, a torrent of coin would be swallowed down, and, as in the case of the gorged reptile, there would be a period of inaction; like the serpent, moreover, he was cold, apathetic, methodical, keeping to his own mysterious times and seasons.

No one could see the man pass without feeling a certain kind of admiration, which was half dread, half respect. The tiger's clutch was like steel, his claws were sharp and swift; was there anyone in Saumur who had not felt them? Such a one, for instance, wanted to borrow money to buy that piece of land which he had set his heart upon; M. Cruchot had found the money for him – at eleven per cent. And there was So-and-so yonder; M. des Grassins had discounted his bills, but it was at a ruinous rate.

There were not many days when M. Grandet's name did not come up in conversation, in familiar talk in the evenings, or in the gossip of the town. There were people who took a kind of patriotic pride in the old vine-grower's wealth. More than one innkeeper or merchant had found occasion to remark to a stranger with a certain complacency, 'There are millionaires in two or three of our firms here, sir; but as for M. Grandet, he himself could hardly tell you how much he was worth!'

In 1816 the shrewdest heads in Saumur set down the value of the cooper's landed property at about four millions; but as, to strike a fair average, he must have drawn something like a hundred thousand francs (they thought) from his property between the years 1793 and 1817, the amount of money he possessed must nearly equal the value of the land. So when M. Grandet's name was mentioned over a game at boston, or a chat about the prospects of the vines, these folk would look wise and remark, 'Who is that you are talking of? Old Grandet? . . . Old Grandet must have five or six millions, there is no doubt about it.'

'Then you are cleverer than I am; I have never been able to find out how much he has,' M. Cruchot or M. des Grassins would put in, if they overheard the talk.

If anyone from Paris mentioned the Rothschilds or M. Laffitte, the good people in Saumur would ask if any of those persons were as rich as M. Grandet. And if the Parisian should answer in the affirmative with a pitying smile, they looked at one another incredulously and flung up their heads. So great a fortune was like a golden mantle; it covered its owner and all that he did. At one time some of the eccentricities of his mode of life gave rise to laughter at his expense; but the satire and the laughter had died out, and M. Grandet still went his way, till at last even his slightest actions came to be taken as precedents, and every trifling thing he said or did carried weight. His remarks, his clothing, his gestures, the way he blinked his eyes, had all been studied with the care with which a naturalist studies the workings of instinct in some wild creature; and no one failed to discern the taciturn and profound wisdom that underlay all these manifestations.

'We shall have a hard winter,' they would say; 'old Grandet has put on his fur gloves, we must gather the grapes.' Or, 'Goodman Grandet is laying in a lot of cask staves; there will be plenty of wine this year.'

M. Grandet never bought either meat or bread. Part of his rents were paid in kind, and every week his tenants brought in poultry, eggs, butter, and wheat sufficient for the needs of his household. Moreover, he owned a mill, and the miller, besides paying rent, came over to fetch a certain quantity of corn, and brought him back both the bran and the flour. Big Nanon, the one maid-servant, baked all the bread once a week, on Saturday mornings (though she was not so young as she had been). Others of the tenants were market gardeners, and M. Grandet had arranged that these were to keep him supplied with fresh vegetables. Of fruit there was no lack; indeed, he sold a good deal of it in the market. Firewood was gathered from his own hedges, or taken from old stumps of trees that grew by the sides of his fields. His tenants chopped up the wood, carted it into the town, and obligingly stacked his faggots for him, receiving in return – his thanks. So he seldom had occasion to spend money. His only known items of expenditure were for sacramental bread, for sittings in the church for his wife and daughter, their dress, Nanon's wages, renewals of the linings of Nanon's saucepans, repairs about the house, candles, rates and taxes, and the necessary outlays of money for improvements. He had recently acquired six hundred acres of woodland, and, being unable to look after it himself, had induced a keeper belonging to a neighbour to attend to it, promising to repay the man for his trouble. After this purchase had been made, and not before, game appeared on the Grandets' table.

Grandet's manners were distinctly homely. He did not say very much. He expressed his ideas, as a rule, in brief, sententious phrases, uttered in a low voice. Since the time of the Revolution when for a while he had attracted some attention, the worthy man had contracted a tiresome habit of stammering as soon as he took part in a discussion or began to speak at any length. He had other peculiarities. He habitually drowned his ideas in a flood of words more or less incoherent; his singular inaptitude for reasoning logically was usually set down to a defective education; but this, like his unwelcome fluency, the trick of stammering, and various other mannerisms, was assumed, and for reasons which, in the course of the story, will be made sufficiently clear. In conversation, moreover, he had other resources: four phrases, like algebraical formulae, which fitted every case, were always forthcoming to solve every knotty problem in business or domestic life – 'I do not know', 'I cannot do it', 'I will have nothing to do with it', and 'We shall see.' He never committed himself; he never said yes or no; he never put anything down in writing. He listened with apparent indifference when he was spoken to, caressing his chin with his right hand, while the back of his left supported his elbow. When once he had formed his opinion in any matter of business, he never changed it; but he pondered long even over the smallest transactions. When in the course of deep and weighty converse he had managed to fathom the intentions of an antagonist, who meanwhile flattered himself that *he* at least knew where to have Grandet, the latter was wont to say: 'I must talk it over with my wife before I can give a definite answer.' In business matters the wife, whom he had reduced to the most abject submission, was unquestionably a most convenient support and screen.

He never paid visits, never dined away from home, nor asked anyone to dinner; his movements were almost noiseless; he seemed to carry out his principles of economy in everything; to make no useless sound, to be chary of spending even physical energy. His respect for the rights of ownership was so habitual that he never displaced nor disturbed anything belonging to another. And yet, in spite of the low tones of his voice, in spite of his discretion and cautious bearing, the cooper's real character showed itself in his language and manners, and this was more especially the case in his own house, where he was less on his guard than elsewhere.

As to Grandet's exterior. He was a broad, square-shouldered, thick-set man, about five feet high; his legs were thin (he measured perhaps twelve inches round the calves), his knee joints large and prominent. He had a bullet-shaped head, a sun-burned face, scarred with the smallpox, and a narrow chin; there was no trace of a curve about the lines of his mouth. He possessed a set of white teeth, eyes with the expression of stony avidity in them with which the basilisk is credited, a deeply-furrowed brow on which there were prominences not lacking in significance, hair that had once been of a sandy hue, but which was now fast turning grey; so that

thoughtless youngsters, rash enough to make jokes on
so serious a subject, would say that M. Grandet's very
hair was 'gold and silver'. On his nose, which was broad
and blunt at the tip, was a variegated wen; gossip af-
firmed, not without some appearance of truth, that
spite and rancour was the cause of this affection. There
was a dangerous cunning about this face, although the
man, indeed, was honest according to the letter of the
law; it was a selfish face; there were but two things in
the world for which its owner cared – the delights of
hoarding wealth in the first place, and in the second,
the only being who counted for anything in his estima-
tion, his daughter Eugénie, his only child, who one day
should inherit that wealth. His attitude, manner, bearing, and everything about him plainly showed that he
had the belief in himself which is the natural outcome
of an unbroken record of successful business specula-
tions. Pliant and smooth-spoken though he might appear to be, M. Grandet was a man of bronze. He was
always dressed after the same fashion; in 1819 he
looked in this respect exactly as he had looked at any
time since 1791. His heavy shoes were secured by
leather laces; he wore thick woollen stockings all the
year round, knee-breeches of chestnut-brown home-
spun, silver buckles, a brown velvet waistcoat adorned
with yellow stripes and buttoned up to the throat, a
loosely-fitting coat with ample skirts, a black cravat, and
a broad-brimmed Quaker-like hat. His gloves, like
those of the gendarmerie, were chosen with a view to
hard wear; a pair lasted him nearly two years. In order to
keep them clean, he always laid them down on the
same place on the brim of his hat, till the action had
come to be mechanical with him. So much, and no
more, Saumur knew of this her citizen.

A few fellow townspeople, six in all, had the right of
entry to Grandet's house and society. First among these

in order of importance was M. Cruchot's nephew. Ever since his appointment as president of the court of first instance, this young man had added the appellation 'de Bonfons' to his original name of Cruchot; in time he hoped that the Bonfons would efface the Cruchot, when he meant to drop the Cruchot altogether, and was at no little pains to compass this end. Already he signed himself C. de Bonfons. Any litigant who was so ill inspired as to address him in court as 'M. Cruchot', was soon made painfully aware that he had blundered. The magistrate was about thirty-three years of age, and the owner of the estate of Bonfons (*Boni Fontis*), which brought in annually seven thousand livres. In addition to this he had prospects; he would succeed some day to the property of his uncle the notary, and there was yet another uncle besides, the Abbé Cruchot, a dignitary of the Chapter of Saint Martin of Tours; both relatives were commonly reported to be men of substance. The three Cruchots, with a goodly number of kinsfolk, connected too by marriage with a score of other houses, formed a sort of party in the town, like the family of the Medici in Florence long ago; and, like the Medici, the Cruchots had their rivals – their Pazzi.

Mme des Grassins, the mother of a son twenty-three years of age, came assiduously to take a hand at cards with Mme Grandet, hoping to marry her own dear Adolphe to Mlle Eugénie. She had a powerful ally in her husband the banker, who had secretly rendered the old miser many a service, and who could give opportune aid on her field of battle. The three des Grassins had likewise their host of adherents, their cousins, and trusty auxiliaries.

The abbé (the Talleyrand of the Cruchot faction), well supported by his brother the notary, closely disputed the ground with the banker's wife; they meant to carry off the wealthy heiress for their nephew the president. The struggle between the two parties for the prize of the hand of Eugénie Grandet was an open secret; all Saumur watched it with the keenest interest. Which would Mlle Grandet marry? Would it be M. le Président or M. Adolphe des Grassins? Some solved the problem by saying that M. Grandet would give his daughter to neither. The old cooper (said they) was consumed with an ambition to have a peer of France for his son-in-law, and he was on the look-out for a peer of France, who for the consideration of an income of three hundred thousand livres would find all the past, present, and future barrels of the Grandets no obstacle to a match. Others demurred to this, and urged that both M. and Mme des Grassins came of a good family, that they had wealth enough for anything, that Adolphe was a very good-looking, pretty-behaved young man, and that unless the Grandets had a pope's nephew somewhere in the background, they ought to be satisfied with a match in every way so suitable; for they were nobodies after all; all Saumur had seen Grandet going about with an adze in his hands, and moreover he had worn the red cap of liberty in his time.

The more astute observers remarked that M. Cruchot de Bonfons was free of the house in the High Street, while his rival only visited there on Sundays. Some maintained that Mme des Grassins, being on more intimate terms with the women of the house, had opportunities of inculcating certain ideas which sooner or later must conduce to her success. Others retorted that the Abbé Cruchot had the most insinuating manner in the world, and that with a churchman on one side and a woman on the other the chances were about even.

'It is gown against cassock,' said a local wit.

Those whose memories went further back, said that the Grandets were too prudent to let all that property go out of the family. Mlle Eugénie Grandet of Saumur

would be married one of these days to the son of the
other M. Grandet of Paris, a rich wholesale wine merchant. To these both Cruchotins and Grassinistes were
wont to reply as follows:

'In the first place, the brothers have not met twice in
thirty years. Then M. Grandet of Paris is ambitious for
that son of his. He himself is mayor of his division of the
department, a deputy, a colonel of the National Guard,
and a judge of the tribunal of commerce. He does not
own to any relationship with the Grandets of Saumur,
and is seeking to connect himself with one of Napoleon's dukes.'

What will not people say of an heiress? Eugénie
Grandet was a stock subject of conversation for twenty
leagues round; nay, in public conveyances, even as far
as Angers on the one hand and Blois on the other!

In the beginning of the year 1811 the Cruchotins
gained a signal victory over the Grassinistes. The young
Marquis de Froidfond being compelled to realize his
capital, the estate of Froidfond, celebrated for its park
and its handsome château, was for sale; together with its
dependent farms, rivers, fishponds, and forest; altogether it was worth three million francs. M. Cruchot,
Président Cruchot, and the Abbé Cruchot by uniting
their forces had managed to prevent a proposed division into small lots. The notary made an uncommonly
good bargain for his client, representing to the young
marquis that the purchase money of the small lots could
only be collected after endless trouble and expense,
and that he would have to sue a large proportion of the
purchasers for it; while here was M. Grandet, a man
whose credit stood high, and who was moreover
ready to pay for the land at once in hard coin; it would
be better to take M. Grandet's offer. In this way the fair
marquisate of Froidfond was swallowed down by
M. Grandet, who, to the amazement of Saumur, paid

for it in ready money (deducting discount of course) as soon as the required formalities were completed. The news of this transaction travelled far and wide; it reached Orleans, it was spoken of at Nantes.

M. Grandet went to see his château, and on this wise: a cart happened to be returning thither, so he embraced this opportunity of visiting his newly-acquired property, and took a look round in the capacity of owner. Then he returned to Saumur, well convinced that this investment would bring him in a clear five per cent, and fired with a magnificent ambition; he would add his own bits of land to the marquisate of Froidfond, and everything should lie within a ring fence. For the present he would set himself to replenish his almost exhausted coffers; he would cut down every stick of timber in his copses and forests, and fell the poplars in his meadows.

It is easy after this explanation to understand all that was conveyed by the words, 'M. Grandet's house' – the cold, dreary, and silent house at the upper end of the town, under the shadow of the ruined ramparts.

Two pillars supported the arch above the doorway, and for these, as also for the building of the house itself, a porous crumbling stone peculiar to the district along the banks of the Loire had been employed, a kind of tufa so soft that at most it scarcely lasts for two hundred years. Rain and frost had gnawed numerous irregular holes in the surface, with a curious effect; the piers and the voussoirs looked as though they were composed of the vermicular stones often met with in French architecture. The doorway might have been the portal of a jail. Above the arch there was a long sculptured bas-relief of harder stone, representing the four seasons, four forlorn figures, aged, blackened, and weather-worn. Above the bas-relief there was a projecting ledge of masonry where some chance-sown plants had taken root; yellow pellitory, bindweed, a plantain or two, and a little cherry tree, that even now had reached a fair height.

The massive door itself was of dark oak, shrunk and warped, and full of cracks; but, feeble as it looked, it was firmly held together by a series of iron nails with huge heads, driven into the wood in a symmetrical design. In the middle there was a small square grating covered with rusty iron bars, which served as an excuse for a door knocker which hung there from a ring, and struck upon the menacing head of a great iron bolt. The knocker itself, oblong in shape, was of the kind that our ancestors used to call a 'jaquemart', and not unlike a huge note of exclamation. If an antiquary had examined it carefully, he might have found some traces of the grotesque human head that it once represented, but the features of the typical clown had long since been effaced by constant wear. The little grating had been made in past times of civil war, so that the household might recognize their friends without before admitting them, but now it afforded to inquisitive eyes a view of a dank and gloomy archway, and a flight of broken steps leading to a not unpicturesque garden shut in by thick walls through which the damp was oozing, and a hedge of sickly-looking shrubs. The walls were part of the old fortifications, and up above upon the ramparts there were yet other gardens belonging to some of the neighbouring houses.

A door beneath the arch of the gateway opened into a large parlour, the principal room on the ground floor. Few people comprehend the importance of this apartment in little towns in Anjou, Berri, and Touraine. The parlour is also the hall, drawing-room, study, boudoir, and dining-room all in one; it is the stage on which the drama of domestic life is played, the very heart and centre of the home. Hither the hairdresser repaired

once in six months to cut M. Grandet's hair. The tenants and the curé, the sous-préfet and the miller's
lad, were all alike shown into this room. There were
two windows which looked out upon the street, the
floor was boarded, the walls were panelled from floor to
ceiling, covered with old carvings, and painted grey.
The rafters were left visible, and were likewise painted
grey, the plaster in intervening spaces was yellow with
age.

An old brass clock case inlaid with arabesques in tor-
toise-shell stood on the chimney-piece, which was of
white stone, and adorned with rude carvings. Above it
stood a mirror of a greenish hue; the edges were bev-
elled in order to display the thickness of the glass, and
reflected a thin streak of coloured light into the room,
which was caught again by the polished surface of another mirror of Damascus steel, which hung upon the
wall.

Two branched sconces of gilded copper which
adorned either end of the chimney-piece answered a
double purpose. The branch roses which served as
candle-sockets were removable, and the main stem,
fitted into an antique copper contrivance on a bluish
marble pedestal, did duty as a candlestick for ordinary
days.

The old-fashioned chairs were covered with tapestry,
on which the fables of La Fontaine were depicted; but
a thorough knowledge of the author was required in
order to make out the subjects, for the colours had
faded badly, and the outlines of the figures were hardly
visible through a multitude of darns. Four sideboards
occupied the four corners of the room, each of these articles of furniture terminating in a tier of very dirty
shelves. An old inlaid card-table with a chess-board
marked out upon its surface stood in the space between
the two windows, and on the wall, above the table,

hung an oval barometer in a dark wooden setting, adorned by a carved bunch of ribbons; they had been gilt ribbons once upon a time, but generations of flies had wantonly obscured the gilding, till its existence had become problematical. Two portraits in pastel hung on the wall opposite the fireplace. One was believed to represent Mme Grandet's grandfather, old M. de la Bertellière, as a lieutenant in the Guards, and the other the late Mme Gentillet, as a shepherdess.

Crimson curtains of *gros de Tours* were hung in the windows and fastened back with silk cords and huge tassels. This luxurious upholstery, so little in harmony with the manners and customs of the Grandets, had been included in the purchase of the house, like the pier-glass, the brass timepiece, the tapestry-covered chairs, and the rosewood corner sideboards. In the further window stood a straw-bottomed chair, raised on blocks of wood, so that Mme Grandet could watch the passers-by as she sat. A work-table of cherry wood, bleached and faded by the light, filled the other window space, and close beside it Eugénie Grandet's little arm-chair was set.

The lives of mother and daughter had flowed on tranquilly for fifteen years. Day after day, from April to November, they sat at work in the windows; but the first day of the latter month found them beside the fire, where they took up their positions for the winter. Grandet would not allow a fire to be lighted in the room before that date, nor again after the 31st of March, let the early days of spring or of autumn be cold as they might. Big Nanon managed by stealth to fill a little brazier with glowing ashes from the kitchen fire, and in this way the chilly evenings of April and October were rendered tolerable for Mme and Mlle Grandet. All the household linen was kept in repair by the mother and daughter; and so conscientiously did they devote their days to this duty (no light task in truth), that if Eugénie wanted to embroider a collarette for her mother she was obliged to steal the time from her hours of slumber, and to resort to a deception to obtain from her father the candle by which she worked. For a long while past it had been the miser's wont to dole out the candles to his daughter and big Nanon in the same way that he gave out the bread and the other matters daily required by the household.

Perhaps big Nanon was the one servant in existence who could and would have endured her master's tyrannous rule. Everyone in the town used to envy M. and Mme Grandet for her. 'Big Nanon', so called on account of her height of five feet eight inches, had been a part of the Grandet household for thirty-five years. She was held to be one of the richest servants in Saumur, and this on a yearly wage of sixty livres! The sixty livres had accumulated for thirty-five years, and quite recently Nanon had deposited four thousand livres with M. Cruchot for the purchase of an annuity. This result of a long and persevering course of thrift appealed to the imagination – it seemed tremendous. There was not a maid-servant in Saumur but was envious of the poor woman, who by the time she had reached her sixtieth year would have scraped together enough to keep herself from want in her old age; but no one thought of the hard life and all the toil which had gone to the making of that little hoard.

Thirty-five years ago, when Nanon had been a home-ly, hard-featured girl of two-and-twenty, she had not been able to find a place because her appearance had been so much against her. Poor Nanon! it was really very hard. If her head had been set on the shoulders of a gre-nadier it would have been greatly admired, but there is a fitness in things, and Nanon's style of beauty was inappropriate. She had been a herdswoman on a farm for a

time, till the farmhouse had been burnt down, and then
it was, that, full of the robust courage that shrinks from
nothing, she came to seek service in Saumur.

At that time M. Grandet was thinking of marriage,
and already determined to set up housekeeping. The
girl, who had been rebuffed from door to door, came
under his notice. He was a cooper, and therefore a good
judge of physical strength; he foresaw at once how useful this feminine Hercules could be, a strongly-made
woman who stood planted as firmly on her feet as an
oak tree rooted in the soil where it has grown for two
generations, a woman with square shoulders, large hips,
and hands like a ploughman's, and whose honesty was
as unquestionable as her virtue. He was not dismayed
by a martial countenance, a disfiguring wart or two, a
complexion like burnt clay, and a pair of sinewy arms;
neither did Nanon's rags alarm the cooper, whose heart
was not yet hardened against misery. He took the poor
girl into his service, gave her food, clothes, shoes, and
wages. Nanon found her hard life not intolerably hard.
Nay, she secretly shed tears of joy at being so treated;
she felt a sincere attachment for this master, who expected as much from her as ever feudal lord required of
a serf.

Nanon did all the work of the house. She did the
cooking and the washing, carrying all the linen down to
the Loire and bringing it back on her shoulders. She
rose at daybreak and went to bed late. It was she who,
without any assistance, cooked for the vintagers in the
autumn, and looked sharply after the market-folk. She
watched over her master's property like a faithful dog,
and with a blind belief in him; she obeyed his most arbitrary commands without a murmur – his whims were
law to her.

After twenty years of service, in the famous year
1811, when the vintage had been gathered in after un-

heard-of toil and trouble, Grandet made up his mind to present Nanon with his old watch, the only gift she had ever received from him. She certainly had the reversion of his old shoes (which happened to fit her), but as a rule they were so far seen into already that they were of little use to anyone else, and could not be looked upon as a present. Sheer necessity had made the poor girl so penurious that Grandet grew quite fond of her at last, and regarded her with the same sort of affection that a man gives to his dog; and as for Nanon, she cheerfully wore the collar of servitude set round with spikes that she had ceased to feel. Grandet might stint the day's allowance of bread, but she did not grumble. The fare might be scanty and poor, but Nanon's spirits did not suffer, and her health appeared to benefit; there was never any illness in that house.

And then Nanon was one of the family. She shared every mood of Grandet's, laughed when he laughed, was depressed when he was out of spirits, took her views of the weather or of the temperature from him, and worked with him and for him. This equality was an element of sweetness which made up for many hardships in her lot. Out in the vineyards her master had never said a word about the small peaches, plums, or nectarines eaten under the trees that are planted between the rows of vines.

'Come, Nanon, take as much as you like,' he would say, in years when the branches were bending beneath their load, and fruit was so abundant that the farmers round about were forced to give it to the pigs.

For the peasant girl, for the outdoor farm servant, who had known nothing but harsh treatment from childhood, for the girl who had been rescued from starvation by charity, old Grandet's equivocal laughter was like a ray of sunshine. Besides, Nanon's simple nature and limited intelligence could only entertain one idea at a time; and during those thirty-five years of service one picture was constantly present to her mind – she saw herself a barefooted girl in rags standing at the gate of M. Grandet's timber yard, and heard the sound of the cooper's voice, saying, 'What is it, lassie?' and the warmth of gratitude filled her heart today as it did then. Sometimes, as he watched her, the thought came up in Grandet's mind how that no syllable of praise or admiration had ever been breathed in her ears, that all the tender feelings that a woman inspires had no existence for her, and that she might well appear before God one day as chaste as the Virgin Mary herself. At such times, prompted by a sudden impulse of pity, he would exclaim, 'Poor Nanon!'

The remark was always followed by an indescribable look from the old servant. The words so spoken from time to time were separate links in a long and unbroken chain of friendship. But in this pity in the miser's soul, which gave a thrill of pleasure to the lonely woman, there was something indescribably revolting; it was a cold-blooded pity that stirred the cooper's heart; it was a luxury that cost him nothing. But for Nanon it meant the height of happiness! Who will not likewise say, 'Poor Nanon!' God will one day know His angels by the tones of their voices and by the sorrow hidden in their hearts.

There were plenty of households in Saumur where servants were better treated, but where their employers, nevertheless, enjoyed small comfort in return. Wherefore people asked, 'What have the Grandets done to that big Nanon of theirs that she should be so attached to them? She would go through fire and water to serve them!'

Her kitchen, with its barred windows that looked out into the yard, was always clean, cold, and tidy, a thorough miser's kitchen, in which nothing was allowed to be wasted. When Nanon had washed her plates and dishes, put the remains of the dinner into the safe, and raked out the fire, she left her kitchen (which was only separated from the dining-room by the breadth of a passage), and sat down to spin hemp in the company of her employers, for a single candle must suffice for the whole family in the evening. The serving-maid slept in a little dark closet at the end of the passage, lit only by a borrowed light. Nanon had an iron constitution and sound health, which enabled her to sleep with impunity year after year in this hole, where she could hear the slightest sound that broke the heavy silence brooding day and night over the house; she lay like a watch-dog, with one ear open; she was never off duty, not even while she slept.

Some description of the rest of the house will be necessary in the course of the story in connection with later events; but the parlour, wherein all the splendour and luxury of the house was concentrated, has been sketched already, and the emptiness and bareness of the upper rooms can be surmised for the present.

It was in the middle of November, in the year 1819, twilight was coming on, and big Nanon was lighting a fire in the parlour for the first time. It was a festival day in the calendar of the Cruchotins and Grassinistes, wherefore the six antagonists were preparing to set forth, all armed cap-à-pie, for a contest in which each side meant to outdo the other in proofs of friendship. The Grandets' parlour was to be the scene of action. That morning Mme and Mlle Grandet, duly attended by Nanon, had repaired to the parish church to hear mass. All Saumur had seen them go, and everyone had been put in mind of the fact that it was Eugénie's birthday. M. Cruchot, and Abbé Cruchot, and M. C. de Bonfons, therefore, having calculated the hour when dinner would be over, were eager to be first in the field, and to arrive before the Grassinistes to congratulate Mlle Grandet. All three carried huge bunches of flowers gathered in their little garden plots, but the stalks of the magistrate's bouquet were ingeniously bound round by a white satin ribbon with a tinsel fringe at the ends.

In the morning M. Grandet had gone to Eugénie's room before she had left her bed, and had solemnly presented her with a rare gold coin. It was her father's wont to surprise her in this way twice every year – once on her birthday, once on the equally memorable day of her patron saint. Mme Grandet usually gave her daughter a winter or a summer dress, according to circumstances. The two dresses and two gold coins, which she received on her father's birthday and on New Year's Day, altogether amounted to an annual income of nearly a hundred crowns; Grandet loved to watch the money accumulating in her hands. He did not part with his money; he felt that it was only like taking it out of one box and putting it into another; and besides, was it not, so to speak, fostering a proper regard for gold in his heiress? She was being trained in the way in which she should go. Now and then he asked for an account of her wealth (formerly swelled by gifts from the La Bertellières), and each time he did so he used to tell her: 'This will be your *dozen* when you are married.'

The *dozen* is an old-world custom which has lost none of its force, and is still religiously adhered to in several midland districts in France. In Berri or Anjou when a daughter is married, it is incumbent upon her parents, or upon her bridegroom's family, to give her a purse containing either a dozen, or twelve dozen, or twelve hundred gold or silver coins, the amount varying with the means of the family. The poorest herd-girl would not be content without her *dozen* when she married, even if she could only bring twelve pence as a dower. They talk even yet at Issoudun of a fabulous dozen once given to a rich heiress, which consisted of a hundred and forty-four Portuguese moidores; and when Catherine de' Medici was married to Henry II, her uncle, Clement VII, gave the bride a dozen antique gold medals of priceless value.

Eugénie wore her new dress at dinner, and looked prettier than usual in it; her father was in high good-humour.

'Let us have a fire,' he cried, 'as it is Eugénie's birth-day! It will be a good omen.'

'Mademoiselle will be married within the year, that's certain,' said big Nanon, as she removed the remains of a goose, that pheasant of the coopers of Saumur.

'There is no one that I know of in Saumur who would do for Eugénie,' said Mme Grandet, with a timid glance at her husband, a glance that revealed how completely her husband's tyranny had broken the poor woman's spirit.

Grandet looked at his daughter, and said merrily, 'We must really begin to think about her; the little girl is twenty-three years old today.'

Neither Eugénie nor her mother said a word, but they exchanged glances; they understood each other.

Mme Grandet's face was thin and wrinkled and yellow as saffron; she was awkward and slow in her movements, one of those beings who seem born to be tyrannized over. She was a large-boned woman, with a large nose, large eyes, and a prominent forehead; there seemed to be, at first sight, some dim suggestion of a resemblance between her and some shrivelled, spongy, dried-up fruit. The few teeth that remained to her were dark and discoloured; there were deep lines fretted about her mouth, and her chin was something after the 'nut-cracker' pattern. She was a good sort of woman, and a La Bertellière to the backbone. The Abbé Cruchot had more than once found occasion to tell her that she had not been so bad looking when she was young, and she did not disagree with him. An angelic sweetness of disposition, the helpless meekness of an insect in the hands of cruel children, a sincere piety, a kindly heart, and an even temper that nothing could ruffle or sour, had gained universal respect and pity for her.

Her appearance might provoke a smile, but she had brought her husband more than three hundred thousand francs, partly as her dowry, partly through bequests. Yet Grandet never gave his wife more than six francs at a time for pocket money, and she always regarded herself as dependent upon her husband. The meek gentleness of her nature forbade any revolt against his tyranny; but so deeply did she feel the humiliation of her position, that she had never asked him for a sou, and when M. Cruchot demanded her signature to any document, she always gave it without a word. This foolish sensitive pride, which Grandet constantly and unwittingly hurt, this magnanimity which he was quite incapable of understanding, were Mme Grandet's dominant characteristics.

Her dress never varied. Her gown was always of the same dull, greenish shade of levantine, and usually lasted her nearly a twelvemonth; the large handkerchief at her throat was of some kind of cotton material; she wore a straw bonnet, and was seldom seen without a black silk apron. She left the house so rarely that her walking shoes were seldom worn out; indeed, her requirements were very few, she never wanted anything for herself. Sometimes it would occur to Grandet that it was a long while since he had given the last six francs to his wife, and his conscience would prick him a little; and after the vintage, when he sold his wine, he always demanded pin-money for his wife over and above the bargain. These four or five louis out of the pockets of the Dutch or Belgian merchants were Mme Grandet's only certain source of yearly income. But although she received her five louis, her husband would often say to her, as if they had had one common purse, 'Have you a few sous that you can lend me?' and she, poor woman, glad that it was in her power to do anything for the man whom her confessor always taught her to regard as her lord and master, used to return to him more than one crown out of her little store in the course of the winter. Every month, when Grandet disbursed the five-franc piece which he allowed his daughter for needles, thread, and small expenses of dress, he remarked to his wife (after he had buttoned up his pocket), 'And how about you, mother; do you want anything?' And with a mother's dignity Mme Grandet would answer, 'We will talk about that by and by, dear.'

Her magnanimity was entirely lost upon Grandet; he considered that he did very handsomely by his wife. The philosophic mind contemplating the Nanons, the Mme Grandets, the Eugénies of this life, holds that the author of the universe is a profound satirist, and who will quarrel with the conclusion of the philosophic mind? After the dinner, when the question of Eugénie's marriage had been raised for the first time, Nanon went up to M. Grandet's room to fetch a bottle of blackcurrant cordial, and very nearly lost her footing on the staircase as she came down.

'Great stupid! Are *you* going to take to tumbling about?' inquired her master.

'It is all along of the step, sir; it gave way. The staircase isn't safe.'

'She is quite right,' said Mme Grandet. 'You ought to have had it mended long ago. Eugénie all but sprained her foot on it yesterday.'

'Here,' said Grandet, who saw that Nanon looked very pale, 'as today is Eugénie's birthday, and you have nearly fallen downstairs, take a drop of blackcurrant cordial; that will put you right again.'

'I deserve it, too, upon my word,' said Nanon. 'Many a one would have broken the bottle in my place; I should have broken my elbow first, holding it up to save it.'

'Poor Nanon!' muttered Grandet, pouring out the blackcurrant cordial for her.

'Did you hurt yourself?' asked Eugénie, looking at her in concern.

'No, I managed to break the fall; I came down on my side.'

'Well,' said Grandet, 'as today is Eugénie's birthday, I will mend your step for you. Somehow, you women-folk cannot manage to put your foot down in the corner, where it is still solid and safe.'

Grandet took up the candle, left the three women without any other illumination in the room than the bright dancing firelight, and went to the bakehouse, where tools, nails, and odd pieces of wood were kept.

'Do you want any help?' Nanon called to him, when the first blow sounded on the staircase.

'No! no! I am an old hand at it,' answered the cooper.

At this very moment, while Grandet was doing the repairs himself to his worm-eaten staircase, and whist-ling with all his might as memories of his young days came up in his mind, the three Cruchots knocked at the house door.

'Oh, it's you, is it, Monsieur Cruchot?' asked Nanon, as she took a look through the small square grating.

'Yes,' answered the magistrate.

Nanon opened the door, and the glow of the firelight shone on the three Cruchots, who were groping in the archway.

'Oh! you have come to help us keep her birthday,' Nanon said, as the scent of flowers reached her.

'Excuse me a moment, gentlemen,' cried Grandet, who recognized the voices of his acquaintances; 'I'll be with you in a moment! There is no pride about me; I am patching up a broken stair here myself.'

'Go on, go on, Monsieur Grandet! The charcoal burner is mayor in his own house,' said the magistrate sententiously. Nobody saw the allusion, and he had his laugh all to himself.

Mme and Mlle Grandet rose to greet them. The magistrate took advantage of the darkness to speak to Eugénie.

'Will you permit me, mademoiselle, on the anniversary of your birthday, to wish you a long succession of prosperous years, and may you for long preserve the health with which you are blessed at present.'

He then offered her such a bouquet of flowers as was seldom seen in Saumur; and taking the heiress by both arms, gave her a kiss on either side of the throat, a fervent salute which brought the colour into Eugénie's face. The magistrate was tall and thin, somewhat resembling a rusty nail; this was his notion of paying court.

'Do not disturb yourselves,' said Grandet, coming back into the room. 'Fine doings these of yours, Monsieur le Président, on high days and holidays!'

'With mademoiselle beside him every day would be a holiday for my nephew,' answered the Abbé Cruchot, also armed with a bouquet; and with that the abbé kissed Eugénie's hand. As for M. Cruchot, he kissed her unceremoniously on both cheeks, saying, 'This sort of thing makes us feel older, eh? A whole year older every twelve months.'

Grandet set down the candle in front of the brass clock on the chimney-piece; whenever a joke amused him he kept on repeating it till it was worn threadbare; he did so now.

'As today is Eugénie's birthday,' he said, 'let us have an illumination.'

He carefully removed the branches from the two sconces, fitted the sockets into either pedestal, took from Nanon's hands a whole new candle wrapped in a scrap of paper, fixed it firmly in the socket, and lighted it. Then he went over to his wife and took up his position beside her, looking by turns at his daughter, his friends, and the two lighted candles.

The Abbé Cruchot was a fat, dumpy little man with a well-worn sandy peruke. His peculiar type of face might have belonged to some old lady whose life is spent at the card table. At this moment he was stretching out his feet and displaying a very neat and strong pair of shoes with silver buckles on them.

'The des Grassins have not come round?' he asked.

'Not yet,' answered Grandet.

'Are they sure to come?' put in the old notary, with various contortions of a countenance as full of holes as a colander.

'Oh! yes, I think they will come,' said Mme Grandet.

'Is the vintage over?' asked Président de Bonfons, addressing Grandet; 'are all your grapes gathered?'

'Yes, everywhere!' answered the old vine-grower, rising and walking up and down the length of the room; he straightened himself up as he spoke with a conscious pride that appeared in that word 'everywhere'.

As he passed by the door that opened into the passage, Grandet caught a glimpse of the kitchen; the fire was still alight, a candle was burning there, and big Nanon was about to begin her spinning by the hearth; she did not wish to intrude upon the birthday party.

'Nanon!' he called, stepping out into the passage, 'Nanon! why ever don't you rake out the fire, put out the candle and come in here! *Goodness!* the room is large enough to hold us all.'

'But you are expecting grand visitors, sir.'

'Have you any objection to them? They are all descended from Adam just as much as you are.'

Grandet went back to the president.

'Have you sold your wine?' he inquired.

'Not I; I am holding it. If the wine is good now, it will be better still in two years' time. The growers, as you know, of course, are in a ring, and mean to keep prices up. The Belgians shall not have it all their own way this year. And if they go away, well and good, let them go; they will come back again.'

'Yes; but we must hold firm,' said Grandet in a tone that made the magistrate shudder.

'Suppose he should sell his wine behind our backs?' he thought.

At that moment another knock at the door announced the des Grassins, and interrupted a quiet talk between Mme Grandet and the Abbé Cruchot.

Mme des Grassins was a dumpy, lively, little person with a pink-and-white complexion, one of those women for whom the course of life in a country town has flowed on with almost claustral tranquillity, and who, thanks to this regular and virtuous existence, are still youthful at the age of forty. They are something like the late roses in autumn, which are fair and pleasant to the sight, but the almost scentless petals have a pinched look, there is a vague suggestion of coming winter about them. She dressed tolerably well, her gowns came from Paris, she was a leader of society in Saumur, and received on certain evenings. Her husband had been a quartermaster in the Imperial Guard, but he had retired from the army with a pension, after being badly wounded at Austerlitz. In spite of his consideration for Grandet, he still retained, or affected to retain, the bluff manners of a soldier.

'Good day, Grandet,' he said, holding out his hand to the cooper with that wonted air of superiority with which he eclipsed the Cruchot faction. 'Mademoiselle,' he added, addressing Eugénie, after a bow to Mme Grandet, 'you are always charming, ever good and fair, and what more can one wish you?'

With that he presented her with a small box, which a servant was carrying, and which contained a Cape heath, a plant only recently introduced into Europe, and very rare.

Mme des Grassins embraced Eugénie very affectionately, squeezed her hand, and said, 'I have commissioned Adolphe to give you my little birthday gift.'

A tall, fair-haired young man, somewhat pallid and weakly in appearance, came forward at this; his manners were passably good, although he seemed to be shy. He had just completed his law studies in Paris, where he had managed to spend eight or ten thousand francs over and above his allowance. He now kissed Eugénie on both cheeks, and laid a workbox with gilded silver fittings before her; it was a showy, trumpery thing enough, in spite of the little shield on the lid, on which an E. G. had been engraved in Gothic characters, a detail which gave an imposing air to the whole. Eugénie raised the lid with a little thrill of pleasure, the happiness was as complete as it was unlooked for – the happiness that brings bright colour into a young girl's face and makes her tremble with delight. Her eyes turned to her father as if to ask whether she might accept the gift; M. Grandet answered the mute inquiry with a 'Take it, my daughter!' in tones which would have made the reputation of an actor. The three Cruchots stood dumbfounded when they saw the bright, delighted glance that Adolphe des Grassins received from the heiress, who seemed to be dazzled by such undreamed-of splendours.

M. des Grassins offered his snuff-box to Grandet, took a pinch himself, brushed off a few stray specks from his blue coat and from the ribbon of the Legion of Honour at his button-hole, and looked at the Cruchots, as who should say, 'Parry that thrust if you can!' Mme des Grassins's eyes fell on the blue glass jars in which the Cruchots' bouquets had been set. She looked at their gifts with the innocent air of pretended interest which a satirical woman knows how to assume upon occasion. It was a delicate crisis. The abbé got up and left the others, who were forming a circle round the fire, and walked with Grandet to the other end of the room. When the two elders had reached the embrasure of the window at the further end, away from the group by the fire, the priest said in the miser's ear: 'Those people yonder are throwing their money out of the windows.'

'What does that matter to me so long as it comes my way?' the old vine-grower answered.

'If you had a mind to give your daughter golden scissors, you could very well afford it,' said the abbé.

'I shall give her something better than scissors,' Grandet answered.

'What an idiot my nephew is!' thought the abbé, as he looked at the magistrate, whose dark, ill-favoured countenance was set off to perfection at that moment by a shock head of hair. 'Why couldn't *he* have hit on some expensive piece of foolery?'

'We will take a hand at cards, Madame Grandet,' said Mme des Grassins.

'But as we are all here, there are enough of us for two tables . . .'

'As today is Eugénie's birthday, why not all play together at lotto?' said old Grandet; 'these two children could join in the game.'

The old cooper, who never played at any game whatever, pointed to his daughter and Adolphe.

'Here, Nanon, move the tables out.'

'We will help you, Mademoiselle Nanon,' said Mme des Grassins cheerfully; she was thoroughly pleased, because she had pleased Eugénie.

'I have never seen anything so pretty anywhere,' the heiress said to her. 'I have never been so happy in my life before.'

'It was Adolphe who chose it,' said Mme des Grassins in the girl's ear; 'he brought it from Paris.'

'Go your ways, accursed scheming woman,' muttered the magistrate to himself. 'If you or your husband ever find yourselves in a court of law, you shall be hard put to it to gain the day.'

The notary, calmly seated in his corner, watched the abbé, and said to himself, 'The des Grassins may do what they like; my fortune and my brother's and my nephew's fortunes altogether mount up to eleven hundred thousand francs. The des Grassins, at the very most, have only half as much, and they have a daughter. Let them give whatever they like, all will be ours some day – the heiress and her presents too.'

Two tables were in readiness by half-past eight o'clock. Mme des Grassins, with her winning ways, had succeeded in placing her son next to Eugénie. The actors in the scene, so commonplace in appearance, so full of interest beneath the surface, each provided with slips of pasteboard of various colours and blue glass counters, seemed to be listening to the little jokes made by the old notary, who never drew a number without making some remark upon it, but they were all thinking of M. Grandet's millions. The old cooper himself eyed the group with a certain self-complacency; he looked at Mme des Grassins with her pink feathers and fresh toilette, at the banker's soldierly face, at Adolphe, at the magistrate, at the abbé and the notary, and within himself he said, 'They are all after my crowns; that is what they are here for. It is for my daughter that they come to be bored here. Aha! and my daughter is for none of them, and all these people are so many harpoons to be used in my fishing.'

The merriment of this family party, the laughter, only sincere when it came from Eugénie or her mother, and to which the low whirring of Nanon's spinning-wheel made an accompaniment, the sordid meanness playing for high stakes, the young girl herself, like some rare bird, the innocent victim of its high value, tracked down and snared by specious pretences of friendship; taken altogether, it was a sorry comedy that was being played in the old grey-painted parlour, by the dim light of the two candles. Was it not, however, a drama of all time, played out everywhere all over the world, but here reduced to its simplest expression? Old Grandet towered above the other actors, turning all this sham affection to his own account, and reaping a rich harvest from this simulated friendship. His face hovered above the scene like the interpretation of an evil dream. He was like the incarnation of the one god who yet finds worshippers in modern times, of Money and the power of wealth.

With him the gentler and sweeter impulses of human life only occupied the second place; but they so filled three purer hearts there, that there was no room in them for other thoughts – the hearts of Nanon, and of Eugénie and her mother. And yet, how much ignorance mingled with their innocent simplicity! Eugénie and her mother knew nothing of Grandet's wealth; they saw everything through a medium of dim ideas peculiar to their own narrow world, and neither desired nor despised money, accustomed as they were to do without it. Nor were they conscious of an uncongenial atmosphere; the strength of their feelings, their inner life, made of them a strange exception in this gathering, wholly in-

tent upon material interest. Appalling is the condition
of man; there is no drop of happiness in his lot but has
its source in ignorance.

Just as Mme Grandet had won sixteen sous, the largest amount that had ever been punted beneath that
roof, and big Nanon was beaming with delight at the
sight of madame pocketing that splendid sum, there
was a knock at the house door, so sudden and so loud
that the women started on their chairs.

'No one in Saumur would knock in that way!' said
the notary.

'What do they thump like that for?' said Nanon. 'Do
they want to break our door down?'

'Who the devil is it?' cried Grandet.

Nanon took up one of the two candles and went to
open the door. Grandet followed her.

'Grandet! Grandet!' cried his wife; a vague terror
seized her, and she hurried to the door of the room.

The players all looked at each other.

'Suppose we go too?' said M. des Grassins. 'That
knock meant no good, it seemed to me.'

But M. des Grassins scarcely caught a glimpse of a
young man's face and of a porter who was carrying two
huge trunks and an assortment of carpet bags, before
Grandet turned sharply on his wife and said:

'Go back to your lotto, Madame Grandet, and leave
me to settle with this gentleman here.'

With that he slammed the parlour door, and the lotto
players sat down again, but they were too much excited
to go on with the game.

'Is it anyone who lives in Saumur, Monsieur des
Grassins?' his wife inquired.

'No; a traveller.'

'Then he must have come from Paris.'

'As a matter of fact,' said the notary, drawing out a
heavy antique watch, a couple of fingers' breadth in

thickness, and not unlike a Dutch punt in shape, 'as a matter of fact, it is nine o'clock. *Peste!* the mail coach is not often behind time.'

'Is he young looking?' put in the Abbé Cruchot.

'Yes,' answered M. des Grassins. 'The luggage he has with him must weight three hundred kilos at least.'

'Nanon does not come back,' said Eugénie.

'It must be some relation of yours,' the president remarked.

'Let us put down our stakes,' said Mme Grandet gently. 'Monsieur Grandet was vexed, I could tell that by the sound of his voice, and perhaps he would be displeased if he came in and found us all discussing his affairs.'

'Mademoiselle,' Adolphe addressed his neighbour, 'it will be your cousin Grandet no doubt, a very nice-looking young fellow whom I once met at a ball at Monsieur de Nucingen's.'

Adolphe went no further, his mother stamped on his foot under the table. Aloud, she asked him for two sous for his stake, adding in an undertone, meant only for his ears, 'Will you hold your tongue, you great silly!'

They could hear the footsteps of Nanon and the porter on the staircase, but Grandet returned to the room almost immediately, and just behind him came the traveller who had excited so much curiosity, and loomed so large in the imaginations of those assembled; indeed, his sudden descent into their midst might be compared to the arrival of a snail in a beehive, or the entrance of a peacock into some humdrum village poultry-yard.

'Take a seat near the fire,' said Grandet, addressing the stranger.

The young man looked round the room and bowed very gracefully before seating himself. The men rose and bowed politely in return, the women curtsied rather ceremoniously.

'You are feeling cold, I expect, sir,' said Mme Grandet; 'you have no doubt come from –'

'Just like the women!' broke in the goodman, looking up from the letter which he held in his hand. 'Do let the gentleman have a little peace.'

'But, father, perhaps the gentleman wants something after his journey,' said Eugénie.

'He has a tongue in his head,' the vine-grower answered severely.

The stranger alone felt any surprise at this scene, the rest were quite used to the worthy man and his arbitrary behaviour. But after the two inquiries had received these summary answers, the stranger rose and stood with his back to the fire, held out a foot to the blaze, so as to warm the soles of his boots, and said to Eugénie, 'Thank you, cousin, I dined at Tours. And I do not require anything,' he added, glancing at Grandet, 'I am not in the least tired.'

'Do you come from Paris?' (it was Mme des Grassins who now put the inquiry).

M. Charles (for this was the name borne by the son of M. Grandet of Paris), hearing someone question him, took out an eyeglass that hung suspended from his neck by a cord, fixed it in his eye, made a deliberate survey of the objects upon the table and of the people sitting round it, eyed Mme des Grassins very coolly, and said (when he had completed his survey), 'Yes, madame. You are playing at lotto, aunt,' he added; 'pray go on with your game, it is too amusing to be broken off . . .'

'I knew it was the cousin,' thought Mme des Grassins, and she gave him a side-glance from time to time.

'Forty-seven,' cried the old abbé. 'Keep count. Madame des Grassins, that is your number, is it not?'

M. des Grassins put down a counter on his wife's card; the lady herself was not thinking of lotto, her mind was full of melancholy forebodings, she was

watching Eugénie and the cousin from Paris. She saw
how the heiress now and then stole a glance at her
cousin, and the banker's wife could easily discover in
those glances a *crescendo* of amazement or of curiosity.

There was certainly a strange contrast between
M. Charles Grandet, a handsome young man of two-
and-twenty, and the worthy provincials, who, tolerably
disgusted already with his aristocratic airs, were scornfully studying the stranger with a view to making game
of him. This requires some explanation.

At two-and-twenty childhood is not so very far away,
and youth, on the borderland, has not finally and for
ever put away childish things; Charles Grandet's vanity
was childish, but perhaps ninety-nine young men out of
a hundred would have been carried away by it and behaved exactly as he did.

Some days previously his father had bidden him to
go on a visit of several months to his uncle in Saumur;
perhaps M. Grandet (of Paris) had Eugénie in his mind.
Charles, launched in this way into a county town for the
first time in his life, had his own ideas. He would make
his appearance in provincial society with all the superiority of a young man of fashion; he would reduce the
neighbourhood to despair by his splendour; he would
inaugurate a new epoch, and introduce all the latest and
most ingenious refinement of Parisian luxury. To be
brief, he meant to devote more time at Saumur than in
Paris to the care of his nails, and to carry out schemes of
elaborate and studied refinements in dress at his
leisure; there should be none of the not ungraceful
negligence of attire which a young man of fashion
sometimes affects.

So Charles took with him into the country the most
charming of shooting costumes, the sweetest thing in
hunting-knives and sheaths, and a perfect beauty of a
rifle. He packed up a most tasteful collection of waist-

coats; grey, white, black, beetle-green shot with gold, speckled and spangled; double waistcoats, waistcoats with rolled collars, stand-up collars, turned-down collars, open at the throat, buttoned up to the chin with a row of gold buttons. He took examples of all the ties and cravats in favour at that epoch. He took two of Buisson's coats. He took his finest linen, and the dressing-case with gold fittings that his mother had given him. He took all his dandy's paraphernalia, not forgetting an enchanting little writing-case, the gift of the most amiable of women (for him at least), a great lady whom he called Annette, and who at that moment was travelling with her husband in Scotland, a victim to suspicions which demanded the temporary sacrifice of her happiness; hence, also, Charles took a great deal of very tasteful letter-paper on which to write to her every fortnight.

In short, his cargo of Parisian frivolities was as complete as it was possible to make it; nothing had been omitted, from the horse-whip, useful for beginning a duel, to the pair of richly chased and mounted pistols that end one. There was all the ploughing gear required by a young idler in the field of life.

His father had told him to travel alone and modestly, and he had obeyed. He had come in the coupé of the diligence, which he secured all to himself; and was not ill-satisfied to save wear, in this way, to a smart and comfortable travelling carriage which he had ordered, and in which he meant to go to meet his Annette, the aforesaid great lady who ... etc., and whom he was to rejoin next June at Baden-Baden.

Charles expected to meet scores of people during his visit to his uncle; he expected to have some shooting on his uncle's land; he expected, in short, to find a large house on a large estate; he had not thought to find his relatives in Saumur at all; he had only found out that they lived there by asking the way at Froidfond, and even after this discovery he expected to see them in a large mansion. But whether his uncle lived in Saumur or at Froidfond, he was determined to make his first appearance properly, so he had assumed a most fascinating travelling costume, made with the simplicity that is the perfection of art, a most *adorable* creation, to use the word which in those days expressed superlative praise of the special qualities of a thing or of a man. At Tours he had summoned a hairdresser, and his handsome chestnut hair was curled afresh. He had changed his linen and put on a black satin cravat, which, in combination with a round collar, made a very becoming setting for a pale and satirical face. A long overcoat, fitting tightly at the waist, gave glimpses of a cashmere waistcoat with a rolled collar, and beneath this again a second waistcoat of some white material. His watch was carelessly thrust into a side pocket, and save in so far as a gold chain secured it to a buttonhole, its continuance there appeared to be purely accidental. His grey trousers were buttoned at the sides, and the seams were adorned with designs embroidered in black silk. A pair of grey gloves had nothing to dread from contact with a gold-headed cane, which he managed to admiration. A discriminating taste was evinced throughout the costume, and shone conspicuous in the travelling cap. Only a Parisian, and a Parisian moreover from some remote and lofty sphere, could trick himself out in such attire, and bring all its absurd details into harmony by coxcombry carried to such a pitch that it ceased to be ridiculous; this young man carried it off, moreover, with a swaggering air befitting a dead shot, conscious of the possession of a handsome pair of pistols and the good graces of an Annette.

If, moreover, you wish to thoroughly understand the surprise with which the Saumurois and the young

Parisian mutually regarded each other, you must behold, as did the former, the radiant vision of this elegant
traveller shining in the gloomy old room, as well as the
figures that composed the family picture that met the
stranger's eyes. There sat the Cruchots; try to imagine
them.

To begin with, all three took snuff, with utter disregard of personal cleanliness or of the black deposit with
which their shirt frills were encrusted. Their limp silk
handkerchiefs were twisted into a thick rope, and
wound tightly about their necks. Their collars were
crumpled and soiled, their linen was dingy; there was
such a vast accumulation of underwear in their presses,
that it was only necessary to wash twice in the year, and
the linen acquired a bad colour with lying by. Age and
ugliness might have wrought together to produce a
masterpiece in them. Their hard-featured, furrowed,
and wrinkled faces were in keeping with their creased
and threadbare clothing, and both they and their gar-
ments were worn, shrunken, twisted out of shape.
Dwellers in country places are apt to grow more or less
slovenly and careless of their appearance; they cease by
degrees to dress for others; the career of a pair of gloves
is indefinitely prolonged, there is a general want of
freshness and a decided neglect of detail. The sloven-
liness of the Cruchots, therefore, was not conspicuous;
they were in harmony with the rest of the company, for
there was one point on which both Cruchotins and
Grassinistes were agreed for the most part – they held
the fashions in horror.

The Parisian assumed his eyeglass again in order to
study the curious accessories of the room; his eyes
travelled over the rafters in the ceiling, over the dingy
panels covered with fly-spots in sufficient abundance to
punctuate the whole of the *Encyclopédie méthodique* and
the *Moniteur* besides. The lotto-players looked up at

this and stared at him; if a giraffe had been in their midst they could hardly have gazed with more eager curiosity. Even M. des Grassins and his son, who had beheld a man of fashion before in the course of their lives, shared in the general amazement; perhaps they felt the indefinable influence of the general feeling about the stranger, perhaps they regarded him not un-approvingly. 'You see how they dress in Paris,' their sat-irical glances seemed to say to their neighbours.

One and all were at liberty to watch Charles at their leisure, without any fear of offending the master of the house, for by this time Grandet was deep in a long letter which he held in his hand. He had taken the only candle from the table beside him, without any re-gard for the convenience of his guests or for their pleasure.

It seemed to Eugénie, who had never in her life be-held such a paragon, that her cousin was some seraphic vision, some creature fallen from the skies. The per-fume exhaled by those shining locks, so gracefully curled, was delightful to her. She would fain have passed her fingers over the delicate, smooth surface of those wonderful gloves. She envied Charles his little hands, his complexion, the youthful refinement of his features. In fact, the sight of her cousin gave her the same sensations of exquisite pleasure that might be aroused in a young man by the contemplation of the fanciful portraits of ladies in English *Keepsakes*, portraits drawn by Westall and engraved by Finden, with a burin so skilful that you fear to breathe upon the vellum sur-face lest the celestial vision should disappear. And yet – how should the impression produced by a young ex-quisite upon an ignorant girl whose life was spent in darning stockings and mending her father's clothes, in the dirty wainscoted window embrasure whence, in an hour, she saw scarcely one passer-by in the silent street, how should her dim impressions be conveyed by such an image as this?

Charles drew from his pocket a handkerchief embroidered by the great lady who was travelling in Scotland. It was a dainty piece of work wrought by love, in hours that were lost to love; Eugénie gazed at her cousin, and wondered, was he really going to use it? Charles's manners, his way of adjusting his eyeglass, his superciliousness, his affectations, his manifest contempt for the little box which had but lately given so much pleasure to the wealthy heiress, and which in his eyes seemed to be a very absurd piece of rubbish; everything, in short, which had given offence to the Cruchots and the Grassinistes pleased Eugénie so much that she lay awake for long that night thinking about this phoenix of a cousin.

Meanwhile the numbers were drawn but languidly, and very soon the lotto came to an end altogether. Big Nanon came into the room and said aloud, 'Madame, you will have to give me some sheets to make the gentleman's bed.'

Mme Grandet disappeared with Nanon, and Mme des Grassins said in a low voice, 'Let us keep our sous, and give up the game.'

Each player took back his coin from the chipped saucer which held the stakes. Then there was a general stir, and a wheeling movement in the direction of the fire.

'Is the game over?' inquired Grandet, still reading his letter.

'Yes, yes,' answered Mme des Grassins, seating herself next to Charles.

Eugénie left the room to help her mother and Nanon, moved by a thought that came with the vague feeling that stirred her heart for the first time. If she had been questioned by a skilful confessor, she would have no doubt admitted that her thought was neither for Nanon nor for her mother, but that she was seized with a restless and urgent desire to see that all was right in her cousin's room, to busy herself on her cousin's account, to see that nothing was forgotten, to think of everything he might require, and to make sure that it was there, to make certain that everything was as neat and pretty as might be. She alone, so Eugénie thought already, could enter into her cousin's ideas and understand his tastes.

As a matter of fact, she came just at the right moment. Her mother and Nanon were about to leave the room in the belief that it was all in readiness; Eugénie convinced them in a moment that everything was yet to do. She filled Nanon's head with these ideas: the sheets had not been aired, Nanon must bring the warming-pan, there were ashes, there was a fire downstairs. She herself covered the old table with a clean white cloth, and told Nanon to mind and be sure to change it every morning. There must be a good fire in the room; she overcame her mother's objections, she induced Nanon to put a good supply of firewood outside in the passage, and to say nothing about it to her father. She ran downstairs into the parlour, sought in one of the sideboards for an old japanned tray which had belonged to the late M. de la Bertellière, and from the same source she procured a hexagonal crystal glass, a little gilt spoon with almost all the gilding rubbed off, and an old slender-necked glass bottle with Cupids engraved upon it; these she deposited in triumph on a corner of the chimney-piece. More ideas had crowded up in her mind during that one quarter of an hour than in all the years since she had come into the world.

'Mamma,' she began, 'he will never be able to bear the smell of a tallow candle. Suppose that we buy a wax candle?'

She fled, lightly as a bird, to find her purse, and drew thence the five francs which she had received for the month's expenses.

'Here, Nanon, be quick.'

'But what will your father say?'

This dreadful objection was raised by Mme Grandet, when she saw her daughter with an old Sèvres china sugar-basin which Grandet had brought back with him from the château at Froidfond.

'And where is the sugar to come from?' she went on. 'Are you mad?'

'Nanon can easily buy the sugar when she goes for the candle, mamma.'

'But how about your father?'

'Is it a right thing that his nephew should not have a glass of *eau sucrée* to drink if he happens to want it? Besides, he will not notice it.'

'Your father always notices things,' said Mme Grandet, shaking her head.

Nanon hesitated; she knew her master.

'Do go, Nanon; it is my birthday today, you know!'

Nanon burst out laughing in spite of herself at the first joke her young mistress had ever been known to make, and did her bidding.

While Eugénie and her mother were doing their best to adorn the room which M. Grandet had allotted to his nephew, Mme des Grassins was bestowing her attention on Charles, and making abundant use of her eyes as she did so.

'You are very brave,' she said, 'to leave the pleasures of the capital in winter in order to come to stay in Saumur. But if you are not frightened away at first sight of us, you shall see that even here we can amuse ourselves.' And she gave him a languishing glance, in true provincial style.

Women in the provinces are wont to affect a demure and staid demeanour, which gives a furtive and eager eloquence to their eyes, a peculiarity which may be noted in ecclesiastics, for whom every pleasure is stolen or forbidden. Charles was so thoroughly out of his element in this room, it was all so far removed from the great château and the splendid surroundings in which he had thought to find his uncle, that, on paying closer attention to Mme des Grassins, she almost reminded him of Parisian faces half obliterated already by these strange, new impressions. He responded graciously to the advances which had been made to him, and naturally they fell into conversation.

Mme des Grassins gradually lowered her voice to tones suited to the nature of her confidences. Both she and Charles Grandet felt a need of mutual confidence, of explanations and an understanding; so after a few minutes spent in coquettish chatter and jests that covered a serious purpose, the wily provincial dame felt free to converse without fear of being overheard, under cover of a conversation on the sale of the vintage, the one all-absorbing topic at that moment in Saumur.

'If you will honour us with a visit,' she said, 'you will certainly do us a pleasure; my husband and I shall be very glad to see you. Our *salon* is the only one in Saumur where you will meet both the wealthy merchant society and the *noblesse*. We ourselves belong in a manner to both; they do not mix with each other at all except at our house; they come to us because they find it amusing. My husband, I am proud to say, is very highly thought of in both circles. So we will do our best to beguile the tedium of your stay. If you are going to remain with the Grandets, what will become of you? Bon Dieu! Your uncle is a miser, his mind runs on nothing but his vine cuttings; your aunt is a saint who cannot put two ideas together; and your cousin is a silly little thing, a common sort of girl, with no breeding and no money, who spends her life in mending dish-cloths.'

''Tis a very pretty woman,' said Charles to himself; Mme des Grassins's coquettish glances had not been thrown away upon him.

'It seems to me that you mean to monopolize the gentleman,' said the big banker, laughing, to his wife, an unlucky observation, followed by remarks more or less spiteful from the notary and the president; but the abbé gave them a shrewd glance, took a pinch of snuff, and handed his snuff-box to the company, while he gave expression to their thoughts. 'Where could the gentleman have found anyone better qualified to do the honours of Saumur?' he said.

'Come, abbé, what do you mean by that?' asked M. des Grassins.

'It is meant, sir, in the most flattering sense for you, for madame, for the town of Saumur, and for this gentleman,' added the shrewd ecclesiastic, turning towards Charles. Without appearing to pay the slightest heed to their talk, he had managed to guess the drift of it.

Adolphe des Grassins spoke at last, with what was meant to be an off-hand manner. 'I do not know,' he said, addressing Charles, 'whether you have any recollection of me; I once had the pleasure of dancing in the same quadrille at a ball given by Monsieur le Baron de Nucingen, and –'

'I remember it perfectly,' answered Charles, surprised to find himself the object of general attention.

'Is this gentleman your son?' he asked of Mme des Grassins.

The abbé gave her a spiteful glance.

'Yes, I am his mother,' she answered.

'You must have been very young when you came to Paris?' Charles went on, speaking to Adolphe.

'We cannot help ourselves, sir,' said the abbé. 'Our babes are scarcely weaned before we send them to Babylon.'

Mme des Grassins gave the abbé a strangely penetrating glance; she seemed to be seeking the meaning of those words.

'You must go into the country,' the abbé went on, 'if you want to find women not much on the other side of thirty, with a grown-up son a licentiate of law, who look as fresh and youthful as Madame des Grassins. It only seems like the other day when the young men and the ladies stood on chairs to see you dance, madame,' the abbé added, turning towards his fair antagonist; 'your triumphs are as fresh in my memory as if they had happened yesterday.'

'Oh! the old wretch!' said Mme des Grassins to herself, 'is it possible that he has guessed?'

'It looks as though I should have a great success in Saumur,' thought Charles. He unbuttoned his overcoat and stood with his hand in his waistcoat pocket, gazing into space, striking the attitude which Chantrey thought fit to give to Byron in his statue of that poet.

Meanwhile Grandet's inattention, or rather his preoccupation, during the reading of his letter had escaped neither the notary nor the magistrate. Both of them tried to guess at the contents by watching the almost imperceptible changes in the worthy man's face, on which all the light of the candle was concentrated. The vine-grower was hard put to it to preserve his wonted composure. His expression must be left to the imagination, but here is the fatal letter:

MY BROTHER,

It is nearly twenty-three years now since we saw each other. The last time we met it was to make arrangements for my marriage, and we parted in high spirits. Little did I then think, when you were congratulating yourself on our prosperity, that one day you would be the sole hope and stay of our family. By the time that this letter reaches your hands, I shall be no more. In my position, I could not survive the disgrace of bankruptcy; I have held up my head above the surface till the last moment, hoping to weather the storm; it is all of no use, I must sink now. Just after the failure of my stockbroker came the failure of Roguin (my notary); my last resources have been swept away, and I have nothing left. It is my heavy misfortune to owe nearly four millions; my assets only amount to twenty-five per cent of my debts. I hold heavy stocks of wine, and owing to the abundance and good quality of your vintages, they have fallen ruinously in value. In three days' time all Paris will say, 'Monsieur Grandet was a rogue!' and I, honest though I am, shall lie wrapped in a winding-sheet of infamy. I have despoiled my own son of his mother's fortune and of the spotless name on which I have brought disgrace. He knows nothing of all this – the unhappy child whom I have idolized. Happily for him, he did not know when we bade each other good-bye, and my heart overflowed with tenderness for him, how soon it should cease to beat. Will he not curse me some day? Oh, my brother, my brother, a child's curse is an awful thing! If we curse our children, they may appeal against us, but their curses cling to us for ever! Grandet, you are my elder brother, you must shield me from this; do not let Charles say bitter things of me when I am lying in my grave. Oh, my brother, if every word in this letter were written in my tears, in my blood, it would not cost me such bitter anguish, for then I should be weeping, bleeding, dying, and the agony would be ended; but now I am still suffering – I see the death before me with dry eyes. You therefore are

Charles's father, now! He has no relations on his mother's side for reasons which you know. Why did I not defer to social prejudices? Why did I yield to love? Why did I marry the natural daughter of a noble? Charles is the last of his family; he is alone in the world. Oh, my unhappy boy, my son! . . . Listen, Grandet, I am asking nothing for myself, and you could scarcely satisfy my creditors if you would; your fortune cannot be sufficient to meet a demand of three millions; it is for my son's sake that I write. You must know, my brother, that as I think of you my petition is made with clasped hands; that this is my dying prayer to you. Grandet, I know that you will be a father to him; I know that I shall not ask in vain, and the sight of my pistols does not cause me a pang.

And then Charles is very fond of me; I was kind to him, I never said him nay; he will not curse me! For the rest, you will see how sweet-tempered and obedient he is; he takes after his mother; he will never give you any trouble, poor boy! He is accustomed to luxurious ways; he knows nothing of the hardships that you and I experienced in the early days when we were poor. . . And now he has not a penny, and he is alone in the world, for all his friends are sure to leave him, and it is I who have brought these humiliations upon him. Ah, if I had only the power to send him straight to heaven now, where his mother is! This is madness! To go back to my misfortunes and Charles's share in them. I have sent him to you so that you may break the news of my death and explain to him what his future must be. Be a father to him; ah, more than that, be an indulgent father! Do not expect him to give up his idle ways all at once; it would kill him. On my knees I beg him to renounce all claims to his mother's fortune; but I need not ask that of him, his sense of honour will prevent him from adding himself to the list of my creditors; see that he resigns his claims when the right time comes. And you must lay everything before him, Grandet – the struggle and the hardships that he will have to face in the life that I have spoiled for him; and then if he has any tenderness still left for me, tell him from me that all is not lost for him – be sure you tell him that. Work, which was our salvation, can restore the fortune which I have lost; and if he will listen to his father's voice, which would fain make itself heard yet a little while from the grave, let him leave this country and go to the Indies. And, brother, Charles is honest and energetic; you will help him with his first trading venture, I know you will; he would die sooner than not repay you; you will do as much as that for him, Grandet, or you will lay up regrets for yourself. Ah! if my boy finds no kindness and no help in you, I shall for ever pray God to punish your hard-heartedness. If I could have withheld a few payments, I might have saved a little sum for him – he surely has a right to some of his mother's fortune – but the payments at the end of the month taxed all my resources, and I could not manage it. I would fain have died with my mind at rest about his future; I wish I could have received your solemn promise, coming straight from your hand, it would have brought warmth with it for me; but time presses. Even while Charles is on his way, I am compelled to file my schedule. My affairs are all in order; I am endeavouring so to arrange everything that it will be evident that my failure is due neither to carelessness nor to dishonesty, but simply to disasters which I could not help. Is it not for Charles's sake that I take these pains? Farewell, my brother. May God bless you in every way for the generosity with which you (as I cannot doubt) will accept and fulfil this trust. There will be one voice that will never cease to pray for you in the world whither we must all go sooner or later, and where I am even now.

VICTOR-ANGE-GUILLAUME GRANDET.

'So you are having a chat?' said old Grandet, folding up the letter carefully in the original creases, and putting it into his waistcoat pocket.

He looked at his nephew in a shy and embarrassed way, seeking to dissemble his feelings and his calculations.

'Do you feel warmer?'

'I am very comfortable, my dear uncle.'

'Well, whatever are the women after?' his uncle went on; the fact that his nephew would sleep in the house had by that time slipped from his memory. Eugénie and Mme Grandet came into the room as he spoke.

'Is everything ready upstairs?' the goodman inquired. He had now quite recovered himself, and recollected the facts of the case.

'Yes, father.'

'Very well, then, nephew, if you are feeling tired, Nanon will show you to your room. Lord! there is nothing very smart about it, but you will overlook that here among poor vine-growers, who never have a penny to bless themselves with. The taxes swallow up everything we have.'

'We don't want to be intrusive, Grandet,' said the banker. 'You and your nephew may have some things to talk over; we will wish you good evening. Good-bye till to-morrow.'

Everyone rose at this, and took leave after their several fashions. The old notary went out under the archway to look for his lantern, lighted it, and offered to see the des Grassins to their house. Mme des Grassins had not been prepared for the event which had brought the evening so early to a close, and her maid had not appeared.

'Will you honour me by taking my arm, madame?' said the Abbé Cruchot, addressing Mme des Grassins.

'Thank you, Monsieur l'Abbé,' said the lady dryly; 'my son is with me.'

'I am not a compromising acquaintance for a lady,' the abbé continued.

'Take Monsieur Cruchot's arm,' said her husband.

The abbé, with the fair lady on his arm, walked on quickly for several paces, so as to put a distance between them and the rest of the party.

'That young man is very good-looking, madame,' he said, with a pressure on her arm to give emphasis to the remark. '''Tis good-bye to the baskets, the vintage is over! You must give up Mademoiselle Grandet; Eugénie is meant for her cousin. Unless he happens to be smitten with some fair face in Paris, your son Adolphe will have yet another rival –'

'Nonsense, Monsieur l'Abbé. It will not be long before the young man will find out that Eugénie is a girl who has nothing to say for herself; and she has gone off in looks. Did you notice her? She was yellow as a quince this evening.'

'Which, possibly, you have already pointed out to her cousin?'

'Indeed, I have not taken the trouble –'

'If you always sit beside Eugénie, madame,' interrupted the abbé, 'you will not need to tell the young man much about his cousin; he can make his own comparisons.'

'He promised me at once to come to dine with us the day after tomorrow.'

'Ah! madame,' said the abbé, 'if you would only . . .'

'Would only what, Monsieur l'Abbé? Do you mean to put evil suggestions into my mind? I have not come to the age of thirty-nine with a spotless reputation (heaven be thanked!) to compromise myself now – not for the empire of the Great Mogul! We are both of us old enough to know what that kind of talk means;

and I must say that your ideas do not square very well with your sacred calling. For shame! this is worthy of *Faublas*.'

'So you have read *Faublas*?'

'No, Monsieur l'Abbé; *Les Liaisons dangereuses* is what I meant to say.'

'Oh! that book is infinitely more moral,' said the abbé, laughing. 'But you would make me out to be as depraved as young men are nowadays. I only meant that you –'

'Do you dare to tell me that you meant no harm? The thing is plain enough. If that young fellow (who certainly is good-looking, that I grant you) paid court to me, it would not be for the sake of my interest with that cousin of his. In Paris, I know, there are tender mothers who sacrifice themselves thus for their children's happiness and welfare, but we are not in Paris, Monsieur l'Abbé.'

'Yes, madame.'

'And,' continued she, 'neither Adolphe nor I would purchase a hundred millions at such a price.'

'Madame, I said nothing about a hundred millions. Perhaps such a temptation might have been too much for either of us. Still, in my opinion, an honest woman may indulge in a little harmless coquetry, in the strictest propriety; it is a part of her social duties, and –'

'You think so?'

'Do we not owe it to ourselves, madame, to endeavour to be as agreeable as possible to others? . . . Permit me to blow my nose. Take my word for it, madame,' resumed the abbé, 'that he certainly regarded you with rather more admiration than he saw fit to bestow on me, but I can forgive him for honouring beauty rather than grey hairs –'

'It is perfectly clear,' said the president in his thick voice, 'why Monsieur Grandet of Paris is sending his son to Saumur; he has made up his mind to make a match –'

'Then why should the cousin have dropped from the skies like this?' answered the notary.

'There is nothing in that,' remarked M. des Grassins, 'old Grandet is so close.'

'Des Grassins,' said his wife, 'I have asked that young man to come and dine with us. So you must go to Monsieur and Madame de Larsonnière, dear, and ask them to come, and the du Hautoys; and they must bring that pretty girl of theirs, of course; I hope she will dress herself properly for once. Her mother is jealous of her, and makes her look such a figure. I hope that you gentlemen will do us the honour of coming too?' she added, stopping the procession in order to turn to the two Cruchots, who had fallen behind.

'Here we are at your door, madame,' said the notary. The three Cruchots took leave of the three des Grassins, and on their way home the talent for pulling each other to pieces, which provincials possess in perfection, was fully called into play; the great event of the evening was exhaustively discussed, and all its bearings upon the respective positions of Cruchotins and Grassinistes were duly considered. Clearly it behoved both alike to prevent Eugénie from falling in love with her cousin, and to hinder Charles from thinking of Eugénie. Sly hints, plausible insinuations, faint praise, vindications undertaken with an air of candid friendliness – what resistance could the Parisian offer when the air hurtled with deceptive weapons such as these?

As soon as the four relatives were left alone in the great room, M. Grandet spoke to his nephew:

'We must go to bed. It is too late to begin to talk tonight of the business that brought you here; tomorrow will be time enough for that. We have breakfast here at eight o'clock. At noon we take a snatch of something, a little fruit, a morsel of bread, and a glass of white wine, and, like Parisians, we dine at five o'clock. That is the way of it. If you care to take a look at the town, or to go into the country round about, you are quite free to do so. You will excuse me if, for business reasons, I cannot always accompany you. Very likely you will be told hereabouts that I am rich: 'tis always Monsieur Grandet here and Monsieur Grandet there. I let them talk. Their babble does not injure my credit in any way. But I have not a penny to bless myself with; and, old as I am, I work like any young journeyman who has nothing in the world but his plane and a pair of stout arms. Perhaps you will find out for yourself some of these days what a lot of work it takes to earn a crown when you have to toil and moil for it yourself. Here, Nanon, bring the candles.'

'I hope you will find everything you want, nephew,' said Mme Grandet; 'but if anything has been forgotten, you will call Nanon.'

'It would be difficult to want anything, my dear aunt, for I believe I have brought all my things with me. Permit me to wish you and my young cousin good night.'

Charles took a lighted wax candle from Nanon; it was a commodity of local manufacture, which had grown old in the shop, very dingy, very yellow, and so like the ordinary tallow variety that M. Grandet had no suspicion of the article of luxury before him; indeed, it never entered into his head to imagine that there could be such a thing in the house.

'I will show you the way,' said the goodman.

One of the doors in the dining-room gave immediate access to the archway and to the staircase; but tonight, out of compliment to his guest, Grandet went by way of the passage which separated the kitchen from the dining-room. A folding door, with a large oval pane of glass let into it, closed in the passage at the end nearest the staircase, an arrangement intended to keep out the blasts of cold air that rushed through the archway. With a like end in view, strips of list had been nailed to the doors; but in winter the east wind found its way in, and whistled none the less shrewdly about the house, and the dining-room was seldom even tolerably warm.

Nanon went out, drew the bolts on the entrance gate, fastened the door of the dining-room, went across to the stable to let loose a great wolf-dog with a cracked voice; it sounded as though the animal was suffering from laryngitis. His savage temper was well known, and Nanon was the only human being who could manage him. There was some wild strain in both these children of the fields; they understood each other.

Charles glanced round at the dingy yellow walls and smoke-begrimed ceiling, and saw how the crazy, worm-eaten stairs shook beneath his uncle's heavy tread; he was fast coming to his senses, this was sober reality indeed! The place looked like a hen-roost. He looked round questioningly at the faces of his aunt and cousin, but they were so thoroughly accustomed to the staircase and its peculiarities that it never occurred to them that it could cause any astonishment; they took his signal of distress for a simple expression of friendliness, and smiled back at him in the most amiable way. That smile was the last straw; the young man was at his wits' end.

'What the devil made my father send me here?' said he to himself.

Arriving on the first landing, he saw before him three doors painted a dull red-brown colour; there were no mouldings round any of them, so that they would have been scarcely visible in the dusty surface of the wall if it had not been for the very apparent heavy bars of iron with which they were embellished, and which terminated in a sort of rough ornamental design, as did the ends of the iron scutcheons which surrounded the keyholes. A door at the head of the stairs, which had once given entrance into the room over the kitchen, was evidently blocked up. As a matter of fact, the only entrance was through Grandet's own room, and this room over the kitchen was the vine-grower's sanctum.

Daylight was admitted into it by a single window which looked out upon the yard, and which, for greater security, was protected by a grating of massive iron bars. The master of the house allowed no one, not even Mme Grandet, to set foot in this chamber; he kept the right of entry to himself, and sat there, undisturbed and alone, like an alchemist in the midst of his crucibles. Here, no doubt, there was some cunningly contrived and secret hiding-place; for here he stored up the title-deeds of his estates; here, too, he kept the delicately adjusted scales in which he weighed his gold louis; and here every night he made out receipts, wrote acknowledgments of sums received, and laid his schemes, so that other businessmen seeing Grandet never busy, and always prepared for every emergency, might have been excused for imagining that he had a fairy or familiar spirit at his beck and call. Here, no doubt, when Nanon's snoring shook the rafters, when the savage watch-dog bayed and prowled about the yard, when Mme Grandet and Eugénie were fast asleep, the old cooper would come to be with his gold, and hug himself upon it, and toy with it, and fondle it, and brood over it, and so, with the intoxication of the gold upon him, at last to sleep. The walls were thick, the closed shutters kept their secret. He alone had the key of this laboratory, where, if reports spoke truly, he pored over plans on which every fruit tree belonging to him was mapped out, so that he could reckon out his crops, so much to every vine stem; and his yield of timber, to a faggot.

The door of Eugénie's room was opposite this closed-up portal; the room occupied by M. and Mme Grandet was at the end of the landing, and consisted of the entire front of the house. It was divided within by a partition; Mme Grandet's chamber was next to Eugénie's, with which it communicated by a glass door; the other half of the room, separated from the mysterious cabinet by a thick wall, belonged to the master of the house. Goodman Grandet had cunningly lodged his nephew on the second storey, in an airy garret immediately above his own room, so that he could hear every sound and inform himself of the young man's goings and comings, if the latter should take it into his head to leave his quarters.

Eugénie and her mother, arrived on the first landing, kissed each other, and said good night; they took leave of Charles in a few formal words, spoken with an apparent indifference, which in her heart the girl was far from feeling, and went to their rooms.

'This is your room, nephew,' said Grandet, addressing Charles as he opened the door. 'If you should wish to go out, you will have to call Nanon; for if you don't, it will be "no more at present from your most obedient", the dog will gobble you down before you know where you are. Good night, sleep well. Ha ha! the ladies have lighted a fire in your room,' he went on.

Just at that moment big Nanon appeared, armed with a warming-pan.

'Did anyone ever see the like?' said M. Grandet. 'Do you take my nephew for a woman in childbed? he is not an invalid. Be off, Nanon! you and your hot ashes.'

'But the sheets are damp, sir, and the gentleman looks as delicate as a woman.'

'All right, get on with it, since you have taken it into your head,' said Grandet, thrusting her in by the shoulders, 'but mind you don't set the place on fire,' and the miser groped his way downstairs, muttering to himself.

Charles, breathless with astonishment, was left among his trunks. He looked round about him, at the sloping roof of the attic, at the wallpaper of a pattern peculiar to little country inns, bunches of flowers symmetrically arranged on a buff-coloured background; he looked at the rough stone chimney-piece full of rifts and cracks (the mere sight of it sent a chill through him, in spite of the fire in the grate), at the ramshackle cane-seated chairs, at the open night-table large enough to hold a fair-sized sergeant-at-arms, at the strip of worn rag-carpet beside the canopied bedstead, at the curtains which shook every moment as if the whole worm-eaten structure would fall to pieces; finally, he turned his attention to big Nanon, and said earnestly:

'Look here, my good girl, am I really in Monsieur Grandet's house? Monsieur Grandet, formerly Mayor of Saumur, and brother of Monsieur Grandet of Paris?'

'Yes, sir, you are; and you are staying with a very kind, a very amiable and excellent gentleman. Am I to help you to unpack those trunks of yours?'

'Faith, yes, old soldier, I wish you would. Did you serve in the horse marines?'

'Oh! oh! oh!' chuckled Nanon. 'What may they be? What are the horse marines? Are they old salts? Do they go to sea?'

'Here, look out my dressing-gown; it is in that portmanteau, and this is the key.'

Nanon was overcome with astonishment at the sight of a green silk dressing-gown, embroidered with gold flowers after an antique pattern.

'Are you going to sleep in *that*?' she inquired.

'Yes.'

'Holy Virgin! What a beautiful altar cloth it would make for the parish church! Oh, my dear young gentleman, you should give it to the Church, and you will save your soul, which you are like to lose for that thing. Oh, how nice you look in it! I will go and call mademoiselle to look at you.'

'Come now, Nanon, since that is your name, will you hold your tongue and let me go to bed? I will set my things straight tomorrow, and as you have taken such a fancy to my gown, you shall have a chance to save your soul. I am too good a Christian to take it away with me when I go; you shall have it, and you can do whatever you like with it.'

Nanon stood stock-still, staring at Charles; she could not bring herself to believe that he really meant what he said.

'You are going to give that grand dressing-gown to *me*!' she said, as she turned to go. 'The gentleman is dreaming already. Good night.'

'Good night, Nanon. – Whatever am I doing here?' said Charles to himself, as he dropped off to sleep. 'My father is no fool; I have not been sent here for nothing. Pooh! "Serious business tomorrow," as some old Greek wiseacre used to say.'

'*Sainte Vierge!* how nice he is!' said Eugénie to herself in the middle of her prayers, and that night they remained unfinished.

Mme Grandet alone lay down to rest with no thought in her quiet mind. Through the door in the thin partition she could hear her husband pacing to and fro in his room. Like all sensitive and timid women, she had thoroughly studied the character of her lord and master. Just as the sea-mew foresees the coming storm, she knew by almost imperceptible signs that a tempest was raging in Grandet's mind, and, to use her own expression, she 'lay like one dead' at such seasons. Grandet's eyes turned towards his sanctum; he looked at the door, which was lined with sheet iron on the inner side (he himself had seen to that), and muttered, 'What a preposterous notion this is of my brother's, to leave his child to me! A pretty legacy! I haven't twenty crowns to spare, and what would twenty crowns be to a popinjay like that, who looked at my weather-glass as if it wasn't fit to light the fire with?'

And Grandet, meditating on the probable outcome of this mournful dying request, was perhaps more perturbed in spirit than the brother who had made it.

'Shall I really have that golden gown?' Nanon said, and she fell asleep wrapped round in her altar cloth, dreaming for the first time in her life of shining embroideries and flowered brocade, just as Eugénie dreamed of love.

In a girl's innocent and uneventful life there comes a mysterious hour of joy when the sunlight spreads through the soul, and it seems to her that the flowers express the thoughts that rise within her, thoughts that are quickened by every heart-beat, only to blend in a vague feeling of longing, when the days are filled with innocent melancholy and delicious happiness. Children smile when they see the light for the first time, and when a girl dimly divines the presence of love in the world she smiles as she smiled in her babyhood. If light is the first thing that we learn to love, is not love like light in the heart? This moment had come for Eugénie; she saw the things of life clearly for the first time.

Early rising is the rule in the country, so, like most other girls, Eugénie was up betimes in the morning; this morning she rose earlier than usual, said her prayers, and began to dress; her toilette was henceforth to possess an interest unknown before. She began by brushing her chestnut hair, and wound the heavy plaits about her head, careful that no loose ends should escape from the braided coronet which made an appropriate setting for a face both frank and shy, a simple coiffure which harmonized with the girlish outlines.

As she washed her hands again and again in the cold spring water that roughened and reddened the skin, she looked down at her pretty rounded arms and wondered what her cousin did to have hands so soft and so white, and nails so shapely. She put on a pair of new stockings, and her best shoes, and laced herself carefully, without passing over a single eyelet-hole. For the first time in her life, in fact, she wished to look her best, and felt that it was pleasant to have a pretty new dress to wear, a becoming dress which was nicely made.

The church clock struck just as she had finished dressing; she counted the strokes, and was surprised to find that it was still only seven o'clock. She had been so anxious to have plenty of time for her toilette, that she had risen too early, and now there was nothing left to do. Eugénie, in her ignorance, never thought of studying the position of a tress of hair, and of altering it a dozen times to criticize its effect; she simply folded her arms, sat down by the window, and looked out upon the yard, the long strip of garden, and the terraced gardens up above upon the ramparts.

It was a somewhat dreary outlook thus shut in by the grim rock walls, but not without a charm of its own, the mysterious beauty of quiet over-shaded gardens, or of wild and solitary places. Under the kitchen window there was a well with a stone coping round it; a pulley was suspened above the water from an iron bracket overgrown by a vine; the vine-leaves were red and faded now that the autumn was nearly at an end, and the crooked stem was plainly visible as it wound its way to the house wall, and crept along the house till it came to an end by the wood stack, where the faggots were arranged with as much neatness and precision as the volumes on some book-lover's shelves. The flag-stones in the yard were dark with age and mosses, and dank with the stagnant air of the place; weeds grew here and there among the chinks. The massive outworks of the old fortifications were green with moss, with here and there a long dark brown streak where water dripped, and the eight tumbledown steps, which gave access to the garden at the further end of the yard, were almost hidden by a tall growth of plants; the general effect of the crumbling stones had a vague resemblance to some crusader's tomb erected by his widow in the days of yore and long since fallen into ruin.

Along the low mouldering stone wall there was a fence of open lattice-work, rotten with age, and fast falling to pieces; overrun by various creeping plants that clambered over it at their own sweet will. A couple of stunted apple trees spread out their gnarled and twisted branches on either side of the wicket gate that led into the garden – three straight gravel walks with strips of border in between, and a line of box-edging on either side; and, at the further end, underneath the ramparts, a sort of arbour of lime trees, and a row of raspberry canes. A huge walnut tree grew at the end nearest to the house, and almost overshadowed the cooper's strong-room with its spreading branches.

It was one of those soft bright autumn mornings peculiar to the districts along the Loire; there was not a trace of mist; the light frosty rime of the previous night was rapidly disappearing as the mild rays of the autumn sun shone on the picturesque surroundings, the old walls, the green tangled growth in the yard and garden.

All these things had been long familiar to Eugénie's eyes, but today it seemed to her that there was a new beauty about them. A throng of confused thoughts filled her mind as the sunbeams overflowed the world without. A vague, inexplicable new happiness stirred within her, and enveloped her soul, as a bright cloud might cling about some object in the material world. The quaint garden, the old walls, every detail in her little world, seemed to be living through this new experience with her; the nature without her was in harmony with her inmost thoughts. The sunlight crept along the wall till it reached a maidenhair fern; the changing hues of a pigeon's breast shone from the thick fronds and glossy stems, and all Eugénie's future grew bright with radiant hopes. Henceforward the bit of wall, its pale flowers, its blue harebells and bleached grasses, was a pleasant sight for her; it called up associations which had all the charm of the memories of childhood.

The rustling sound made by the leaves as they fell to the earth, the echoes that came up from the court, seemed like answers to the girl's secret questionings as she sat and mused; she might have stayed there by the window all day and never have noticed how the hours went by, but other thoughts surged up within her soul. Again and again she rose and stood before the glass, and looked at herself, as a conscientious writer scrutinizes his work, criticizes it, and says hard things about it to himself.

'I am not pretty enough for him!'

This was what Eugénie thought, in her humility, and the thought was fertile in suffering. The poor child did not do herself justice; but humility, or more truly, fear, is born with love. Eugénie's beauty was of a robust type often found among the lower middle classes, a type which may seem somewhat wanting in refinement, but in her the beauty of the Venus of Milo was ennobled and purified by the beauty of Christian sentiment, which invests woman with a dignity unknown to ancient sculptors. Her head was very large; the masculine but delicate outlines of her forehead recalled the Jupiter of Phidias; all the radiance of her pure life seemed to shine from the clear grey eyes. An attack of smallpox, so mild that it had left no scars on the oval face or features, had yet somewhat blurred their fresh fair colouring, and coarsened the smooth and delicate surface, still so fine and soft that her mother's gentle kiss left a passing trace of faint red on her cheek. Perhaps her nose was a little too large, but it did not contradict the kindly and affectionate expression of the mouth, and the red lips covered with finely etched lines. Her throat was daintily rounded. There was something that attracted attention and stirred the imagination in the curving lines of her figure, covered to the throat by her high-necked dress; no doubt she possessed little of the grace that is due to the toilette, and her tall frame was strong rather than lissom, but this was not without its charm for judges of beauty.

For Eugénie was both tall and strongly built. She had nothing of the prettiness that ordinary people admire; but her beauty was unmistakable, and of a kind in which artists alone delight. A painter in quest of an exalted and spiritual type, searching women's faces for the beauty which Raphael dreamed of and conjured into being, the eyes full of proud humility, the pure outlines, often due to some chance inspiration of the artist, but which a virtuous and Christian life can alone acquire or preserve – a painter haunted by this ideal would have seen at once in Eugénie Grandet's face her unconscious and innate nobility of soul, a world of love behind the quiet brow, and in the way she had with her eyelids and in her eyes that divine something which baffles description. There was a serene tranquillity about her features, unspoiled and unwearied by the expression of pleasure; it was as if you watched, across some placid lake, the shadowy outlines of hills far off against the sky. The beauty of Eugénie's face, so quiet and so softly coloured, was like that of some fair, half-opened flower about which the light seems to hover; in its quality of restfulness, its subtle revelation of a beautiful nature, lay the charm that attracted beholders.

Eugénie was still on the daisied brink of life, where illusions blossom and joys are gathered which are not known in later days. So she looked in the glass, and with no thought of love as yet in her mind, she said, 'He will not give me a thought; I am too ugly!'

Then she opened her door, went out on to the landing, and bent over the staircase to hear the sounds in the house.

'He is not getting up yet,' she thought. She heard Nanon's morning cough as the good woman went to and fro, swept out the dining-room, lit the kitchen fire, chained up the dog, and talked to her friends the brutes in the stable.

Eugénie fled down the staircase, and ran over to Nanon, who was milking the cow.

'Nanon,' she cried, 'do let us have some cream for my cousin's coffee, there's a dear.'

'But, mademoiselle, you can't have cream off this morning's milk,' said Nanon, as she burst out laughing. 'I can't make cream for you. Your cousin is as charming as charming can be, that he is! You haven't seen him in that silk night-rail of his, all flowers and gold! I did though! The linen he wears is every bit as fine as Monsieur le Curé's surplice.'

'Nanon, make some cake for us.'

'And who is to find the wood to heat the oven and the flour and the butter?' asked Nanon, who in her capacity of Grandet's prime minister was a person of immense importance in Eugénie's eyes, and even in Eugénie's mother's. 'Is *he* to be robbed to make a feast for your cousin? Ask for the butter and the flour and the firewood; he is your father, go and ask him, he may give them to *you*. There! there he is, just coming downstairs to see after the provisions –'

But Eugénie had escaped into the garden; the sound of her father's footsteps on the creaking staircase terrified her. She was conscious of a modesty that shrank from the observation of others, and a happiness which, as we are apt to think, and perhaps not without reason, shines from our eyes, and is written at large upon our foreheads. And not only so, she was conscious of other thoughts. The bleak discomfort of her father's house had struck her for the first time, and, with a dim feeling of vexation, the poor child wished that she could alter it all, and bring it more into harmony with her cousin's elegance. She felt a passionate longing to do something for him, without the slightest idea what that something should be. The womanly instinct awakened in her at the first sight of her cousin was only the stronger because she had reached her three-and-twentieth year, and mind and heart were fully developed; and she was so natural and simple that she acted on the promptings of her angelic nature without submitting herself, her impressions, or her feelings to any introspective process.

For the first time in her life the sight of her father struck a sort of terror into her heart; she felt that he was the master of her fate, and that she was guiltily hiding some of her thoughts from him. She began to walk hurriedly up and down, wondering how it was that the air was so fresh; there was a reviving force in the sunlight, it seemed to be within her as well as without. It was as if a new life had begun.

While she was still thinking how to gain her end concerning the cake, a quarrel came to pass between Nanon and Grandet, a thing as rare as a winter swallow. The goodman had just taken his keys, and was about to dole out the provisions required for the day.

'Is there any bread left over from yesterday?' he asked of Nanon.

'Not a crumb, sir.'

Grandet took up a large loaf, round in form and close in consistence, shaped in one of the flat baskets which they use for baking in Anjou, and was about to cut it, when Nanon broke in upon him with:

'There are five of us today, sir.'

'True,' answered Grandet; 'but these loaves of yours weigh six pounds apiece; there will be some left over. Besides, these young fellows from Paris never touch bread, as you will soon see.'

'Then do they eat *kitchen*?' asked Nanon.

This word *kitchen* in the Angevin dictionary signifies anything which is spread upon bread; from butter, the commonest variety, to preserved peaches, the most distinguished of all *kitchens*; and those who, as small children, have nibbled off the *kitchen* and left the bread, will readily understand the bearing of Nanon's remark.

'No,' replied Grandet with much gravity, 'they eat neither bread nor *kitchen*; they are like a girl in love, as you may say.'

Having at length cut down the day's rations to the lowest possible point, the miser was about to go to his fruit-loft, first carefully locking up the cupboards of his store-room, when Nanon stopped him.

'Just give me some flour and butter, sir,' she said, 'and I will make a cake for the children.'

'Are you going to turn the house upside down because my nephew is here?'

'Your nephew was no more in my mind than your dog, no more than he was in yours. . . . There, now! you have only put out six lumps of sugar, and I want eight.'

'Come, come, Nanon; I have never seen you like this before. What has come over you? Are you mistress here? You will have six lumps of sugar and no more.'

'Oh, very well; and what is your nephew to sweeten his coffee with?'

'He can have two lumps; I shall go without it myself.'

'*You* go without sugar! and at your age! I would sooner pay for it out of my own pocket.'

'Mind your own business.'

In spite of the low price of sugar, it was, in Grandet's eyes, the most precious of all colonial products. For him it was always something to be used sparingly; it was still worth six francs a pound, as in the time of the Empire, and this pet economy had become an inveterate habit with him. But every woman, no matter how simple she may be, can devise some shift to gain her ends; and Nanon allowed the question of the sugar to drop, in order to have her way about the cake.

'Mademoiselle,' she called through the window, 'wouldn't you like some cake?'

'No, no,' answered Eugénie.

'Stay, Nanon,' said Grandet as he heard his daughter's voice; 'there!'

He opened the flour-bin, measured out some flour, and added a few ounces of butter to the piece which he had already cut.

'And firewood; I shall want firewood to heat the oven,' said the inexorable Nanon.

'Ah, well, you can take what you want,' he answered ruefully; 'but you will make a fruit tart at the same time, and you must bake the dinner in the oven, that will save lighting another fire.'

'*Quien!*' cried Nanon; 'there is no need to tell me that!'

Grandet gave his trusty prime minister a glance that was almost paternal.

'Mademoiselle,' cried the cook, 'we are going to have a cake.'

Grandet came back again with the fruit, and began by setting down a plateful on the kitchen table.

'Just look here, sir,' said Nanon, 'what lovely boots your nephew has! What leather, how nice it smells! What are they to be cleaned with? Am I to put your egg-blacking on them?'

'No, Nanon,' said Eugénie; 'I expect the egg would spoil the leather. You had better tell him that you have no idea how to clean black morocco. . . Yes, it is morocco, and he himself will buy you something in Saumur to clean his boots with. I have heard it said that they put sugar into their blacking, and that is what makes it so shiny.'

'Then is it good to eat?' asked the maid, as she picked up the boots and smelt them. '*Quien, quien!* they smell of madame's eau-de-Cologne! Oh, how funny!'

'*Funny!*' said her master; 'people spend more money on their boots than they are worth that stand in them, and you think it funny!' He had just returned from a second and final expedition to the fruit-loft, carefully locking the door after him.

'You will have soup once or twice a week while your nephew is here, sir, will you not?'

'Yes.'

'Shall I go round to the butcher's?'

'You will do nothing of the kind. You can make some chicken broth; the tenants will keep you going. But I shall tell Cornoiller to kill some ravens for me. That kind of game makes the best broth in the world.'

'Is it true, sir, that they live on dead things?'

'You are a fool, Nanon! They live, like everybody else, on anything that they can pick up. Don't we all live on dead things? What about legacies?' And goodman Grandet, having no further order to give, drew out his watch, and finding that there was yet half an hour to spare before breakfast, took up his hat, gave his daughter a kiss, and said, 'Would you like to take a walk along the Loire? I have something to see after in the meadows down there.'

Eugénie put on her straw hat lined with rose-coloured silk; and then father and daughter went down the crooked street towards the market-place.

'Where are you off to so early this morning?' said the notary Cruchot, as he met the Grandets.

'We are going to take a look at something,' responded his friend, in no wise deceived by this early move on the notary's part.

Whenever Grandet was about to 'take a look at something', the notary knew by experience that there was something to be gained by going with him. With him, therefore, he went.

'Come along, Cruchot,' said Grandet, addressing the notary. 'You are one of my friends; I am going to show you what a piece of folly it is to plant poplars in good soil –'

'Then the sixty thousand francs that you got hold of for those poplars of yours in the meadows by the Loire are a mere trifle to you?' said Cruchot, opening his eyes wide in his bewilderment. 'And such luck as you had too! . . . Felling your timber just when there was no white wood to be had in Nantes, so that every trunk fetched thirty francs!'

Eugénie heard and did not hear, utterly unconscious that the most critical moment of her life was rapidly approaching, that a paternal and sovereign decree was about to be pronounced, and that the old notary was to bring all this about. Grandet had reached the magnificent meadow-land by the Loire, which had come into his hands in his Republican days. Some thirty labourers were busy digging out the roots of the poplars that once stood there, filling up the holes that were left, and levelling the ground.

'Now, Monsieur Cruchot, see how much space a poplar takes up,' said he, addressing the notary. 'Jean,' he called to a workman, 'm-m-measure r-round the sides with your rule.'

'Eight feet four times over,' said the workman when he had finished.

'Thirty-two feet of loss,' said Grandet to Cruchot. 'Now along that line there were three hundred poplars, weren't there? Well, then, three hundred t-t-times thirty-two f-feet will eat up five hundredweight of hay, allow twice as much again for the space on either side, and you get fifteen hundredweight; then there is the intervening space – say a thousand t-t-trusses of hay altogether.'

'Well,' said Cruchot, helping his friend out, 'and a thousand trusses of that hay would fetch something like six hundred francs.'

'S-s-say t-twelve hundred, because the s-second crop is worth three or four hundred francs. Good, then reckon up what t-t-twelve hundred francs per annum d-d-during f-forty years comes to, at compound interest of course.'

'Sixty thousand francs, or thereabouts,' said the notary.

'That is what I make it! Sixty thousand f-f-francs. Well,' the vine-grower went on without stammering, 'two thousand poplars will not bring in fifty thousand francs in forty years. So you lose on them. That *I* found out,' said Grandet, who was vastly pleased with himself. 'Jean,' he continued, turning to the labourer, 'fill up all the holes except those along the riverside, where you can plant those poplar saplings that I bought. If you set them along by the Loire, they will grow there finely at the expense of the Government,' he added, and as he looked round at Cruchot the wen on his nose twitched slightly; the most sardonic smile could not have said more.

'Yes, it is clear enough, poplars should only be planted in poor soil,' said Cruchot, quite overcome with amazement at Grandet's astuteness.

'Y-e-s, sir,' said the cooper laconically.

Eugénie was looking out over the glorious landscape

and along the Loire, without heeding her father's arithmetic; but Cruchot's talk with his client took another turn, and her attention was suddenly aroused.

'So you have a son-in-law come from Paris; they are talking about nothing but your nephew in all Saumur. I shall soon have settlements to draw up; eh, père Grandet?'

'Did you come out early to t-t-tell me that?' inquired Grandet, and again the wen twitched. 'Very well, you are an old crony of mine; I will be p-plain with you, and t-t-tell you what you w-want to know. I would rather fling my d-d-daughter into the Loire, look you, than g-give her to her cousin. You can give that out. But, no; l-l-let people gossip.'

Everything swam before Eugénie's eyes. Her vague hopes of distant happiness had suddenly taken definite shape, had sprung up and blossomed, and then her harvest of flowers had been as suddenly cut down and lay on the earth. Since yesterday she had woven the bonds of happiness that unite two souls, and henceforward sorrow, it seemed, was to strengthen them. Is it not written in the noble destiny of woman that the grandeur of sorrow should touch her more closely than all the pomp and splendour of fortune?

How came it that a father's feelings had been extinguished (as it seemed) in her father's heart? What crime could be laid at Charles's door? Mysterious questions! Mysterious and sad forebodings already surrounded her growing love, that mystery within her soul. When they turned to go home again, she trembled in every limb; and as they went up the shady street, along which she had lately gone so joyously, the shadows looked gloomy, the air she breathed seemed full of the melancholy of autumn, everything about her was sad. Love, that had brought these keener perceptions, was quick to interpret every boding sign. As they neared home, she walked on ahead of her father, knocked at the house door, and stood waiting beside it. But Grandet, seeing that the notary carried a newspaper still in its wrapper, asked, 'How are consols?'

'I know you will not take my advice, Grandet,' Cruchot replied. 'You should buy at once; the chance of making twenty per cent on them in two years is still open to you, and they pay a very fair rate of interest besides, five thousand livres is not a bad return on eighty thousand francs. You can buy now at eighty francs fifty centimes.'

'We shall see,' remarked Grandet pensively, rubbing his chin.

'*Mon Dieu!*' exclaimed the notary, who by this time had unfolded his newspaper.

'Well, what is it?' cried Grandet as Cruchot put the paper in his hands and said:

'Read that paragraph.'

'M. Grandet, one of the most highly respected merchants in Paris, shot himself through the head yesterday afternoon, after putting in an appearance on Change as usual. He had previously sent in his resignation to the Président of the Chamber of Deputies, resigning his position as Judge of the Tribunal of Commerce at the same time. His affairs had become involved through the failures of his stockbroker and notary, MM. Roguin and Souchet. M. Grandet, whose character was very greatly esteemed, and whose credit stood high, would no doubt have found temporary assistance on the market which would have enabled him to tide over his difficulties. It is to be regretted that a man of such high character should have given way to the first impulse of despair' – and so forth, and so forth.

'I knew it,' the old vine-grower said.

Phlegmatic though Cruchot was, he felt a horrible shudder run through him at the words; perhaps Grandet of Paris had stretched imploring hands in vain to the millions of Grandet of Saumur; the blood ran cold in his veins.

'And his son?' he asked presently; 'he was in such spirits yesterday evening.'

'His son knows nothing as yet,' Grandet answered, imperturbable as ever.

'Good morning, Monsieur Grandet,' said Cruchot. He understood the position now, and went to reassure the Président de Bonfons.

Grandet found breakfast ready. Mme Grandet was already seated in her chair, mounted on the wooden blocks, and was knitting woollen cuffs for the winter. Eugénie ran to her mother and put her arms about her, with the eager hunger for affection that comes of a hidden trouble.

'You can get your breakfast,' said Nanon, bustling downstairs in a hurry; 'he is sleeping like a cherub. He looks so nice with his eyes shut! I went in and called him, but it was all one, he never heard me.'

'Let him sleep,' said Grandet; 'he will wake soon enough to hear bad news, in any case.'

'What is the matter?' asked Eugénie. She was putting into her cup two small lumps of sugar, weighing goodness knows how many grains; her worthy parent was wont to amuse himself by cutting up sugar whenever he had nothing better to do.

Mme Grandet, who had not dared to put the question herself, looked at her husband.

'His father has blown his brains out.'

'*My uncle?*' said Eugénie.

'Oh! that poor boy!' cried Mme Grandet.

'Poor indeed!' said Grandet; 'he has not a penny.'

'Ah, well, he is sleeping as if he were the king of all the world,' said Nanon pityingly.

Eugénie could not eat. Her heart was wrung as a woman's heart can be when for the first time her whole soul is filled with compassion for the sorrow of one she loves. She burst into tears.

'You did not know your uncle, so what is there to cry about?' said her father with a glance like a hungry tiger's; just such a glance as he would give, no doubt, to his heaps of gold.

'But who wouldn't feel sorry for the poor young man, sir?' said the serving-maid; 'sleeping there like a log, and knowing nothing of his fate.'

'I did not speak to you, Nanon! Hold your tongue.'

In that moment Eugénie learned that a woman who loves must dissemble her feelings. She was silent.

'Until I come back, Madame Grandet, you will say nothing about this to him, I hope,' the old cooper continued. 'They are making a ditch in my meadows along the road, and I must go and see after it. I shall come back for the second breakfast at noon, and then my nephew and I will have a talk about his affairs. As for you, Mademoiselle Eugénie, if you are crying over that popinjay, let us have no more of it, child. He will be off post-haste to the Indies directly, and you will never set eyes on *him* any more.'

Her father took up his gloves, which were lying on the rim of his hat, put them on in his cool, deliberate way, inserting the fingers of one hand between those of the other, dovetail fashion, so as to thrust them down well into the tips of the gloves, and then he went out.

'Oh, mamma, I can scarcely breathe!' cried Eugénie when she was alone with her mother; 'I have never suffered like this!'

Mme Grandet, seeing her daughter's white face, opened the window and let fresh air into the room.

'I feel better now,' said Eugénie after a little.

This nervous excitement in one who was usually so quiet and self-possessed produced an effect on Mme Grandet. She looked at her daughter, and her mother's love and sympathetic instinct told her everything. But, in truth, the celebrated Hungarian twin sisters, united to each other by one of nature's errors, could scarcely have lived in closer sympathy than Eugénie and her mother. Were they not always together; together in the window where they sat the livelong day, together at church; did they not breathe the same air even when they slept?

'My poor little girl!' said Mme Grandet, drawing Eugénie's head down till it rested upon her bosom.

Her daughter lifted her face, and gave her mother a questioning look which seemed to read her inmost thoughts.

'Why must he be sent to the Indies?' said the girl. 'If he is in trouble, ought he not to stay here with us? Is he not our nearest relation?'

'Yes, dear child, that would only be natural; but your father has reasons for what he does, and we must respect them.'

Mother and daughter sat in silence; the one on her chair mounted on the wooden blocks, the other in her little arm-chair. Both women took up their needlework. Eugénie felt that her mother understood her, and her heart was full of gratitude for such tender sympathy.

'How kind you are, dear mamma!' she said as she took her mother's hand and kissed it.

The worn, patient face, aged with many sorrows, lighted up at the words.

'Do you like him?' asked Eugénie.

For all answer, Mme Grandet smiled. Then after a moment's pause she murmured, 'You cannot surely love him already? That would be a pity.'

'Why would it be a pity?' asked Eugénie. 'You like him, Nanon likes him, why should I not like him too? Now then, mamma, let us set the table for his breakfast.'

She threw down her work, and her mother followed her example, saying as she did so, 'You are a mad girl!'

But none the less did she sanction her daughter's freak by assisting in it.

Eugénie called Nanon.

'Haven't you all you want yet, mam'selle?'

'Nanon, surely you will have some cream by twelve o'clock?'

'By twelve o'clock? Oh, yes,' answered the old servant.

'Very well, then, let the coffee be very strong. I have heard Monsieur des Grassins say that they drink their coffee very strong in Paris. Put in plenty.'

'And where is it to come from?'

'You must buy some.'

'And suppose the master meets me?'

'He is down by the river.'

'I will just slip out then. But Monsieur Fessard asked me when I went about the candle if the Three Holy Kings were paying us a visit. Our goings-on will be all over the town.'

'Your father would be quite capable of beating us,' said Mme Grandet, 'if he suspected anything of all this.'

'Oh, well, then, never mind; he will beat us, we will take the beating on our knees.'

At this Mme Grandet raised her eyes to heaven, and said no more. Nanon put on her sun-bonnet and went out. Eugénie spread a clean linen table-cloth, then she went upstairs in quest of some bunches of grapes which she had amused herself by hanging from some strings up in the attic. She tripped lightly along the corridor, so as not to disturb her cousin, and could not resist the temptation to stop a moment before the door to listen to his even breathing.

'Trouble wakes while he is sleeping,' she said to herself.

She arranged her grapes on the few last green vine leaves as daintily as any experienced *chef d'office*, and set them on the table in triumph. She levied contributions on the pears which her father had counted out, and piled them up pyramid-fashion, with autumn leaves among them. She came and went, and danced in and out. She might have ransacked the house; the will was in no wise lacking, but her father kept everything under lock and key, and the keys were in his pocket. Nanon came back with two new-laid eggs. Eugénie could have flung her arms round the woman's neck.

'The farmer from La Lande had eggs in his basket; I asked him for some, and to please me he let me have these, the nice man.'

After two hours of industrious application, Eugénie succeeded in preparing a very simple meal; it cost but little, it is true, but it was a terrible infringement of the immemorial laws and customs of the house. No one sat down to the midday meal, which consisted of a little bread, some fruit or butter, and a glass of wine. Twenty times in those two hours Eugénie had left her work to watch the coffee boil, or to listen for any sound announcing that her cousin was getting up; now looking round on the table drawn up to the fire, with one of the arm-chairs set beside it for her cousin, on the two plates of fruit, the egg-cups, the bottle of white wine, the bread, and the little pyramid of white sugar in a saucer; Eugénie trembled from head to foot at the mere thought of the glance her father would give her if he should happen to come in at that moment. Often, therefore, did she look at the clock, to see if there was yet time for her cousin to finish his breakfast before her parent's return.

'Never mind, Eugénie, if your father comes in, I will take all the blame,' said Mme Grandet.

Eugénie could not keep back the tears. 'Oh, my kind mother,' she cried, 'I have not loved you enough!'

Charles, after making innumerable pirouettes round his room, came down at last, singing gay little snatches of song. Luckily it was only eleven o'clock after all. He had taken as much pains with his appearance (the Parisian!) as if he had been staying in the château belonging to the high-born fair one who was travelling in Scotland; and now he came in with that gracious air of condescension which sits not ill on youth, and which gave Eugénie a melancholy pleasure. He had come to regard the collapse of his castles in Anjou as a very good joke, and went up to his aunt quite gaily.

'I hope you slept well, dear aunt? And you, too, cousin?'

'Very well, sir; how did you sleep?'

'Soundly.'

'Cousin, you must be hungry,' said Eugénie; 'sit down.'

'Oh! I never breakfast before twelve o'clock, just after I rise. But I have fared so badly on my journey, that I will yield to persuasion. Besides –' He drew out the daintiest little watch that ever issued from Bréguet's workshop. 'Dear me, it is only eleven o'clock; I have been up betimes.'

'Up betimes?' asked Mme Grandet.

'Yes, but I wanted to set my things straight. Well, I am quite ready for something, something not very substantial, a fowl or a partridge.'

'Holy Virgin!' exclaimed Nanon, hearing these words.

'A partridge,' Eugénie said to herself. She would willingly have given all she had for one.

'Come and take your seat,' said Mme Grandet, addressing her nephew.

The dandy sank into the arm-chair in a graceful attitude, much as a pretty woman might recline on her sofa. Eugénie and her mother drew their chairs to the fire and sat near him.

'Do you always live here?' Charles inquired, thinking that the room looked even more hideous by daylight than by candlelight.

'Always,' Eugénie answered, watching him as she spoke. 'Always, except during the vintage. Then we go to help Nanon, and we all stay at the Abbey at Noyers.'

'Do you never take a walk?'

'Sometimes, on Sundays after vespers, when it is fine, we walk down as far as the bridge,' said Mme Grandet, 'or we sometimes go to see them cutting the hay.'

'Have you a theatre here?'

'Go to the play!' cried Mme Grandet; 'go to see play-actors! Why, sir, do you not know that that is a mortal sin?'

'There, sir,' said Nanon, bringing in the eggs, 'we will give you chickens in the shell.'

'Oh, new-laid eggs!' said Charles, who, after the manner of those accustomed to luxury, had quite forgotten all about his partridge. 'Delicious! Do you happen to have any butter, eh, my good girl?'

'Butter? If you have butter now, you will have no cake by and by,' said the handmaid.

'Yes, of course, Nanon; bring some butter,' cried Eugénie.

The young girl watched her cousin while he cut his bread and butter into strips, and felt happy. The most romantic shop-girl in Paris could not more thoroughly enjoy the spectacle of innocence triumphant in a melodrama. It must be conceded that Charles, who had been brought up by a graceful and charming mother, and had received his 'finishing education' from an accomplished woman of the world, was as dainty, neat, and elegant in his ways as any coxcomb of the gentler sex. The girl's quiet sympathy produced an almost magnetic effect. Charles, finding himself thus waited upon by his cousin and aunt, could not resist the influence of their overflowing kindness. He was radiant with good humour, and the look he gave Eugénie was almost a smile. As he looked at her more closely he noticed her pure, regular features, her unconscious attitude, the wonderful clearness of her eyes, in which love sparkled, though she as yet knew nothing of love but its pain and a wistful longing.

'Really, my dear cousin,' he said, 'if you were in a box at the opera and in evening dress, I would answer for it, my aunt's remark about deadly sin would be justified, all the men would be envious, and all the women jealous.'

Eugénie's heart beat fast with joy at this compliment, though it conveyed no meaning whatever to her mind.

'You are laughing at a poor little country cousin,' she said.

'If you knew me better, cousin, you would know that I detest banter; it sears the heart and deadens the feelings.' And he swallowed down a strip of bread and butter with perfect satisfaction.

'No,' he continued, 'I never make fun of others, very likely because I have not wit enough, a defect which puts me at a great disadvantage. They have a deadly trick in Paris of saying, "He is *so* good-natured", which, being interpreted, means, "The poor youth is as stupid as a rhinoceros." But as I happen to be rich, and it is known that I can hit the bull's-eye straight off at thirty paces with any kind of pistol anywhere, these witticisms are not levelled at me.'

'It is evident from what you say, nephew,' said Mme Grandet gravely, 'that you have a kind heart.'

'That is a very pretty ring of yours,' said Eugénie; 'is there any harm in asking to see it?'

Charles took off the ring and held it out; Eugénie reddened as her cousin's rose-pink nails came in contact with her finger-tips.

'Mother, only see how fine the work is!'

'Oh, what a lot of gold there is in it!' said Nanon, who brought in the coffee.

'What is that?' asked Charles, laughing, as he pointed to an oval pipkin, made of glazed brown earthenware, ornamented without by a circular fringe of ashes. It was full of a brown boiling liquid, in which coffee grounds were visible as they rose to the surface and fell again.

'Coffee; boiling hot!' answered Nanon.

'Oh, my dear aunt, I must at least leave some beneficent trace of my stay here. You are a long way behind the times! I will show you how to make decent coffee in a *cafetière à la Chaptal.*' Forthwith he endeavoured to explain the principles on which this utensil is constructed.

'Bless me! if there is all that to-do about it,' said Nanon, 'you would have to give your whole time to it. I'll never make coffee that way, I know. Who is to cut the grass for our cow while I am looking after the coffee-pot?'

'I would do it,' said Eugénie.

'*Child!*' said Mme Grandet, with a look at her daughter; and at the word came a swift recollection of the misery about to overwhelm the unconscious young man, and the three women were suddenly silent, and gazed pityingly at him. He could not understand it.

'What is it, cousin?' he asked Eugénie.

'Hush!' said Mme Grandet, seeing that the girl was about to reply. 'You know that your father means to speak to the gentleman –'

'Say "Charles",' said young Grandet.

'Oh, is your name Charles?' said Eugénie. 'It is a nice name.'

Evil forebodings are seldom vain.

Just at that moment Mme Grandet, Eugénie, and Nanon, who could not think of the cooper's return without shuddering, heard the familiar knock at the door.

'That is papa!' cried Eugénie.

She took away the saucer full of sugar, leaving one or two lumps on the tablecloth. Nanon hurried away with the egg-cups. Mme Grandet started up like a frightened fawn. There was a sudden panic of terror, which amazed Charles, who was quite at a loss to account for it.

'Why, what is the matter?' he asked.

'My father is coming in,' explained Eugénie.

'Well, and what then?'

M. Grandet entered the room, gave one sharp glance at the table, and another at Charles. He saw how it was at once.

'Aha! you are making a fête for your nephew. Good, very good, oh! very good, indeed!' he said, without stammering. 'When the cat is away, the mice may play.'

'Fête?' thought Charles, who had not the remotest conception of the state of affairs in the Grandet household.

'Bring me my glass, Nanon,' said the goodman.

Eugénie went for the glass. Grandet drew from his waistcoat pocket a large clasp-knife with a stag's horn handle, cut a slice of bread, buttered it slowly and sparingly, and began to eat as he stood. Just then Charles put some sugar into his coffee; this called Grandet's attention to the pieces of sugar on the table; he looked hard at his wife, who turned pale, and came a step or two towards him; he bent down and said in the poor woman's ear:

'Where did all that sugar come from?'

'Nanon went out to Fessard's for some; there was none in the house.'

It is impossible to describe the painful interest that this dumb show possessed for the three women; Nanon had left her kitchen, and was looking into the dining-room to see how things went there. Charles meanwhile tasted his coffee, found it rather strong, and looked round for another piece of sugar, but Grandet had already pounced upon it and taken it away.

'What do you want, nephew?' the old man inquired.

'The sugar.'

'Pour in some more milk if your coffee is too strong,' answered the master of the house.

Eugénie took up the saucer of sugar, of which Grandet had previously taken possession, and set it on the table, looking quietly at her father the while. Truly, the fair Parisian who exerts all the strength of her weak arms to help her lover to escape by a ladder of silken cords, displays less courage than Eugénie showed when she put the sugar back upon the table. The Parisian will have her reward. She will proudly exhibit the bruises on a round white arm, her lover will bathe them with tears and cover them with kisses, and pain will be extinguished in bliss; but Charles had not the remotest conception of what his cousin endured for him, or of the horrible dismay that filled her heart as she met her father's angry eyes; he would never even know of her sacrifice.

'You are eating nothing, wife?'

The poor bond-slave went to the table, cut a piece of bread in fear and trembling, and took a pear. Eugénie, grown reckless, offered the grapes to her father, saying as she did so:

'Just try some of my fruit, papa! You will take some, will you not, cousin? I brought those pretty grapes down on purpose for you.'

'Oh! if they could have their way, they would turn Saumur upside down for you, nephew! As soon as you have finished we will take a turn in the garden together; I have some things to tell you that would take a deal of sugar to sweeten them.'

Eugénie and her mother both gave Charles a look, which the young man could not mistake.

'What do you mean by that, uncle? Since my mother died' – here his voice softened a little – 'there is no misfortune possible for me . . .'

'Who can know what afflictions God may send to make trial of us, nephew,' said his aunt.

'Tut, tut, tut,' muttered Grandet, 'here you are beginning with your folly already! I am sorry to see that you have such white hands, nephew.'

He displayed the fists, like shoulders of mutton, with which nature had terminated his own arms.

'That is the sort of hand to rake the crowns together! You put the kind of leather on your feet that we used to make pocket-books of to keep bills in. That is the way you have been brought up. That's bad! that's bad!'

'What do you mean, uncle? I'll be hanged if I understand one word of this.'

'Come along,' said Grandet.

The miser shut his knife with a snap, drained his glass, and opened the door.

'Oh! keep up your courage, cousin!'

Something in the girl's voice sent a sudden chill through Charles; he followed his formidable relative with dreadful misgivings. Eugénie and her mother and Nanon went into the kitchen; an uncontrollable anxiety led them to watch the two actors in the scene which was about to take place in the damp little garden.

Uncle and nephew walked together in silence at first. Grandet felt the situation to be a somewhat awkward one; not that he shrank at all from telling Charles of his father's death, but he felt a kind of pity for a young man left in this way without a penny in the world, and he cast about for phrases that should break this cruel news as gently as might be. 'You have lost your father!' – he could say that; there was nothing in that; fathers usually predecease their children. But, 'You have not a penny!' All the woes of the world were summed up in those words, so for the third time the worthy man walked the whole length of the path in the centre of the garden, crunching the gravel beneath his heavy boots, and no word was said.

At all great crises in our lives, any sudden joy or great sorrow, there comes a vivid consciousness of our surroundings that stamps them on the memory for ever; and Charles, with every faculty strained and intent, saw the box-edging to the borders, the falling autumn leaves, the mouldering walls, the gnarled and twisted boughs of the fruit trees, and till his dying day every picturesque detail of the little garden came back with the memory of the supreme hour of that early sorrow.

'It is very fine, very warm,' said Grandet, drawing in a deep breath of air.

'Yes, uncle, but why –'

'Well, my boy,' his uncle resumed, 'I have some bad news for you. Your father is very ill . . .'

'What am I doing here?' cried Charles. 'Nanon!' he shouted, 'order post-horses! I shall be sure to find a carriage of some sort in the place, I suppose,' he added, turning to his uncle, who had not stirred from where he stood.

'Horses and a carriage are of no use,' Grandet answered, looking at Charles, who immediately stared straight before him in silence. 'Yes, my poor boy, you guess what has happened; he is dead. But that is nothing; there is something worse; he has shot himself through the head –'

'*My father?*'

'Yes, but that is nothing either. The newspapers are discussing it, as if it were any business of theirs. There, read for yourself.'

Grandet had borrowed Cruchot's paper, and now he laid the fatal paragraph before Charles. The poor young fellow – he was only a lad as yet – made no attempt to hide his emotion, and burst into tears.

'Come, that is better,' said Grandet to himself. 'That look in his eyes frightened me. He is crying; he will pull through. Never mind, my poor nephew,' Grandet resumed aloud, not knowing whether Charles heard him or no, 'that is nothing, you will get over it, but –'

'Never! never! My father! my father!'

'He has ruined you; you are penniless.'

'What is that to me? Where is my father? . . . my father!' The sound of his sobbing filled the little garden, reverberated in ghastly echoes from the walls. Tears are as infectious as laughter; the three women wept with pity for him. Charles broke from his uncle without waiting to hear more, and sprang into the yard, found the staircase, and fled to his own room, where he flung himself across the bed and buried his face in the bedclothes, that he might give way to his grief in solitude as far as possible from these relations.

'Let him alone till the first shower is over,' said Grandet, going back to the parlour. Eugénie and her mother had hastily returned to their places, had dried their eyes, and were sewing with cold trembling fingers.

'But that fellow is good for nothing,' went on Grandet; 'he is so taken up with dead folk that he doesn't even think about the money.'

Eugénie shuddered to hear the most sacred of sorrows spoken of in such a way; from that moment she began to criticize her father. Charles's sobs, smothered though they were, rang through that house of echoes;

the sounds seemed to come from under the earth, a heart-rending wail that grew fainter towards the end of the day, and only ceased as night drew on.

'Poor boy!' said Mme Grandet.

It was an unfortunate remark! Goodman Grandet looked at his wife, then at Eugénie, then at the sugar basin; he recollected the sumptuous breakfast prepared that morning for their unhappy kinsman, and planted himself in the middle of the room.

'Oh, by the by,' he said, in his usual cool, deliberate way, 'I hope you will not carry your extravagance any further, Madame Grandet; I do not give you MY money for you to squander it on sugar for that young rogue.'

'Mother had nothing whatever to do with it,' said Eugénie. 'It was I –'

'Because you are come of age,' Grandet interrupted his daughter, 'you think you can set yourself to thwart me, I suppose? Mind what you are about, Eugénie –'

'But, father, your own brother's son ought not to have to go without sugar in your house.'

'Tut, tut, tut, tut!' came from the cooper in a cadence of four semitones. ''Tis "my nephew" here, and "my brother's son" there; Charles is nothing to us, he has not a brass farthing. His father is a bankrupt, and when the young sprig has cried as much as he wishes, he shall clear out of this; I will not have my house turned topsy-turvy for him.'

'What is a bankrupt, father?' asked Eugénie.

'A bankrupt,' replied her father, 'is guilty of the most dishonourable action that can dishonour a man.'

'It must be a very great sin,' said Mme Grandet, 'and our brother will perhaps be eternally lost.'

'There you are with your preachments,' her husband retorted, shrugging his shoulders. 'A bankrupt, Eugénie,' her father continued, 'is a thief whom the law unfortunately takes under its protection. People trusted

Guillaume Grandet with their goods, confiding in his character for fair dealing and honesty; he has taken all they have, and left them nothing but their eyes to weep with. A bankrupt is worse than a highwayman; a highwayman sets upon you, and you have a chance to defend yourself; he risks his life besides, while the other – Charles is disgraced in fact.'

The words filled the poor girl's heart; they weighed upon her with all their weight; she herself was so scrupulously conscientious; no flower in the depths of a forest had grown more delicately free from spot or stain; she knew none of the maxims of worldly wisdom, and nothing of its quibbles and its sophistries. So she accepted her father's cruel definition and sweeping statements as to bankrupts; he drew no distinction between a fraudulent bankruptcy and a failure from unavoidable causes, and how should she?

'But, father, could you not have prevented this misfortune?'

'My brother did not ask my advice; besides, his liabilities amount to four millions.'

'How much is a million, father?' asked Eugénie, with the simplicity of a child who would fain have its wish fulfilled at once.

'A million?' queried Grandet. 'Why, it is a million francs, four hundred thousand five-franc pieces; there are twenty sous in a franc, and it takes five francs of twenty sous each to make a five-franc piece.'

'*Mon Dieu! Mon Dieu!*' cried Eugénie, 'how came my uncle to have four millions of his own? Is there really anybody in France who has so many millions as that?'

Grandet stroked his daughter's chin and smiled. The wen seemed to grow larger.

'What will become of cousin Charles?'

'He will set out for the East Indies, and try to make a fortune. That is his father's wish.'

'But has he any money to go with?'

'I shall pay his passage out as far as . . . yes . . . as far as Nantes.'

Eugénie sprang up and flung her arms about her father's neck.

'Oh! father,' she said, 'you are good!'

Her warm embrace embarrassed Grandet somewhat; perhaps, too, his conscience was not quite at ease.

'Does it take a long while to make a million?' she asked.

'Lord! yes,' said the cooper; 'you know what a napoleon is; well, then, it takes fifty thousand of them to make a million.'

'Mamma, we will have a *novena* said for him.'

'That was what I was thinking,' her mother replied.

'Just like you! always thinking how to spend money. Really, one might suppose that we had any amount of money to throw away!'

As he spoke, a sound of low hoarse sobbing, more ominous than any which had preceded it, came from the garret. Eugénie and her mother shuddered.

'Nanon,' called Grandet, 'go up and see that he is not killing himself.'

'Look here! you two,' he continued, turning to his wife and daughter, whose cheeks grew white at his tones, 'there is to be no nonsense, mind! I am leaving the house. I am going round to see the Dutchmen who are going today. Then I shall go to Cruchot's and have a talk with him about all this.'

He went out. As soon as the door closed upon Grandet, Eugénie and her mother breathed more freely. The girl had never felt constraint in her father's presence until that morning; but a few hours had wrought rapid changes in her ideas and feelings.

'Mamma, how many louis is a hogshead of wine worth?'

'Your father gets something between a hundred and a hundred and fifty francs for his; sometimes two hundred, I believe, from what I have heard him say.'

'And would there be fourteen hundred hogsheads in a vintage?'

'I don't know how many there are, child, upon my word; your father never talks about business to me.'

'But, anyhow, papa must be rich.'

'Maybe. But M. Cruchot told me that your father bought Froidfond two years ago. That would be a heavy pull on him.'

Eugénie, now at a loss as to her father's wealth, went no further with her arithmetic.

'He did not even so much as see me, the poor dear!' said Nanon on her return. 'He is lying there on his bed like a calf, crying like a Magdalen, you never saw the like! Poor young man, what can be the matter with him?'

'Let us go up at once and comfort him, mamma; if we hear a knock, we will come downstairs.'

There was something in the musical tones of her daughter's voice which Mme Grandet could not resist. Eugénie was sublime; she was a girl no longer, she was a woman. With beating hearts they climbed the stairs and went together to Charles's room. The door was open. The young man saw nothing, and heard nothing; he was absorbed in his grief, an inarticulate cry broke from him now and again.

'How he loves his father!' said Eugénie in a low voice, and in her tone there was an unmistakable accent which betrayed the passion in her heart, and hopes of which she herself was unaware. Mme Grandet, with the quick instinct of a mother's love, glanced at her daughter and spoke in a low voice in her ear.

'Take care,' she said, 'or you may love him.'

'Love him!' said Eugénie. 'Ah! if you only knew what my father said.'

Charles moved slightly as he lay, and saw his aunt and cousin.

'I have lost my father,' he cried; 'my poor father! If he had only trusted me and told me about his losses, we might have worked together to repair them. Mon Dieu! my kind father! I was so sure that I should see him again, and I said good-bye so carelessly, I am afraid, never thinking –'

His words were interrupted by sobs.

'We will surely pray for him,' said Mme Grandet. 'Submit yourself to the will of God.'

'Take courage, cousin,' said Eugénie gently; 'nothing can give your father back to you; you must now think how to save your honour –'

A woman always has her wits about her, even in her capacity of comforter, and with instinctive tact Eugénie sought to divert her cousin's mind from his sorrow by leading him to think about himself.

'My honour?' cried the young man, hastily pushing back the hair from his eyes. He sat upright upon the bed, and folded his arms. 'Ah! true. My uncle said that my father had failed.'

He hid his face in his hands with a heart-rending cry of pain.

'Leave me, leave me, cousin Eugénie!' he entreated. 'O God! forgive my father, for he must have been terribly unhappy!'

There was something in the sight of this young sorrow, this utter abandonment of grief, that was horribly engaging. It was a sorrow that shrank from the gaze of others, and Charles's gesture of entreaty that they should leave him to himself was understood by Eugénie and her mother. They went silently downstairs again, took their places by the great window, and sewed on for nearly an hour without a word to each other.

Eugénie had looked round the room; it was a stolen glance. In one of those hasty surveys, by which a girl sees everything in a moment, she had noticed the pretty trifles on the toilette table – the scissors, the razors mounted with gold. The gleams of splendour and luxury, seen amidst all this misery, made Charles still more interesting in her eyes, perhaps by the very force of the contrast. Their life had been so lonely and so quiet; such an event as this, with its painful interest, had never broken the monotony of their lives, little had occurred to stir their imaginations, and now this tragical drama was being enacted under their eyes.

'Mamma,' said Eugénie, 'shall we wear mourning?'

'Your father will decide that,' replied Mme Grandet, and once more they sewed in silence. Eugénie's needle moved with a mechanical regularity, which betrayed her preoccupation of mind. The first wish of this adorable girl was to share her cousin's mourning. About four o'clock a sharp knock at the door sent a sudden thrill of terror through Mme Grandet.

'What can have brought your father back?' she said to her daughter.

The vine-grower came in in high good humour. He rubbed his hands so energetically that nothing but a skin like leather could have borne it, and indeed his hands were tanned like Russia leather, though the fragrant pine-rosin and incense had been omitted in the process. For a time he walked up and down and looked at the weather, but at last his secret escaped him.

'I have hooked them, wife,' he said, without stammering; 'I have them safe. Our wine is sold! The Dutchmen and Belgians were setting out this morning; I hung about in the market-place in front of their inn, looking as simple as I could. What's-his-name – you know the man – came up to me. All the best growers are hanging off and holding their vintages; they wanted to wait, and so they can, I have not hindered them. Our Belgian was at his wits' end, I saw that. So the bargain was struck; he is taking the whole of our vintage at two hundred francs the hogshead, half of it paid down at once in gold, and I have promissory notes for the rest. There are six louis for you. In three months' time prices will go down.'

The last words came out quietly enough, but there was something so sardonic in the tone that if the little knots of growers, then standing in the twilight in the market-place of Saumur in dismay at the news of Grandet's sale, had heard him speak, they would have shuddered; there would have been a panic on the market – wines would have fallen fifty per cent.

'You have a thousand hogsheads this year, father, have you not?' asked Eugénie.

'Yes, little girl.'

These words indicated that the cooper's joy had indeed reached high-water mark.

'That will mean two hundred thousand francs?'

'Yes, Mademoiselle Grandet.'

'Well, then, father, you can easily help Charles.'

The surprise, the wrath and bewilderment with which Belshazzar beheld *Mene Mene Tekel Upharsin* written upon his palace wall were as nothing compared with Grandet's cold fury; he had forgotten all about Charles, and now he found that all his daughter's inmost thoughts were of his nephew, and that this arithmetic of hers referred to him. It was exasperating.

'Look here!' he thundered; 'ever since that scapegrace set foot in *my* house everything has gone askew. You take it upon yourselves to buy sugar-plums, and make a great set-out for him. I will not have these doings. I should think, at my age, I ought to know what is right and proper to do. At any rate, I have no need to take lessons from my daughter, nor from anyone else. I shall do for my nephew whatever it is right and proper for me to do; it is no business of yours, you need not meddle in it. And now, as for you, Eugénie,' he added, turning towards her, 'if you say another word about it, I will send you and Nanon off to the Abbey at Noyers, see if I don't. Where is that boy? Has he come down-stairs yet?'

'No, dear,' answered Mme Grandet.

'Why, what is he doing then?'

'He is crying for his father,' Eugénie said.

Grandet looked at his daughter, and found nothing to say. There was some touch of the father even in him. He took one or two turns up and down, and then went straight to his strong-room to think over possible invest-ments. He had thoughts of buying consols. Those two thousand acres of woodland had brought him in six hundred thousand francs; then there was the money from the sale of the poplars, there was last year's income from various sources, and this year's savings, to say nothing of the bargain which he had just concluded; so that, leaving those two hundred thousand francs out of the question, he possessed a lump sum of nine hundred thousand livres. That twenty per cent, to be made in so short a time upon his outlay, tempted him. Consols stood at seventy. He jotted down his calculations on the margin of the paper that had brought the news of his brother's death; the moans of his nephew sounded in his ears the while, but he did not hear them; he went on with his work till Nanon thumped vigorously on the thick wall to summon her master to dinner. On the last step of the staircase beneath the archway, Grandet paused and thought.

'There is the interest beside the eight per cent – I will do it. Fifteen hundred thousand francs in two years' time, in gold from Paris, too, full weight. . . Well, what has become of my nephew?'

'He said he did not want anything,' replied Nanon. 'He ought to eat, or he will fall ill.'

'It is so much saved,' was her master's comment.

'Lord! yes,' she replied.

'Pooh! he will not keep on crying for ever. Hunger drives the wolf from the wood.'

Dinner was a strangely silent meal. When the cloth had been removed, Mme Grandet spoke to her husband.

'We ought to go into mourning, dear.'

'Really, Madame Grandet, you must be hard up for ways of getting rid of money. Mourning is in the heart; it is not put on with clothes.'

'But for a brother mourning is indispensable, and the Church bids us –'

'Then buy mourning out of your six louis; a band of crêpe will do for me; you can get me a band of crêpe.'

Eugénie said nothing, and raised her eyes to heaven. Her generous instincts, so long repressed and dormant, had been suddenly awakened, and every kindly thought had been harshly checked as it had arisen. Outwardly this evening passed just as thousands of others had passed in their monotonous lives, but for the two women it was the most painful that they had ever spent. Eugénie sewed without raising her head; she took no notice of the workbox which Charles had looked at so scornfully yesterday evening. Mme Grandet knitted away at her cuffs. Grandet sat twirling his thumbs, absorbed in schemes which should one day bring about results that would startle Saumur. Four hours went by. Nobody dropped in to see them. As a matter of fact, the whole town was ringing with the news of Grandet's sharp practice, following on the news of his brother's failure and his nephew's arrival. So imperatively did Saumur feel the need to thrash these matters thoroughly out, that all the vine-growers, great or small, were assembled beneath the des Grassins' roof, and frightful were the imprecations which were launched at the head of their late mayor.

Nanon was spinning; the whirr of her wheel was the only sound in the great room beneath the grey-painted rafters.

'Our tongues don't go very fast,' she said, showing her large teeth, white as blanched almonds.

'There is no call for them to go,' answered Grandet, roused from his calculations.

He beheld a vision of the future – he saw eight millions in three years' time – he had set forth on a long voyage upon a golden sea.

'Let us go to bed. I will go up and wish my nephew a good night from you all, and see if he wants anything.'

Mme Grandet stayed on the landing outside her room door to hear what her worthy husband might say to Charles. Eugénie, bolder than her mother, went a step or two up the second flight.

'Well, nephew, you are feeling unhappy? Yes, cry, it is only natural, a father is a father. But we must bear our troubles patiently. Whilst you have been crying, I have been thinking for you; I am a kind uncle, you see. Come, don't lose heart. Will you take a little wine? Wine costs nothing at Saumur; it is common here; they offer it as they might offer you a cup of tea in the Indies. But you are all in the dark,' Grandet went on. 'That's bad, that's bad; one ought to see what one is doing.'

Grandet went to the chimney-piece.

'What!' he cried, 'a wax candle! Where the devil have they fished that from? I believe the wenches would pull up the floor of my house to cook eggs for that boy.'

Mother and daughter, hearing these words, fled to their rooms, and crept into their beds like frightened mice.

'Madame Grandet, you have a lot of money some-where, it seems,' said the vine-grower, walking into his wife's room.

'I am saying my prayers, dear; wait a little,' faltered the poor mother.

'The devil take your pious notions!' growled Grandet.

Misers have no belief in a life to come, the present is all in all to them. But if this thought gives an insight into the miser's springs of action, it possesses a wider application, it throws a pitiless light upon our own era – for money is the one all-powerful force, ours is pre-eminently the epoch when money is the lawgiver, so-cially and politically. Books and institutions, theories and practice, all alike combine to weaken the belief in a future life, the foundation on which the social edifice has been slowly reared for eighteen hundred years. The grave has almost lost its terrors for us. That future which awaited us beyond the *Requiem* has been trans-ported into the present, and one hope and one ambition possesses us all – to pass *per fas et nefas* into this earthly paradise of luxury, vanity, and pleasure, to deaden the soul and mortify the body for a brief possession of this promised land, just as in other days men were found willing to lay down their lives and to suffer martyrdom for the hope of eternal bliss. This thought can be read at large; it is stamped upon our age, which asks of the man who makes the laws, not 'What do you think?' but 'What can you pay?' And what will become of us when this doctrine has been handed down from the *bourgeoisie* to the people?

'Madame Grandet, have you finished?' asked the cooper.

'I am praying for you, dear.'

'Very well, good night. Tomorrow morning I shall have something to say to you.'

Poor woman! she betook herself to sleep like a schoolboy who has not learned his lessons, and sees before him the angry face of the master when he wakes. Sheer terror led her to wrap the sheets about her head to shut out all sounds, but just at that moment she felt a kiss on her forehead; it was Eugénie who had slipped into the room in the darkness, and stood there barefooted in her night-dress.

'Oh, mother, my kind mother!' she said, 'I shall tell him tomorrow morning that it was all my doing.'

'No, don't; if you do, he will send you away to Noyers. Let me manage it; he will not eat me, after all.'

'Oh, mamma, do you hear?'

'What?'

'*He* is crying still.'

'Go back to bed, dear. The floor is damp, it will strike cold to your feet.'

So ended the solemn day, which had brought for the poor wealthy heiress a lifelong burden of sorrow; never again would Eugénie Grandet sleep as soundly or as lightly as heretofore. It not seldom happens that at some time in their lives this or that human being will act literally 'unlike himself', and yet in very truth in accordance with his nature. Is it not rather that we form our hasty conclusions of him without the aid of such light as psychology affords, without attempting to trace the mysterious birth and growth of the causes which led to these unforeseen results? And this passion, which had its roots in the depths of Eugénie's nature, should perhaps be studied as if it were the delicate fibre of some living organism to discover the secret of its growth. It was a passion that would influence her whole life, so that one day it would be sneeringly called a malady. Plenty of people would prefer to consider a catastrophe improbable rather than undertake the task of tracing the sequence of the events that led to it, of discovering how the links of the chain were forged one by one in the mind of the actor. In this case Eugénie's past life will suffice to keen observers of human nature; her artless impulsiveness, her sudden outburst of tenderness will be no surprise to them. Womanly pity, that treacherous feeling, had filled her soul but the more completely because her life had been so uneventful that it had never been so called forth before.

So the trouble and excitement of the day disturbed her rest; she woke again and again to listen for any sound from her cousin's room, thinking that she still heard the moans that all day long had vibrated through her heart. Sometimes she seemed to see him lying up there, dying of grief; sometimes she dreamed that he was being starved to death. Towards morning she distinctly heard a terrible cry. She dressed herself at once, and in the dim light of the dawn fled noiselessly up the stairs to her cousin's room. The door stood open, the wax candle had burned itself down to the socket. Nature had asserted herself; Charles, still dressed, was sleeping in the arm-chair, with his head fallen forward on the bed; he had been dreaming as famished people dream. Eugénie admired the fair young face. It was flushed and tear-stained; the eyelids were swollen with weeping; he seemed to be still crying in his sleep, and Eugénie's own tears fell fast. Some dim feeling that his cousin was present awakened Charles; he opened his eyes, and saw her distress.

'Pardon me, cousin,' he said dreamily. Evidently he had lost all reckoning of time, and did not know where he was.

'There are hearts here that feel for you, cousin, and *we* thought that you might perhaps want something. You should go to bed; you will tire yourself out if you sleep like that.'

'Yes,' he said, 'that is true.'

'Good-bye,' she said, and fled, half in confusion, half glad that she had come. Innocence alone dares to be thus bold, and virtue armed with knowledge weighs its actions as carefully as vice.

Eugénie had not trembled in her cousin's presence, but when she reached her own room again she could scarcely stand. Her ignorant life had suddenly come to an end; she remonstrated with herself, and blamed herself again and again. 'What will he think of me? He will believe that I love him.' Yet she knew that this was exactly what she wished him to believe. Love spoke plainly within her, knowing by instinct how love calls forth love. The moment when she stole into her cousin's room became a memorable event in the girl's lonely life. Are there not thoughts and deeds which, in love, are for some souls like a solemn betrothal?

An hour later she went to her mother's room, to help her to dress, as she always did. Then the two women went downstairs and took their places by the window, and waited for Grandet's coming in the anxiety which freezes or burns. Some natures cower, and others grow reckless, when a scene or painful agitation is in prospect; the feeling of dread is so widely felt that domestic animals will cry out when the slightest pain is inflicted on them as a punishment, while the same creature if hurt inadvertently will not utter a sound.

The cooper came downstairs, spoke in an absentminded way to his wife, kissed Eugénie, and sat down to table. He seemed to have forgotten last night's threats.

'What has become of my nephew? The child is not much in the way.'

'He is asleep, sir,' said Nanon.

'So much the better, he won't want a wax candle for that,' said Grandet facetiously.

His extraordinary mildness and satirical humour puzzled Mme Grandet; she looked earnestly at her husband. The goodman – here perhaps it may be observed that in Touraine, Anjou, Poitou, and Brittany the designation *goodman* (*bonhomme*), which has been so often applied to Grandet, conveys no idea of merit; it is allowed to people of the worst temper as well as to good-natured idiots, and is applied without distinction to any man of a certain age – the goodman, therefore, took up his hat and gloves with the remark:

'I am going to have a look round in the market-place; I want to meet the Cruchots.'

'Eugénie, your father certainly has something on his mind.'

As a matter of fact, Grandet always slept but little, and was wont to spend half the night in revolving and maturing schemes, a process by which his views, observations, and plans gained amazingly in clearness and precision; indeed, this was the secret of that constant success which was the admiration of Saumur. Time and patience combined will effect most things, and the man who accomplishes much is the man with the strong will who can wait. The miser's life is a constant exercise of every human faculty in the service of a personality. He believes in self-love and interest, and in no other motives of action, but interest is in some sort another form of self-love, to wit, a practical form dealing with the tangible and the concrete, and both forms are comprised in one master-passion, for self-love and interest are but two manifestations of egoism. Hence perhaps the prodigious interest which a miser excites when cleverly put upon the stage. What man is utterly without ambition? And what social ambition can be obtained without money? Everyone has something in common with this being; he is a personification of humanity, and yet is revolting to all the feelings of humanity.

Grandet really 'had something on his mind', as his wife used to say. In Grandet, as in every miser, there was a keen relish for the game, a constant craving to play men off one against another for his own benefit, to mulct them of their crowns without breaking the law. And did not every victim who fell into his clutches renew his sense of power, his just contempt for the weak of the earth who let themselves fall such an easy prey? Ah! who has understood the meaning of the lamb that lies in peace at the feet of God, that most touching symbol of meek victims who are doomed to suffer here below, and of the future that awaits them hereafter, of weakness and suffering glorified at last? But here on earth it is quite otherwise; the lamb is the miser's legitimate prey, and by him (when it is fat enough) it is contemptuously penned, killed, cooked, and eaten. On money and on this feeling of contemptuous superiority the miser thrives.

During the night this excellent man's ideas had taken an entirely new turn; hence his unusual mildness. He had been weaving a web to entangle them in Paris; he would envelop them in its toils, they should be as clay in his hands; they should hope and tremble, come and go, toil and sweat, and all for his amusement, all for the old cooper in the dingy room at the head of the wormeaten staircase in the old house at Saumur; it tickled his sense of humour.

He had been thinking about his nephew. He wanted to save his dead brother's name from dishonour in a way that should not cost a penny either to his nephew or to himself. He was about to invest his money for three years, his mind was quite at leisure from his own affairs; he really needed some outlet for his malicious energy, and here was an opportunity supplied by his brother's failure. The claws were idle, he had nothing to squeeze between them, so he would pound the Parisians for Charles's benefit, and exhibit himself in the light of an excellent brother at a very cheap rate. As a matter of fact, the honour of the family name counted for very little with him in this matter; he looked at it from the purely impersonal point of view of the gambler, who likes to see a game well played although it is no affair of his. The Cruchots were necessary to him, but he did not mean to go in search of them; they should come to him. That very evening the comedy should begin, the main outlines were decided upon already, tomorrow he would be held up as an object of admiration all over the town, and his generosity should not cost him a farthing!

Eugénie, in her father's absence, was free to busy herself openly for her cousin, to feel the pleasure of pouring out for him in many ways the wealth of pity that filled her heart; for in pity alone women are content that we should feel their superiority, and the sublimity of devotion is the one height which they can pardon us for leaving to them.

Three or four times Eugénie went to listen to her cousin's breathing, that she might know whether he was awake or still sleeping; and when she was sure that he was rising, she turned her attention to his breakfast, and cream, coffee, fruit, eggs, plates, and glasses were all in turn the objects of her especial care. She softly climbed the rickety stairs to listen again. Was he dressing? Was he still sobbing? She went to the door at last and spoke:

'Cousin!'

'Yes, cousin?'

'Would you rather have breakfast downstairs or up here in your room?'

'Whichever you please.'

'How do you feel?'

'I am ashamed to say that I am hungry.'

This talk through the closed door was like an episode in a romance for Eugénie.

'Very well, then, we will bring your breakfast up to your room, so that my father may not be vexed about it.'

She sprang downstairs, and ran into the kitchen with the swiftness of a bird.

'Nanon, just go and set his room straight.'

The familiar staircase which she had gone up and down so often, and which echoed with every sound, seemed no longer old in Eugénie's eyes; it was radiant with light, it seemed to speak a language which she understood, it was young again as she herself was, young like the love of her heart. And the mother, the kind, indulgent mother, was ready to lend herself to her daughter's whims, and as soon as Charles's room was ready they both went thither to sit with him. Does not Christian charity bid us comfort the mourner? Little religious sophistries were not wanting by which the women justified themselves.

Charles Grandet received the most tender and affectionate care. Such delicate tact and sweet kindness touched him very closely in his desolation; and as for these two souls, they found a moment's freedom from the restraint under which they lived; they were at home in an atmosphere of sorrow; they could give him the quick sympathy of fellowship in misfortune. Eugénie could avail herself of the privilege of relationship to set his linen in order, and to arrange the trifles that lay on the dressing-table; she could admire the wonderful knick-knacks at her leisure; all the paraphernalia of luxury, the delicately wrought gold and silver passed through her hands, her fingers dwelt lingeringly on them under the pretext of looking closely at the workmanship.

Charles was deeply touched by the generous interest which his aunt and cousin took in him. He knew Parisian life quite sufficiently to know that under these circumstances his old acquaintances and friends would have grown cold and distant at once. But his trouble had brought out all the peculiar beauty of Eugénie's character, and he began to admire the simplicity of manner which had provoked his amusement but yesterday. So when Eugénie waited on her cousin with such frank goodwill, taking from Nanon the earthenware bowl full of coffee and cream to set it before him herself, the Parisian's eyes filled with tears; and when he met her kind glance, he took her hand in his and kissed it.

'Well, what is the matter now?' she asked.

'Oh! they are tears of gratitude,' he answered.

Eugénie turned hastily away, took the candles from the chimney-piece, and held them out to Nanon.

'Here,' she said, 'take these away.'

When she could look at her cousin again, the flush was still on her face, but her eyes at least did not betray her, and gave no sign of the excess of joy that flooded her heart; yet the same thought was dawning in both their souls, and could be read in the eyes of either, and they knew that the future was theirs. This thrill of happiness was all the sweeter to Charles in his great sorrow, because it was so little expected.

There was a knock at the door, and both the women hurried down to their places by the window. It was lucky for them that their flight downstairs was sufficiently precipitate, and that they were at their work when Grandet came in, for if he had met them beneath the archway, all his suspicions would be aroused at once. After the midday meal, which he took standing, the keeper, who had not yet received his promised reward, appeared from Froidfond, bringing with him a hare, some partridges shot in the park, a few eels, and a couple of pike sent by him from the miller's.

'Aha! so here is old Cornoiller; you come just when you are wanted, like salt fish in Lent. Is all that fit to eat?'

'Yes, sir; all killed the day before yesterday.'

'Come, Nanon, look alive! Just take this, it will do for dinner today; the two Cruchots are coming.'

Nanon opened her eyes with amazement, and stared first at one and then at another.

'Oh! indeed,' she said; 'and where are the herbs and the bacon to come from?'

'Wife,' said Grandet, 'let Nanon have six francs, and remind me to go down into the cellar to look out a bottle of good wine.'

'Well, then, Monsieur Grandet,' the gamekeeper began (he wished to see the question of his salary properly settled, and was duly primed with a speech), 'Monsieur Grandet –'

'Tut, tut, tut,' said Grandet, 'I know what you are going to say; you are a good fellow, we will see about that tomorrow, I am very busy today. Give him five francs, wife,' he added, looking at Mme Grandet, and with that he beat a retreat. The poor woman was only too happy to purchase peace at the price of eleven francs. She knew by experience that Grandet usually kept quiet for a fortnight after he had made her disburse coin by coin the money which he had given her.

'There, Cornoiller,' she said, as she slipped ten francs into his hand; 'we will repay you for your services one of these days.'

Cornoiller had no answer ready, so he went.

'Madame,' said Nanon, who had by this time put on her black bonnet and had a basket on her arm, 'three francs will be quite enough; keep the rest. I shall manage just as well with three.'

'Let us have a good dinner, Nanon; my cousin is coming downstairs,' said Eugénie.

'There is something very extraordinary going on, I am sure,' said Mme Grandet. 'This makes the third time since we were married that your father has asked anyone here to dinner.'

It was nearly four o'clock in the afternoon; Eugénie and her mother had laid the cloth and set the table for six persons, and the master of the house had brought up two or three bottles of the exquisite wines, which are jealously hoarded in the cellars of the vine-growing district.

Charles came into the dining-room looking white and sad; there was a pathetic charm about his gestures, his face, his looks, the tones of his voice; his sorrow was no mere pretence, but a deeply-felt grief, and it had given him the interesting look that women like so well. Eugénie only loved him the more because his features were worn with pain. Perhaps, too, this trouble had brought them nearer in other ways. Charles was no longer the rich and handsome young man who lived in a sphere far beyond her ken; he was a kinsman in deep and terrible distress, and sorrow is a great leveller. Woman has this in common with the angels – all suffering creatures are under her protection.

Charles and Eugénie understood each other without a word being spoken on either side. The poor dandy of yesterday, fallen from his high estate, today was an orphan, who sat in a corner of the room, quiet, composed, and proud; but from time to time he met his cousin's eyes, her kind and affectionate glance rested on him, and compelled him to shake off his dark and sombre broodings, and to look forward with her to a future full of hope, in which she loved to think that she might share.

The news of Grandet's dinner-party caused even greater excitement in Saumur than the sale of his vintage, although this latter proceeding had been a crime of the blackest dye, an act of high treason against the vine-growing interest. If Grandet's banquet to the Cruchots had been prompted by the same idea which on a memorable occasion cost Alcibiades' dog its tail, history might perhaps have heard of the miser; but he felt himself to be above public opinion in this town which he exploited; he held Saumur too cheap.

It was not long before the des Grassins heard of Guillaume Grandet's violent end and impending bankruptcy. They determined to pay a visit to their client that evening, to condole with him in his affliction, and to show a friendly interest; while they endeavoured to discover the motives which could have led Grandet to invite the Cruchots to dinner at such a time.

Precisely at five o'clock Président C. de Bonfons and his uncle the notary arrived, dressed up to the nines this time. The guests seated themselves at table, and began by attacking their dinner with remarkably good appetites. Grandet was solemn, Charles was silent, Eugénie was dumb, and Mme Grandet said no more than usual; if it had been a funeral repast, it could not well have been less lively. When they rose from the table, Charles addressed his aunt and uncle:

'Will you permit me to withdraw? I have some long and difficult letters to write.'

'By all means, nephew.'

When Charles had left the room, and his amiable relative could fairly assume that he was out of earshot and deep in his correspondence, Grandet gave his wife a sinister glance.

'Madame Grandet, what we are going to say will be Greek to you; it is half-past seven o'clock, you ought to be off to bed by this time. Good night, my daughter.'

He kissed Eugénie, and mother and daughter left the room.

Then the drama began. Now, if ever in his life, Grandet displayed all the shrewdness which he had acquired in the course of his long experience of men and business, and all the cunning which had gained him the nickname of 'old fox' among those who had felt his

teeth a little too sharply. Had the ambition of the late
Mayor of Saumur soared a little higher; if he had had
the luck to rise to a higher social sphere, and destiny
had sent him to mingle in some congress in which the
fate of nations is at stake, the genius which he was now
devoting to his own narrow ends would doubtless have
done France glorious service. And yet, after all, the
probability is that once away from Saumur the worthy
cooper would have cut but a poor figure, and that
minds, like certain plants and animals, are sterile when
removed to a distant climate and an alien soil.

'M-M-Monsieur le P-P-Président, you were s-s-
saying that b-b-bankruptcy –'

Here the trick of stammering which it had pleased
the vine-grower to assume so long ago that everyone
believed it to be natural to him (like the deafness of
which he was wont to complain in rainy weather), grew
so unbearably tedious for the Cruchot pair, that as they
strove to catch the syllables, they made unconscious
grimaces, moving their lips as if they would fain finish
the words in which the cooper entangled both himself
and them at his pleasure.

And here, perhaps, is the fitting place to record the
history of Grandet's deafness and the impediment in
his speech. No one in Anjou had better hearing or could
speak Angevin French more clearly and distinctly than
the wily vine-grower – when he chose. Once upon a
time, in spite of all his shrewdness, a Jew had got the
better of him. In the course of their discussion the
Israelite had applied his hand to his ear, in the manner
of an ear-trumpet, the better to catch what was said, and
had gibbered to such purpose in his search for a word,
that Grandet, a victim to his own humanity, felt con-
strained to suggest to that crafty Hebrew the words and
ideas of which the Israelite appeared to be in search, to
finish himself the reasonings of the said Hebrew, to say

for that accursed alien all that he ought to have said for himself, till Grandet ended by fairly changing places with the Jew.

From this curious contest of wits the vine-grower did not emerge triumphant; indeed, for the first and last time in his business career he made a bad bargain. But loser though he was from a money point of view, he had received a great practical lesson, and later on he reaped the fruits of it. Wherefore in the end he blessed the Jew who had shown him how to wear out the patience of an opponent, and to keep him so closely employed in expressing his adversary's ideas that he completely lost sight of his own. The present business required more deafness, more stammering, more of the mazy circumlocutions in which Grandet was wont to involve himself, than any previous transaction in his life; for, in the first place, he wished to throw the responsibility of his ideas on someone else; someone else was to suggest his own schemes to him, while he was to keep himself to himself, and leave everyone in the dark as to his real intentions.

'Mon-sieur de B-B-Bonfons.' (This was the second time in three years that he had called the younger Cruchot 'Monsieur de Bonfons', and the president might well consider that this was almost tantamount to being acknowledged as the crafty cooper's son-in-law.)

'You were s-s-s-saying that in certain cases, p-p-p-proceedings in b-b-bankruptcy might be s-s-s-stopped b-b-by –'

'At the instance of a Tribunal of Commerce. That is done every day of the year,' said M. C. de Bonfons, guessing, as he thought, at old Grandet's idea, and running away with it. 'Listen!' he said, and in the most amiable way he prepared to explain himself.

'I am l-listening,' replied the older man meekly, and his face assumed a demure expression; he looked like

some small boy who is laughing in his sleeve at his
schoolmaster while appearing to pay the most respectful attention to every word.

'When anybody who is in a large way of business and
is much looked up to, like your late brother in Paris, for
instance –'

'My b-b-brother, yes.'

'When anyone in that position is likely to find himself insolvent –'

'Ins-s-solvent, do they call it?'

'Yes. When his failure is imminent, the Tribunal of
Commerce, to which he is amenable (do you follow
me?) has power by a judgment to appoint liquidators to
wind up the business. Liquidation is not bankruptcy, do
you understand? It is a disgraceful thing to be a bankrupt, but a *liquidation* reflects no discredit on a man.'

'It is quite a d-d-d-different thing, if only it d-d-does
not cost any more,' said Grandet.

'Yes. But a liquidation can be privately arranged
without having recourse to the Tribunal of Commerce,'
said the president as he took a pinch of snuff. 'How is a
man declared bankrupt?'

'Yes, how?' inquired Grandet. 'I have n-n-never
thought about it.'

'In the first place, he may himself file a petition and
leave his schedule with the clerk of the court, the debt-
or himself draws it up or authorizes someone else to do
so, and it is duly registered. Or, in the second place, his
creditors may make him a bankrupt. But supposing the
debtor does not file a petition, and none of his creditors
make application to the court for a judgment declaring
him bankrupt; now let us see what happens then!'

'Yes, let us s-s-see.'

'In that case, the family of the deceased, or his repre-
sentatives, or his residuary legatee, or the man himself
(if he is not dead), or his friends for him (if he has ab-

sconded), liquidate his affairs. Now, possibly, *you* may intend to do this in your brother's case?' inquired the president.

'Oh! Grandet,' exclaimed the notary, 'that would be acting very handsomely. We in the provinces have our notions of honour. If you saved your name from dishonour, for it is your name, you would be –'

'Sublime!' cried the president, interrupting his uncle.

'Of course, my b-b-brother's n-n-name was Grandet, th-that is certain sure, I d-d-don't deny it, and anyhow this l-l-l-l-liquidation would be a very g-good thing for my n-n-nephew in every way, and I am very f-f-fond of him. But we shall see. I know n-n-nothing of those sharpers in P-Paris, and their t-tricks. And here am I at S-Saumur, you see! There are my vine-cuttings, m-my d-d-draining; in sh-sh-short, there are my own af-f-fairs, to s-s-see after. *I* have n-n-never accepted a bill. What is a bill? I have t-t-taken many a one, b-b-but I have n-n-never put my n-n-name to a piece of p-paper. You t-t-take 'em and you can d-d-d-discount 'em, and that is all I know. I have heard s-s-say that you can b-b-b-buy them –'

'Yes,' assented the president. 'You can buy bills on the market, less so much per cent. Do you understand?'

Grandet held his hand to his ear, and the president repeated his remark.

'But it s-s-seems there are t-t-two s-sides to all this,' replied the vine-grower. 'At my age, I know n-n-n-nothing about this s-s-s-sort of thing. I must st-top here to l-look after the g-g-grapes, the vines d-d-don't stand still, and the g-g-grapes have to p-pay for everything. The vintage m-must be l-l-looked after before anything else. Then I have a g-great d-d-deal on my hands at Froidfond that I can't p-p-possibly l-l-l-leave to anyone else. I don't underst-t-tand a word of all this; it is a p-p-

pretty kettle of fish, confound it; I can't l-l-leave home
to s-see after it. You s-s-s-say that to bring about a l-l-
liquidation I ought to be in Paris. Now you can't be in
t-t-two p-places at once unless you are a b-b-bird.'

'*I* see what you mean,' cried the notary. 'Well, my old
friend, you have friends, friends of long standing ready
to do a great deal for you.'

'Come, now!' said the vine-grower to himself, 'so
you are making up your minds, are you?'

'And if someone were to go to Paris, and find out your
brother Guillaume's largest creditor, and say to him –'

'Here, just l-l-listen to me a moment,' the cooper
struck in. 'Say to him – what? S-s-something like this:
"Monsieur Grandet of Saumur th-this, Monsieur Grandet of Saumur th-th-that. He l-l-loves his brother, he
has a r-r-regard for his n-nephew; Grandet thinks a l-l-
lot of his f-family, he means to d-do well by them. He
has just s-s-sold his vintage uncommonly well. Don't
drive the thing into b-b-b-bankruptcy, call a meeting of
the creditors, and ap-p-point l-l-liquidators. Then s-see
what Grandet will do. You will do a great d-deal b-b-
better for yourselves by coming to an arrangement than
by l-l-letting the l-l-l-lawyers poke their noses into it."
That is how it is, eh?'

'Quite so!' said the president.

'Because, look you here, Monsieur de Bon-Bon-Bon-
fons, you must l-l-look before you l-l-l-leap. And you
can't d-do more than you can. A big af-f-fair like this
wants l-l-l-looking into, or you may ru-ru-ruin yourself.
That is so, isn't it, eh?'

'Certainly,' said the president. 'I myself am of the
opinion that in a few months' time you could buy up
the debts for a fixed sum and pay by instalments. Aha!
you can trail a dog a long way with a bit of bacon. When
there has been no actual bankruptcy, as soon as the bills
are in your hands, you are as white as snow.'

'As s-s-s-snow?' said Grandet, holding his hand to his ear. 'S-s-s-snow? I don't underst-t-tand.'

'Why, then, just listen to me!' cried the president.

'I am l-l-listening –'

'A bill of exchange is a commodity subject to fluctu-ations in value. This is a deduction from Jeremy Ben-tham's theory of interest. He was a publicist who showed conclusively that the prejudices entertained against moneylenders were irrational.'

'Bless me!' put in Grandet.

'And seeing that, according to Bentham, money it-self is a commodity, and that that which money repre-sents is no less a commodity,' the president went on; 'and since it is obvious that the commodity called a bill of exchange is subject to the same laws of supply and demand that control production of all kinds, a bill of ex-change bearing this or that signature, like this or that article of commerce, is scarce or plentiful in the market, commands a high premium or is worth nothing at all. Wherefore the decision of this court – There! how stupid I am, I beg your pardon; I mean I am of the opi-nion that you could easily buy up your brother's debts for twenty-five per cent of their value.'

'You m-m-m-mentioned Je-Je-Je-Jeremy Ben –'

'Bentham, an Englishman.'

'That is a Jeremiah who will save us many lamenta-tions in business matters,' said the notary, laughing.

'The English s-s-sometimes have s-s-s-sensible no-tions,' said Grandet. 'Then, according to B-Bentham, how if my b-b-brother's b-bills are worth n-n-n-noth-ing? If I am right, it looks to me as if . . . the creditors would . . . n-no, they wouldn't. . . I underst-t-tand.'

'Let me explain all this to you,' said the president. 'In law, if you hold all the outstanding bills of the firm of Grandet, your brother, his heirs and assigns, would owe no one a penny. So far, so good.'

'Good,' echoed Grandet.

'And in equity; suppose that your brother's bills were negotiated upon the market (negotiated, do you understand the meaning of that term?) at a loss of so much per cent; and suppose one of your friends happened to be passing, and bought up the bills; there would have been no physical force brought to bear upon the creditors, they gave them up of their own free will, and the estate of the late Grandet of Paris would be clear in the eye of the law.'

'True,' stuttered the cooper, 'b-b-business is business. So that is s-s-s-settled. But, for all that, you underst-tand that it is a d-d-difficult matter. I have not the m-m-money, nor have I the t-t-t-time, nor –'

'Yes, yes; you cannot be at the trouble. Well, now, I will go to Paris for you if you like (you must stand the expenses of the journey, that is a mere trifle). I will see the creditors, and talk to them, and put them off; it can all be arranged; you will be prepared to add something to the amount realized by the liquidation so as to get the bills into your hands.'

'We shall s-see about that; I cannot and *will* not under-t-t-take anything unless I know. . . . You can't d-d-do more than you can, you know.'

'Quite so, quite so.'

'And I am quite bewildered with all these head-splitting ideas that you have sp-prung upon me. Th-this is the f-f-f-first t-time in my l-l-life that I have had to th-th-think about such th –'

'Yes, yes, you are not a consulting barrister.'

'I am a p-p-poor vine-grower, and I know n-n-nothing about what you have just t-t-told me; I m-m-must th-think it all out.'

'Well, then,' began the president, as if he meant to reopen the discussion.

'Nephew!' interrupted the notary reproachfully.

'Well, uncle?' answered the president.

'Let Monsieur Grandet explain what he means to do. It is a very important question, and you are to receive his instructions. Our dear friend might now very pertinently state –'

A knock at the door announced the arrival of the des Grassins; their coming and exchange of greetings prevented Cruchot senior from finishing his sentence. Nor was he ill-pleased with this diversion; Grandet was looking askance at him already, and there was that about the wen on the cooper's face which indicated that a storm was brewing within. And on sober reflection it seemed to the cautious notary that a president of a court of first instance was not exactly the person to dispatch to Paris, there to open negotiations with creditors, and to lend himself to a more than dubious transaction which, however you looked at it, hardly squared with notions of strict honesty; and not only so, but he had particularly noticed that goodman Grandet had shown not the slightest inclination to disburse anything whatever, and he trembled instinctively at the thought of his nephew becoming involved in such a business. He took advantage of the entrance of the des Grassins, took his nephew by the arm, and drew him into the embrasure of the window.

'You have gone quite as far as there is any need,' he said, 'that is quite enough of such zeal; you are overreaching yourself in your eagerness to marry the girl. The devil! You should not rush into a thing openmouthed, like a crow at a walnut. Leave the steering of the ship to me for a bit, and just shift your sails according to the wind. Now, is it a part you ought to play, compromising your dignity as magistrate in such a –'

He broke off suddenly, for he heard M. des Grassins saying to the old cooper, as he held out his hand:

'Grandet, we have heard of the dreadful misfortunes

which have befallen your family – the ruin of the firm of Guillaume Grandet and your brother's death; we have come to express our sympathy with you in this sad calamity.'

'There is only one misfortune,' the notary inter-rupted at this point – 'the death of the younger Mon-sieur Grandet; and if he had thought to ask his brother for assistance, he would not have taken his own life. Our old friend here, who is a man of honour to his finger-tips, is prepared to discharge the debts con-tracted by the firm of Grandet in Paris. In order to spare our friend the worry of what is, after all, a piece of law-yer's business, my nephew the president offers to start immediately for Paris, so as to arrange with the credi-tors, and duly satisfy their claims.'

The three des Grassins were thoroughly taken aback by these words; Grandet appeared to acquiesce in what had been said, for he was pensively stroking his chin. On their way to the house the family had commented very freely upon Grandet's niggardliness, and indeed had almost gone so far as to accuse him of fratricide.

'Ah! just what I expected!' cried the banker, looking at his wife. 'What was I saying to you only just now as we came along, Madame des Grassins? Grandet, I said, is a man who will never swerve a hair's breadth from the strict course of honour; he will not endure the thought of the slightest spot on his name! Money without honour is a disease. Oh! we have a keen sense of honour in the provinces! This is noble – really noble of you, Grandet. I am an old soldier, and I do not mince matters, I say what I think straight out; and great heavens! this is sublime!'

'Then the s-s-sub-sublime costs a great d-d-deal,' stuttered the cooper, as the banker shook him warmly by the hand.

'But this, my good Grandet (no offence to you, Mon-sieur le Président), is simply a matter of business,' des

Grassins went on, 'and requires an experienced man of business to deal with it. There will have to be accounts kept of sales and outgoing expenses; you ought to have tables of interest at your finger-ends. I must go to Paris on business of my own, and I could undertake –'

'Then we must s-s-see about it, and t-t-t-try to arrange between us to p-p-provide for anything that m-may t-t-turn up, but I d-d-don't want to be d-d-drawn into anything that I would rather not d-d-d-do,' continued Grandet, 'because, you see, Monsieur le Président naturally wants me to pay his expenses.' The goodman did not stammer over these last words.

'Eh?' said Mme des Grassins. 'Why, it is a pleasure to stay in Paris! For my part, I should be glad to go there at my own expense.'

She made a sign to her husband, urging him to seize this opportunity of discomfiting their enemies and cheat them of their mission. Then she flung a withering glance at the now crestfallen and miserable Cruchots. Grandet seized the banker by the buttonhole and drew him aside.

'I should feel far more confidence in you than in the president,' he remarked; 'and besides that,' he added (and the wen twitched a little), 'there are other fish to fry. I want to make an investment. I have several thousand francs to put into consols, and I don't mean to pay more than eighty for them. Now, from all I can hear, that machine always runs down at the end of the month. You know all about these things, I expect?'

'Rather! I should think I did. Well, then, I shall have to buy several thousand livres' worth of consols for you?'

'Just by way of a beginning. But mum, I want to play at this game without letting anyone know about it. You will buy them for me at the end of the month, and say nothing to the Cruchots; it would only annoy them.

Since you are going to Paris, we might as well see at the same time what trumps are, for my poor nephew's sake.'

'That is an understood thing. I shall travel post to Paris tomorrow,' said des Grassins aloud, 'and I will come round to take your final instructions at – when shall we say?'

'At five o'clock, before dinner,' said the vine-grower, rubbing his hands.

The two factions for a little while remained facing each other. Des Grassins broke the silence again, clapping Grandet on the shoulder, and saying:

'It is a fine thing to have a good uncle like –'

'Yes, yes,' returned Grandet, falling into the stammer again, 'without m-making any p-p-parade about it; I am a good uncle; I l-l-loved my brother; I will give p-p-p-proof of it, if-if-if it d-doesn't cost –'

Luckily the banker interrupted him at this point.

'We must go, Grandet. If I am to set out sooner than I intended, I shall have to see after some business at once before I go.'

'Right, quite right. I myself, in connection with you know what, must p-p-put on my cons-s-sidering cap, as P-Président Cruchot s-s-says.'

'Plague take it! I am no longer Monsieur de Bonfons,' thought the magistrate moodily, and his face fell; he looked like a judge who is bored by the cause before him.

The heads of the rival clans went out together. Both had completely forgotten Grandet's treacherous crime of that morning; his disloyal behaviour had faded from their minds. They sounded each other, but to no purpose, as to the goodman's real intentions (if intentions he had) in this new turn that matters had taken.

'Are you coming with us to Madame Dorsonval's?' des Grassins asked the notary.

'We are going there later on,' replied the president. 'With my uncle's permission, we will go first to see Mademoiselle de Gribeaucourt; I promised just to look in on her to say good night.'

'We shall meet again, then,' smiled Mme des Grassins.

But when the des Grassins were at some distance from the two Cruchots, Adolphe said to his father, 'They are in a pretty stew, eh?'

'Hush!' returned his mother, 'they can very likely hear what we are saying, and besides, that remark of yours was not in good taste; it sounds like one of your law-school phrases.'

'Well, uncle!' cried the magistrate, when he saw the des Grassins were out of earshot, 'I began by being Président de Bonfons, and ended as plain Cruchot.'

'I saw myself that you were rather put out about it; and the des Grassins took the wind out of our sails. How stupid you are, for all your sharpness! Let *them* set sail, on the strength of a "We shall see" from Grandet; be easy, my boy, Eugénie shall marry you for all that.'

A few moments later, and the news of Grandet's magnanimity was set circulating in three houses at once; the whole town talked of nothing but Grandet's devotion to his brother. The sale of his vintage in utter disregard of the agreement made among the vine-growers was forgotten; everyone fell to praising his scrupulous integrity, and to lauding his generosity, a quality which no one had suspected him of possessing. There is that in the French character which is readily excited to fury or to passionate enthusiasm by any meteor that appears above their horizon, that is captivated by the bravery of a blatant fact. Can it be that collectively men have no memories?

As soon as Grandet had bolted the house door he called to Nanon.

'Don't go to bed,' he said, 'and don't unchain the dog; there is something to be done, and we must do it together. Cornoiller will be round with the carriage from Froidfond at eleven o'clock. You must sit up for him, and let him in quietly; don't let him rap at the door, and tell him not to make a noise. You get into trouble with the police if you raise a racket at night. And besides, there is no need to let all the quarter know that I am going out.'

Having thus delivered himself, Grandet went up to his laboratory, and Nanon heard him stirring about, rummaging, going and coming, all with great caution. Clearly he had no wish to waken his wife or daughter, and above all things he desired in no wise to excite any suspicion in the mind of his nephew; he had seen that a light was burning in the young man's room, and had cursed his relative forthwith.

In the middle of the night Eugénie heard a sound like the groan of a dying man; her cousin was always in her thoughts, and for her the dying man was Charles. How white and despairing he had looked when he wished her good night; perhaps he had killed himself. She hastily wrapped herself in her capuchin, a sort of long cloak with a hood to it, and determined to go to see for herself. Some rays of bright light streaming through the cracks of her door frightened her not a little at first, perhaps the house was on fire; but she was soon reassured. She could hear Nanon's heavy footsteps outside, and the sounds of the old servant's voice mingled with the neighing of several horses.

'Can my father be taking Charles away?' she asked herself, as she set her door ajar, cautiously for fear the hinges should creak, so that she could watch all that was going on in the corridor.

All at once her eyes met those of her father, and, absent and indifferent as they looked, a cold shudder ran through her. The cooper and Nanon were coming along carrying something which hung by a chain from a stout cudgel, one end of which rested on the right shoulder of either; the something was a little barrel such as Grandet sometimes amused himself by making in the bake-house, when he had nothing better to do.

'Holy Virgin! how heavy it is, sir!' said Nanon in a whisper.

'What a pity it is only full of pence!' replied the cooper. 'Look out! or you will knock down the candle-stick.'

The scene was lighted by a single candle set between two balusters.

'Cornoiller,' said Grandet to his gamekeeper *in partibus*, 'have you your pistols with you?'

'No, sir. Lord love you! What can there be to fear for a keg of coppers?'

'Oh! nothing, nothing,' said Goodman Grandet.

'Besides, we shall get over the ground quickly,' the keeper went on; 'your tenants have picked out their best horses for you.'

'Well, well! You did not let them know where I was going?'

'I did not know that myself.'

'Right. Is the carriage strongly built?'

'That's all right, mister. Why, what is the weight of a few paltry barrels like those of yours? It would carry two or three thousand of the like of them.'

'Well,' said Nanon, 'I know there's pretty well eighteen hundredweight *there*, that there is!'

'Will you hold your tongue, Nanon! You tell my wife that I have gone into the country, and that I shall be back to dinner. Hurry up, Cornoiller; we must be in Angers before nine o'clock.'

The carriage started. Nanon bolted the gateway, let the dog loose, and lay down and slept in spite of her

bruised shoulder; and no one in the quarter had any suspicion of Grandet's journey or of its object. The worthy
man was a miracle of circumspection. Nobody ever saw
a penny lying about in that house full of gold. He had
learned that morning from the gossip on the quay that
some vessels were being fitted out at Nantes, and that
in consequence gold was so scarce there that it was
worth double its ordinary value, and speculators were
buying it in Angers. The old cooper, by the simple device of borrowing his tenants' horses, was prepared to
sell his gold at Angers, receiving in return an order upon
the Treasury from the Receiver-General for the sum
destined for the purchase of his consols, and an addition
in the shape of the premium paid on his gold.

'My father is going out,' said Eugénie to herself. She
had heard all that had passed from the head of the staircase.

Silence reigned once more in the house. The rattle
of the wheels in the streets of sleeping Saumur grew
more and more distant, and at last died away. Then it
was that a sound seemed to reach Eugénie's heart before it fell on her ears, a wailing sound that rang through
the thin walls above – it came from her cousin's room.
There was a thin line of light, scarcely wider than a
knife edge, beneath his door; the rays slanted through
the darkness and left a bright gleaming bar along the
balusters of the crazy staircase.

'He is unhappy,' she said, as she went up a little
further.

A second moan brought her to the landing above. The
door stood ajar; she thrust it open. Charles was sleeping in
the rickety old arm-chair, his head drooped over to one
side, his hand hung down and nearly touched the floor,
the pen that he had let fall lay beneath his fingers. Lying
in this position, his breath came in quick, sharp jerks that
startled Eugénie. She entered hastily.

'He must be very tired,' she said to herself, as she saw a dozen sealed letters lying on the table. She read the addresses: 'MM. Farry, Breilman & Co., carriage builders,' 'M. Buisson, tailor'; and so forth.

'Of course, he has been settling his affairs, so that he may leave France as soon as possible,' she thought.

Her eyes fell upon two unsealed letters. One of them began, 'My dear Annette . . .' She felt dazed, and could see nothing more for a moment. Her heart beat fast, her feet seemed glued to the floor.

'*His dear Annette!* He loves, he is beloved! . . . Then there is no more hope! . . . What does he say to her?' These thoughts flashed through her heart and brain. She read the words everywhere: on the walls, on the very floor, in letters of fire.

'Must I give up already? No, I will not read the letter. I ought not to stay. . . . And yet, even if I did read it?'

She looked at Charles, gently took his head in her hands, and propped it against the back of the chair. He submitted like a child, who even while he is sleeping knows that it is his mother who is bending over him, and, without waking, feels his mother's kisses. Like a mother, Eugénie raised the drooping hand, and, like a mother, laid soft a kiss on his hair. '*Dear Annette!*' A mocking voice shrieked the words in her ear.

'I know that perhaps I may be doing wrong, but I will read that letter,' she said.

Eugénie turned her eyes away; her high sense of honour reproached her. For the first time in her life there was a struggle between good and evil in her soul. Hitherto she had never done anything for which she needed to blush. Love and curiosity silenced her scruples. Her heart swelled higher with every phrase as she read; her quickened pulses seemed to send a sharp, tingling glow through her veins, and to heighten the vivid emotions of her first love.

My dear Annette,

Nothing should have power to separate us save this overwhelming calamity that has befallen me, a calamity that no human foresight could have predicted. My father has died by his own hand; his fortune and mine are both irretrievably lost. I am left an orphan at an age when, with the kind of education I have received, I am almost a child; and, nevertheless, I must now endeavour to show myself a man, and to rise from the dark depths into which I have been hurled. I have been spending part of my time tonight in revolving plans for my future. If I am to leave France as an honest man, as of course I mean to do, I have not a hundred francs that I can call my own with which to tempt fate in the Indies or in America. Yes, my poor Anna, I am going in quest of fortune to the most deadly foreign climes. Beneath such skies, they say, fortunes are rapidly and surely made. As for living on in Paris, I could not bring myself to do it. I could not face the coldness, the contempt, and the affronts that a ruined man, the son of a bankrupt, is sure to receive. Great heaven! to owe two millions! . . . I should fall in a duel before a week had passed. So I shall not return to Paris. Your love – the tenderest, the most devoted love that ever ennobled the heart of man – would not seek to draw me back. Alas! my darling, I have not money enough to take me to you, that I might give and receive one last kiss, a kiss that should put strength into me for the task that lies before me. . .

'Poor Charles, I did well to read this. I have money, and he shall have it,' said Eugénie. She went on with the letter when she could see for her tears.

I have not even begun to think of the hardships of poverty. Supposing that I find I have the hundred louis to pay for my passage out, I have not a sou to lay out on a trading venture. Yet, no; I shall not have a hundred louis, nor yet a hundred sous; I have no idea whether anything will be left when I have settled all my debts in Paris. If there is nothing, I shall simply go to Nantes and work my passage out. I will begin at the bottom of the ladder, like many another man of energy who has gone out to the Indies as a penniless youth, to return thence a rich man. This morning I began to look my future steadily in the face. It is far harder for me than for others; I have been the petted child of a mother who idolized me, indulged by the best and kindest of fathers; and at my very entrance into the world I met with the love of an Anna! As yet I have only known the primrose paths of life; such happiness could not last. Yet, dear Annette, I have more fortitude than could be looked for from a thoughtless youth; above all, from a young man thus lapped round in happiness from the cradle, spoiled and flattered by the most delightful woman in Paris, the darling of Fortune, whose wishes were as law to a father who . . . Oh! my father! He is dead, Annette! . . . Well, I have thought seriously over my position, and I have likewise thought over yours. I have grown much older in the last twenty-four hours. Dear Anna, even if, to keep me beside you, you were to give up all the luxuries that you enjoy, your box at the opera, and your toilette, we should not have nearly sufficient for the necessary expenses of the extravagant life that I am accustomed to; and besides, I could not think of allowing you to make such sacrifices for me. Today, therefore, we part for ever.

'Then this is to take leave of her! Sainte-Vierge! what happiness!'

Eugénie started and trembled for joy. Charles stirred

in his chair, and Eugénie felt a chill of dread. Luckily, however, he did not wake. She went on reading.

When shall I come back? I cannot tell. Europeans grow old before their time in those tropical countries, especially Europeans who work hard. Let us look forward and try to see ourselves in ten years' time. In ten years from now your little girl will be eighteen years old; she will be your constant companion; that is, she will be a spy upon you. If the world will judge you very harshly, your daughter will probably judge more harshly still; such ingratitude on a young girl's part is common enough, and we know how the world regards these things. Let us take warning and be wise. Only, keep the memory of those four years of happiness in the depths of your soul, as I shall keep them buried in mine; and be faithful, if you can, to your poor friend. I shall not be too exacting, dear Annette; for, as you can see, I must submit to my altered lot; I am compelled to look at life in a business-like way, and to base my calculations on dull, prosaic fact. So I ought to think of marriage as a necessary step in my new existence; and I will confess to you that here, in my uncle's house in Saumur, there is a cousin whose manners, face, character, and heart you would approve; and who, moreover, has, it appears –

'How tired he must have been to break off like this when he was writing to *her*!' said Eugénie to herself, as the letter ended abruptly in the middle of a sentence. She was ready with excuses for him.

How was it possible that an inexperienced girl should discover the coldness and selfishness of this letter? For young girls, religiously brought up as she had been, are innocent and unsuspecting, and can see nothing but love when they have set foot in love's enchanted kingdom. It is as if a light from heaven shone in their own souls, shedding its beams upon their path; their lover shines transfigured before them in reflected glory, radiant with fair colours from love's magic fires, and endowed with noble thoughts which perhaps in truth are none of his. Women's errors spring, for the most part, from a belief in goodness, and a confidence in truth. In Eugénie's heart the words, 'My dear Annette – my beloved', echoed like the fairest language of love; they stirred her soul like organ music – like the divine notes of the *Venite adoremus* falling upon her ears in childhood.

Surely the tears, not dry even yet upon her cousin's eyelids, betokened the innate nobility of nature that never fails to attract a young girl. How could she know that Charles's love and grief for his father, albeit genuine, was due rather to the fact that his father had loved him than to a deeply rooted affection on his own part for his father? M. and Mme Guillaume Grandet had indulged their son's every whim; every pleasure that wealth could bestow had been his; and thus it followed that he had never been tempted to make the hideous calculations that are only too common among the younger members of a family in Paris, when they see around them all the delights of Parisian life, and reflect with disgust that, so long as their parents are alive, all these enjoyments are not for them. The strange result of the father's lavish kindness had been a strong affection on the part of his son, an affection unalloyed by any afterthought. But, for all that, Charles was a thorough child of Paris, with the Parisian's habit of mind; Annette herself had impressed upon him the importance of thinking out all the consequences of every step; he was not youthful, despite the mask of youth.

He had received the detestable education of a world in which more crimes (in thought and word at least) are committed in one evening than come before a court of justice in the course of a whole session; a world in which great ideas perish, done to death by a witticism, and where it is reckoned a weakness not to see things as they are. To see things as they are – that means, believe in nothing, put faith in nothing and in no man, for there is no such thing as sincerity in opinion or affection; mistrust events, for even events at times have been known to be manufactured. To see things as they are you must weigh your friend's purse morning by morning; you must know by instinct the right moment to interfere for your own profit in every matter that turns up; you must keep your judgment rigorously suspended, be in no hurry to admire a work of art or a noble deed, and give everyone credit for interested motives on every possible occasion.

After many follies, the great lady, the fair Annette, compelled Charles to think seriously; she talked to him of his future, passing a fragrant hand through his hair, and imparted counsel to him on the art of getting on in the world, while she twisted a stray curl about her fingers. She had made him effeminate, and now she set herself to make a materialist of him, a twofold work of demoralization, a corruption none the less deadly because it never offended against the canons of good society, good manners, and good taste.

'You are a simpleton, Charles,' she would say; 'I see that it will be no easy task to teach you the ways of the world. You were very naughty about Monsieur des Lupeaulx. Oh! he is not over-fastidious, I grant you, but you should wait until he falls from power, and then you may despise him as much as you like. Do you know what Madame Campan used to say to us? "My children, so long as a man is a minister, adore him; if he falls, help to drag him to the shambles. He is a kind of deity so long as he is in power, but after he is fallen and ruined he is viler than Marat himself, for he is still alive, while

Marat is dead and out of sight. Life is nothing but a series of combinations, which must be studied and followed very carefully if a good position is to be successfully maintained." '

Charles had no very exalted aims; he was too much of a worldling; he had been too much spoiled by his father and mother, too much flattered by the society in which he moved, to be stirred by any lofty enthusiasm. In the clay of his nature there was a grain of gold, due to his mother's teaching; but it had been passed through the Parisian draw-plate, and beaten out into a thin surface gilding which must soon be worn away by contact with the world.

At this time Charles, however, was only one-and-twenty, and it is taken for granted that freshness of heart accompanies the freshness of youth; it seems so unlikely that the mind within should be at variance with the young face, and the young voice, and the candid glance. Even the hardest judge, the most sceptical attorney, the flintiest-hearted moneylender will hesitate to believe that a wizened heart and a warped and corrupted nature can dwell beneath a young exterior, when the forehead is smooth and tears come so readily to the eyes. Hitherto Charles had never had occasion to put his Parisian maxims in practice; his character had not been tried, and consequently had not been found wanting; but, all unknown to him, egoism had taken deep root in his nature. The seeds of this baneful political economy had been sown in his heart; it was only a question of time, they would spring up and flower so soon as the soil was stirred, as soon as he ceased to be an idle spectator and became an actor in the drama of real life.

A young girl is nearly always ready to believe unquestioningly in the promise of a fair exterior; but even if Eugénie had been as keenly observant and as cautious as girls in the provinces sometimes are, how could she have brought herself to mistrust her cousin, when all he did and said, and everything about him, seemed to be the spontaneous outcome of a noble nature? This was the last outburst of real feeling, the last reproachful sigh of conscience in Charles's life; fate had thrown them together at that moment, and, unfortunately for her, all her sympathies had been aroused for him.

So she laid down the letter that seemed to her so full of love, and gave herself up to the pleasure of watching her sleeping cousin; the dreams and hopes of youth seemed to hover over his face, and then and there she vowed to herself that she would love him always. She glanced over the other letter; there could be no harm in reading it, she thought; she should only receive fresh proofs of the noble qualities with which, womanlike, she had invested the man whom she had idealized.

MY DEAR ALPHONSE [so it began],

By the time this letter is in your hands I shall have no friends left; but I will confess that though I put no faith in the worldly-minded people who use the word so freely, I have no doubts of your friendship for me. So I am commissioning you to settle some matters of business. I look to you to do the best you can for me in this, for all I have in the world is involved in it. By this time you must know how I am situated. I have nothing, and have made up my mind to go out to the Indies. I have just written to all the people to whom any money is owing, and the enclosed list is as accurate as I can make it from memory. I think the sale of my books, furniture, carriages, horses, and so forth ought to bring in sufficient to pay my debts. I only mean to keep back a few trinkets of little value, which will go some way towards a trading venture. I will send you a power of attorney in due form for this sale, my dear Alphonse, in case any difficulty should arise. You might send my guns and everything of that sort to me here. And you must take 'Briton'; no one would ever give me anything like as much as the splendid animal is worth; I would rather give him to you, you must regard him as the mourning ring which a dying man leaves in his will to his executor. Farry, Breilman & Co. have been building a very comfortable travelling carriage for me, but they have not sent it home yet; get them to keep it if you can, and if they decline to have it left on their hands, make the best arrangement you can for me, and do all you can to save my honour in the position in which I am placed. I lost six louis at play to that fellow from the British Isles, mind that he is . . .

'Dear cousin,' murmured Eugénie, letting the sheet fall, and, seizing one of the lighted candles, she hastened on tiptoe to her own room.

Once there, it was not without a keen feeling of pleasure that she opened one of the drawers in an old oak chest – a most beautiful specimen of the skill of the craftsmen of the Renaissance, you could still make out the half-effaced royal salamander upon it. From this drawer she took a large red velvet money-bag, with gold tassels, and the remains of a golden fringe about it, a bit of faded splendour that had belonged to her grandmother. In the pride of her heart she felt its weight, and joyously set to work to reckon up the value of her little hoard, sorting out the different coins. *Imprimis*, twenty Portuguese moidores as new and fresh as when they were struck in 1725, in the reign of John V; each was nominally worth five lisbonines, or a hundred and sixty-eight francs, but actually they were worth a hundred and eighty francs (so her father used to tell her), a fancy value on account of the rarity and beauty of the afore-

said coins, which shone like the sun. *Item*, five geno-
vines, rare Genoese coins of a hundred livres each, their
current value was perhaps about eighty-seven francs,
but collectors would give a hundred for them. These
had come to her from old M. de la Bertellière. *Item*, three
Spanish quadruples of the time of Philip V, bearing the
date 1729. Mme Gentillet had given them to her, one by
one, always with the same little speech: 'There's a little
yellow bird, there's a buttercup for you, worth ninety-
eight livres! Take great care of it, darling; it will be the
flower of your flock.' *Item* (and those were the coins that
her father thought most of, for the gold was a fraction
over the twenty-three carats), a hundred Dutch ducats,
struck at The Hague in 1756, and each worth about thirteen francs. *Item*, a great curiosity! . . . a few coins dear to
a miser's heart, three rupees bearing the sign of the Bal-
ance, and five with the sign of the Virgin stamped upon
them, all pure gold of twenty-four carats – the magnificent coins of the Great Mogul. The weight of metal in
them alone was worth thirty-seven francs forty centimes, but amateurs who love to finger gold would give
fifty francs for such coins as those. *Item*, the double napoleon that had been given to her the day before, and
which she had carelessly slipped into the red velvet bag.

There were new gold pieces fresh from the mint
among her treasures, real works of art, which old Grandet liked to look at from time to time, so that he might
count them over and tell his daughter of their intrinsic
value, expatiating also upon the beauty of the border-
ing, the sparkling field, the ornate lettering with its
sharp, clean, flawless outlines. But now she gave not a
thought to their beauty and rarity; her father's mania,
and the risks she ran by despoiling herself of a hoard so
precious in his eyes, were all forgotten. She thought of
nothing but her cousin, and managed at last to discover,
after many mistakes in calculation, that she was the

owner of five thousand eight hundred francs all told, or of nearly two thousand crowns if the coins were sold for their actual value as curiosities.

She clapped her hands in exultation at the sight of her riches, like a child who is compelled to find some outlet for his overflowing glee and dances for joy. Father and daughter had both counted their wealth that night; he in order to sell his gold, she that she might cast it abroad on the waters of love. She put the money back into the old purse, took it up, and went upstairs with it without a moment's hesitation. Her cousin's distress was the one thought in her mind; she did not even remember that it was night, conventionalities were utterly forgotten; her conscience did not reproach her, she was strong in her happiness and her love.

As she stood upon the threshold with the candle in one hand and the velvet bag in the other, Charles awoke, saw his cousin, and was struck dumb with astonishment. Eugénie came forward, set the light on the table, and said with an unsteady voice:

'Cousin Charles, I have to ask your forgiveness for something I have done; it was very wrong, but if you will overlook it, God will forgive me.'

'What can it be?' asked Charles, rubbing his eyes.

'I have been reading those two letters.'

Charles reddened.

'Do you ask how I came to do it?' she went on, 'and why I came up here? Indeed, I do not know now; and I am almost tempted to feel glad that I read the letters, for through reading them I have come to know your heart, your soul, and –'

'And what?' asked Charles.

'And your plans – the difficulty that you are in for want of money –'

'My *dear* cousin –'

'Hush! hush! do not speak so loud, do not let us

wake anybody. Here are the savings of a poor girl who has no wants,' she went on, opening the purse. 'You must take them, Charles. This morning I did not know what money was; you have taught me that it is simply a means to an end, that is all. A cousin is almost a brother; surely you may borrow from your sister.'

Eugénie, almost as much a woman as a girl, had not foreseen a refusal, but her cousin was silent.

'Why, are you going to refuse me?' asked Eugénie. The silence was so deep that the beating of her heart was audible. Her pride was wounded by her cousin's hesitation, but the thought of his dire need came vividly before her, and she fell on her knees.

'I will not rise,' she said, 'until you have taken that money. Oh, cousin, say something, for pity's sake! . . . so that I may know that you respect me, that you are generous, that . . .'

This cry, wrung from her by a noble despair, brought tears to Charles's eyes; he would not let her kneel, she felt his hot tears on her hands, and sprang to her purse, which she emptied out upon the table.

'Well, then, it is *Yes*, is it not?' she said, crying for joy. 'Do not scruple to take it, cousin: you will be quite rich. That gold will bring you luck, you know. Some day you shall pay it back to me, or, if you like, we will be partners; I will submit to any conditions that you may impose. But you ought not to make so much of this gift.'

Charles found words at last.

'Yes, Eugénie, I should have a little soul indeed if I would not take it. But nothing for nothing, confidence for confidence.'

'What do you mean?' she asked, startled.

'Listen, dear cousin, I have there –'

He interrupted himself for a moment to show her a square box in a leather case, which stood on the chest of drawers.

'There is something there that is dearer to me than life. That box was a present from my mother. Since this morning I have thought that if she could rise from her tomb she herself would sell the gold that in her tenderness she lavished on this dressing-case, but I cannot do it – it would seem like sacrilege.'

Eugénie grasped her cousin's hand tightly in hers at these last words.

'No,' he went on after a brief pause, during which they looked each at each with tearful eyes, 'I do not want to pull it to pieces, nor to risk taking it with me on my wanderings. I will leave it in your keeping, dear Eugénie. Never did one friend confide a more sacred trust to another; but you shall judge for yourself.'

He drew the box from its leather case, opened it, and displayed before his cousin's astonished eyes a dressing-case resplendent with gold – the curious skill of the craftsman had only added to the value of the metal.

'All that you are admiring is nothing,' he said, pressing the spring of a secret drawer. 'There is something which is worth more than all the world to me,' he added sadly.

He took out two portraits, two of Mme de Mirbel's masterpieces, handsomely set in pearls.

'How lovely she is! Is not this the lady to whom you were writing?'

'No,' he said, with a little smile; 'that is my mother, and this is my father – your aunt and uncle. Eugénie, I could beg and pray of you on my knees to keep this treasure safe for me. If I should die, and lose your little fortune, the gold will make good your loss; and to you alone can I leave those two portraits, for you alone are worthy to take charge of them, but do not let them pass into any other hands, rather destroy them. . .'

Eugénie was silent.

'Well, "it is *Yes*, is it not?"' he said, and there was a winning charm in his manner.

As the last words were spoken, she gave him for the first time such a glance as a loving woman can, a bright glance that reveals a depth of feeling within her. He took her hand and kissed it.

'Angel of purity! what is money henceforward between us two? It is nothing, is it not? But the feeling, which alone gave it worth, will be everything.'

'You are like your mother. Was her voice as musical as yours, I wonder?'

'Oh! far more sweet. . .'

'Yes, for you,' she said, lowering her eyelids. 'Come, Charles, you must go to bed; I wish it. You are very tired. Good night.'

Her cousin had caught her hand in both of his; she drew it gently away, and went down to her room, her cousin lighting the way. In the doorway of her room they both paused.

'Oh! why am I a ruined man?' he said.

'Pshaw! my father is rich, I believe,' she returned.

'My poor child,' said Charles, as he set one foot in her room, and propped himself against the wall by the doorway, 'if your father had been rich, he would not have let my father die, and you would not be lodged in such a poor place as this; he would live altogether in quite a different style.'

'But he has Froidfond.'

'And what may Froidfond be worth?'

'I do not know; but there is Noyers too.'

'Some miserable farm-house!'

'He has vineyards and meadows –'

'They are not worth talking about,' said Charles scornfully. 'If your father had even twenty-four thousand livres a year, do you suppose that you would sleep in a bare, cold room like this?' he added, as he made a step forward with his left foot. 'That is where my treasures will be,' he went on, nodding towards the old chest, a device by which he tried to conceal his thoughts from her.

'Go,' she said, 'and try to sleep,' and she barred his entrance into an untidy room. Charles drew back; and the cousins bade each other a smiling good night.

They fell asleep, to dream the same dream; and from that time forward Charles found that there were still roses to be gathered in the world in spite of his mourning. The next morning Mme Grandet saw her daughter walking with Charles before breakfast. He was still sad and subdued; how, indeed, should he be otherwise than sad? He had been brought very low in his distress; he was gradually finding out how deep the abyss was into which he had fallen, and the thought of the future weighed heavily upon him.

'My father will not be back before dinner,' said Eugénie, in reply to an anxious look in her mother's eyes.

The tones of Eugénie's voice had grown strangely sweet; it was easy to see from her face and manner that the cousins had some thought in common. Their souls had rushed together, while perhaps as yet they scarcely knew the power or the nature of this force which was binding them each to each.

Charles sat in the dining-room; no one intruded upon his sorrow. Indeed, the three women had plenty to do. Grandet had gone without any warning, and his work-people were at a standstill. The slater came, the plumber, the bricklayer, and the carpenter followed; so did labourers, tenants, and vine-dressers, some came to pay their dues, and others to receive them, and yet others to make bargains for the repairs which were being done. Mme Grandet and Eugénie, therefore, were continually coming and going; they had to listen to interminable histories from labourers and country people.

Everything that came into the house Nanon promptly and securely stowed away in her kitchen. She always waited for her master's instructions as to what should be kept, and what should be sold in the market. The worthy cooper, like many little country squires, was wont to drink his worst wine, and to reserve his spoiled or wind-fallen orchard fruit for home consumption.

Towards five o'clock that evening Grandet came back from Angers. He had made fourteen thousand francs on his gold, and carried a Government certificate bearing interest until the day when it should be transferred into *rentes*. He had left Cornoiller also in Angers to look after the horses, which had been nearly foundered by the night journey, and had given instructions to bring them back leisurely after they had had a thorough rest.

'I have been to Angers, wife,' he said; 'and I am hungry.'

'Have you had nothing to eat since yesterday?' called Nanon from her kitchen.

'Nothing whatever,' said the worthy man.

Nanon brought in the soup. Des Grassins came to take his client's instructions just as the family were sitting down to dinner. Grandet had not so much as seen his nephew all this time.

'Go on with your dinner, Grandet,' said the banker. 'We can have a little chat. Have you heard what gold is fetching in Angers, and that people from Nantes are buying it there? I am going to send some over.'

'You need not trouble yourself,' answered his worthy client; 'they have quite enough there by this time. I don't like you to lose your labour when I can prevent it; we are too good friends for that.'

'But gold is at thirteen francs fifty centimes premium.'

'Say *was* at a premium.'

'How the deuce did you get to know that?'

'I went over to Angers myself last night,' Grandet told him in a low voice.

The banker started, and a whispered conversation followed; both des Grassins and Grandet looked at Charles from time to time, and once more a gesture of surprise escaped the banker, doubtless at the point when the old cooper commissioned him to purchase *rentes* to bring in a hundred thousand livres.

'Monsieur Grandet,' said des Grassins, addressing Charles, 'I am going to Paris, and if there is anything I can do for you –'

'Thank you, sir, there is nothing,' Charles replied.

'You must thank him more heartily than that, nephew. This gentleman is going to wind up your father's business and settle with his creditors.'

'Then is there any hope of coming to an arrangement?' asked Charles.

'Why, are you not my nephew?' cried the cooper, with a fine assumption of pride. 'Our honour is involved; is not your name Grandet?'

Charles rose from his chair, impulsively flung his arms about his uncle, turned pale, and left the room. Eugénie looked at her father with affection and pride in her eyes.

'Well, let us say good-bye, my good friend,' said Grandet. 'I am very much at your service. Try to get round those fellows over yonder.'

The two diplomatists shook hands, and the cooper went to the door with his neighbour; he came back to the room again when he had closed the door on des Grassins, flung himself down in his easy-chair, and said to Nanon, 'Bring me some cordial.'

But he was too much excited to keep still; he rose and looked at old M. de la Bertellière's portrait, and began to 'dance a jig', in Nanon's phrase, singing to himself:

> Once in the *Gardes françaises*
> I had a grandpapa . . .

Nanon, Mme Grandet, and Eugénie all looked at each other in silent dismay. The vine-grower's ecstasies never boded any good.

The evening was soon over. Old Grandet went off early to bed, and no one was allowed to stay up after that; when he slept, everyone else must likewise sleep, much as in Poland, in the days of Augustus the Strong, whenever the king drank all his subjects were loyally tipsy. Wherefore, Nanon, Charles, and Eugénie were no less tired than the master of the house; and as for Mme Grandet, she slept or woke, ate or drank, as her husband bade her. Yet during the two hours allotted to the digestion of his dinner the cooper was more facetious than he had ever been in his life before, and uttered not a few of his favourite aphorisms; one example will serve to plumb the depths of the cooper's mind. When he had finished his cordial, he looked pensively at the glass, and thus delivered himself:

'You have no sooner set your lips to a glass than it is empty! Such is life. You cannot have your cake and eat it too, and you can't turn over your money and keep it in your purse: if you could only do that, life would be too glorious.'

He was not only jocose, he was good-natured, so that when Nanon came in with her spinning-wheel, 'You must be tired,' he said; 'let the hemp alone.'

'And if I did,' the servant answered, '*quien*! I should have to sit with my hands before me.'

'Poor Nanon! would you like some cordial?'

'Cordial? Oh! I don't say no. Madame makes it much better than the apothecaries do. The stuff they sell is like physic.'

'They spoil the flavour with putting too much sugar in it,' said the goodman.

The next morning, at the eight o'clock breakfast, the party seemed, for the first time, almost like one family. Mme Grandet, Eugénie, and Charles had been drawn together by these troubles, and Nanon herself unconsciously felt with them. As for the old vine-grower, he scarcely noticed his nephew's presence in the house, his greed of gold had been satisfied, and he was very shortly to be quit of this young sprig by the cheap and easy expedient of paying his nephew's travelling expenses as far as Nantes.

Charles and Eugénie meanwhile were free to do what seemed to them good. They were under Mme Grandet's eyes, and Grandet reposed complete faith in his wife in all matters of conduct and religion. Moreover, he had other things to think of; his meadows were to be drained, and a row of poplars was to be planted along the Loire, and there was all the ordinary winter work at Froidfond and elsewhere; in fact, he was exceedingly busy.

And now began the springtime of love for Eugénie. Since that hour in the night when she had given her gold to her cousin, her heart had followed the gift. They shared a secret between them; they were conscious of this understanding whenever they looked at each other; and this knowledge, that brought them more and more closely together, drew them in a manner out of the current of everyday life. And did not relationship justify a certain tenderness in the voice and kindness in the eyes? Eugénie therefore set herself to make her cousin forget his grief in the childish joys of growing love.

For the beginnings of love and the beginnings of life are not unlike. Is not the child soothed by smiles and cradle songs, and fairy tales of a golden future that lies before him? Above him, too, the bright wings of hope are always spread, and does he not shed tears of joy or of sorrow, wax petulant over trifles and quarrelsome over the pebbles with which he builds a tottering palace, or the flowers that are no sooner gathered than forgotten? Is he not also eager to outstrip Time, and to live in the future? Love is the soul's second transformation.

Love and childhood were almost the same thing for Charles and Eugénie; the dawn of love and its childish beginnings were all the sweeter because their hearts were full of gloom; and this love, that from its birth had been enveloped in crêpe, was in keeping with their homely surroundings in the melancholy old house. As the cousins interchanged a few words by the well in the silent courtyard, or sat out in the little garden towards sunset time, wholly absorbed by the momentous nothings that each said to each, or wrapped in the stillness that always brooded over the space between the ramparts and the house, Charles learned to think of love as something sacred. Hitherto, with his great lady, his 'dear Annette', he had experienced little but its perils and storms; but that episode in Paris was over, with its coquetry and passion, its vanity and emptiness, and he turned to this love in its purity and truth.

He came to feel a certain fondness for the old house, and their way of life no longer seemed absurd to him. He would come downstairs early in the morning so as to snatch a few words with Eugénie before her father gave out the stores; and when the sound of Grandet's heavy footstep echoed on the staircase, he fled into the garden.

Even Eugénie's mother did not know of this morning tryst of theirs, and Nanon made as though she did not see it; it was a small piece of audacity that gave the keen relish of a stolen pleasure to their innocent love. Then when breakfast was over, and goodman Grandet had gone to see after his business and his improvements, Charles sat in the grey parlour between the mother and daughter, finding a pleasure unknown before in holding skeins of thread for them to wind, in listening to their talk, and watching them sew. There was something that appealed to him strongly in the almost monastic simplicity of the life, which had led him to discover the nobleness of the natures of these two unworldly women. He had not believed that such lives as these were possible in France; in Germany he admitted that old-world manners lingered still, but in France they were only to be found in fiction and in Auguste Lafontaine's novels. It was not long before Eugénie became an embodiment of his ideal, Goethe's Marguerite without her error.

Day after day, in short, the poor girl hung on his words and looks, and drifted further along the stream of love. She snatched at every happiness as some swimmer might catch at an overhanging willow branch, that so he might reach the bank and rest there for a little while.

Was not the time of parting very near now? The shadow of that parting seemed to fall across the brightest hours of those days that fled so fast; and not one of them went by but something happened to remind her how soon it would be upon them.

For instance, three days after des Grassins had started for Paris, Grandet had taken Charles before a magistrate with the funereal solemnity with which such acts are performed by provincials, and in the presence of that functionary the young man had had to sign a declaration that he renounced all claim to his father's property. Dreadful repudiation! An impiety amounting to apostasy! He went to M. Cruchot to procure two powers of attorney, one for des Grassins, the other for the friend who was commissioned to sell his own personal effects. There were also some necessary formalities in connection with his passport; and finally, on the arrival of the plain suit of mourning which Charles had ordered from Paris, he sent for a clothier in Saumur, and disposed of his now useless wardrobe. This transaction was peculiarly pleasing to old Grandet.

'Ah! *Now* you look like a man who is ready to set out, and means to make his way in the world,' he said, as he saw his nephew in a plain, black overcoat of rough cloth. 'Good, very good!'

'I beg you to believe, sir,' Charles replied, 'that I shall face my position with proper spirit.'

'What does this mean?' asked his worthy relative; there was an eager look in the goodman's eyes at the sight of a handful of gold which Charles held out to him.

'I have gathered together my studs and rings and everything of any value that I have; I am not likely to want them now; but I know of nobody in Saumur, and this morning I thought I would ask you –'

'To buy it?' Grandet broke in upon him.

'No, uncle, to give me the name of some honest man who –'

'Give it to me, nephew; I will take it upstairs and find out what it is worth, and let you know the value to a centime. Jeweller's gold,' he commented, after an examination of a long chain, 'jeweller's gold, eighteen to nineteen carats, I should say.'

The worthy soul held out his huge hand for it, and carried off the whole collection.

'Cousin Eugénie,' said Charles, 'permit me to offer you these two clasps; you might use them to fasten ribbons round your wrists, that sort of bracelet is all the rage just now.'

'I do not hesitate to take it, cousin,' she said, with a look of intelligence.

'And, aunt, this is my mother's thimble; I have treasured it up till now in my dressing-case,' and he gave a pretty gold thimble to Mme Grandet, who for the past ten years had longed for one.

'It is impossible to thank you in words, dear nephew,' said the old mother, as her eyes filled with tears. 'But morning and evening I shall repeat the prayer for travellers, and pray most fervently for you. If anything should happen to me, Eugénie shall take care of it for you.'

'It is worth nine hundred and eighty-nine francs seventy-five centimes, nephew,' said Grandet, as he came in at the door. 'But to save you the trouble of selling it, I will let you have the money in livres.'

This expression 'in livres' means, in the districts along the Loire, that a crown of six livres is to be considered worth six francs, without deduction.

'I did not venture to suggest such a thing,' Charles answered, 'but I shrank from hawking my trinkets about in the town where you are living. Dirty linen ought not to be washed in public, as Napoleon used to say. Thank you for obliging me.'

Grandet scratched his ear, and there was a moment's silence in the room.

'And, dear uncle,' Charles went on, somewhat nervously, and as though he feared to wound his uncle's susceptibilities, 'my cousin and aunt have consented to receive trifling mementoes from me; will you not in your turn accept these sleeve-links, which are useless to me now? they may perhaps recall to your memory a poor boy, in a far-off country, whose thoughts will certainly often turn to those who are all that remain to him now of his family.'

'Oh! my boy, my boy, you must not strip yourself like that for us –'

'What have you there, wife?' said the cooper, turning eagerly towards her. 'Ah! a gold thimble? And you, little girl? Diamond clasps; what next! Come, I will accept your studs, my boy,' he continued, squeezing Charles's hand. 'But . . . you must let me pay . . . your . . . yes, your passage out to the Indies. Yes, I mean to pay your passage. Besides, my boy, when I estimated your jewellery I only took it at its value as metal, you see, without reckoning the workmanship, and it may be worth a trifle more on that account. So that is settled. I will pay you fifteen hundred francs . . . in livres; Cruchot will lend it me, for I have not a brass farthing in the house; unless Perrotet, who is getting behindhand with his dues, will pay me in coin. There! there! I will go and see about it,' and he took up his hat, put on his gloves, and went forthwith.

'Then you are going?' said Eugénie, with sad, admiring eyes.

'I cannot help myself,' he answered, with his head bent down.

For several days Charles looked, spoke, and behaved like a man who is in deep trouble, but who feels the weight of such heavy obligations, that his misfortunes only brace him for greater effort. He had ceased to pity himself; he had become a man. Never had Eugénie augured better of her cousin's character than she did on the day when she watched him come downstairs in his plain, black mourning suit, which set off his pale, sad face to such advantage. The two women had also gone into mourning, and went with Charles to the *Requiem* mass celebrated in the parish church for the soul of the late Guillaume Grandet.

Charles received letters from Paris as they took the midday meal; he opened and read them.

'Well, cousin,' said Eugénie in a low voice, 'are your affairs going on satisfactorily?'

'Never put questions of that sort, my girl,' remarked Grandet. 'I never talk to you about my affairs, and why the devil should you meddle in your cousin's? Just let the boy alone.'

'Oh, I have no secrets of any sort,' said Charles.

'Tut, tut, tut. You will find out that you must bridle your tongue in business, nephew.'

When the two lovers were alone in the garden, Charles drew Eugénie to the old bench under the walnut tree where they so often sat of late.

'I felt sure of Alphonse, and I was right,' he said; 'he has done wonders, and has settled my affairs prudently and loyally. All my debts in Paris are paid, my furniture sold well, and he tells me that he has acted on the advice of an old sea captain who had made the voyage to the Indies, and has invested the surplus money in ornaments and odds and ends for which there is a great demand out there. He has sent my packages to Nantes, where an East Indiaman is taking freight for Java, and so, Eugénie, in five days we must bid each other farewell, for a long while at any rate, and perhaps for ever. My trading venture and the ten thousand francs which two of my friends have sent me, are a very poor start; I cannot expect to return for many years. Dear cousin, let us not consider ourselves bound in any way; I may die, and very likely some good opportunity for settling yourself –'

'You love me? . . .' she asked.

'Oh, yes, indeed!' he replied, with an earnestness of manner that betokened a like earnestness in his feelings.

'Then I will wait for you, Charles. Dear me! my father is looking out of his window,' she exclaimed, evading her cousin, who had drawn closer to embrace her.

She fled to the archway; and seeing that Charles followed her thither, she retreated further, flung back the folding door at the foot of the staircase, and with no very clear idea, save that of flight, she rushed towards the darkest corner of the passage, outside Nanon's sleeping hole; and there Charles, who was close beside her, grasped both hands in his and pressed her to his heart; his arms went round her waist, Eugénie resisted no longer, and leaning against her lover she received and gave the purest, sweetest, and most perfect of all kisses.

'Dear Eugénie, a cousin is better than a brother; he can marry you,' said Charles.

'Amen, so be it!' cried Nanon, opening the door behind them, and emerging from her den. Her voice startled the two lovers, who fled into the dining-room, where Eugénie took up her sewing, and Charles seized on Mme Grandet's prayer-book, opened it at the litanies of the Virgin, and began to read industriously.

'*Quien*!' said Nanon, 'so we are all saying our prayers!'

As soon as Charles fixed the day for his departure, Grandet bustled about and affected to take the greatest interest in the whole matter. He was liberal with advice, and with anything else that cost him nothing, first seeking out a packer for Charles, and then, saying that the man wanted too much for his cases, setting to work with all his might to make them himself, using odd planks for the purpose. He was up betimes every morning, planing, fitting, nailing deal boards together, squaring, and shaping; and, in fact, he made some strong cases, packed all Charles's property in them, and undertook to send them by steamer down the Loire to Nantes in time to go by the merchant ship, and to insure them during the voyage.

Since that kiss given and taken in the passage, the hours sped with terrible rapidity for Eugénie. At times she thought of following her cousin; for of all ties that bind one human being to another, this passion of love is the closest and strongest, and those who know this, and know how every day shortens love's allotted span, and how not time alone but age and mortal sickness and all the untoward accidents of life combine to menace it – these will know the agony that Eugénie suffered. She shed many tears as she walked up and down the little garden; it had grown so narrow for her now; the court-yard, the old house, and the town had all grown narrow, and her thoughts fared forth already across vast spaces of sea.

It was the day before the day of departure. That morning, while Grandet and Nanon were out of the house, the precious casket that held the two portraits was solemnly deposited in Eugénie's chest, beside the now empty velvet bag in the only drawer that could be locked, an installation which was not effected without many tears and kisses. When Eugénie locked the drawer and hid the key in her bosom, she had not the courage to forbid the kiss by which Charles sealed the act.

'The key shall always stay there, dear.'

'Ah, well! my heart will always be there with it too.'

'Oh, Charles, you should not say that!' she said a little reproachfully.

'Are we not married?' he replied. 'I have your word; take mine.'

'Thine for ever!' they said together, and repeated it a second time. No holier vow was ever made on earth; for Charles's love had received a moment's consecration in the presence of Eugénie's simple sincerity.

It was a melancholy group round the breakfast-table next morning. Even Nanon herself, in spite of Charles's gift of a new robe and a gilt cross, had a tear in her eye; but she was free to express her feelings, and did so.

'Oh, that poor, delicate young gentleman who is going to sea! May God take care of him!' ran her discourse.

At half-past ten the whole family left the house to see Charles start for Nantes in the diligence. Nanon had let the dog loose, and locked the door, and meant to carry Charles's handbag. Every shopkeeper in the ancient street was in the doorway to watch the little procession pass. M. Cruchot joined them in the market-place.

'Eugénie,' whispered her mother, 'mind you do not cry!'

They reached the gateway of the inn, and there Grandet kissed Charles on both cheeks. 'Well, nephew,' he said, 'set out poor and come back rich; you leave your father's honour in safe keeping. I – Grandet – will answer to you for that; you will only have to do your part –'

'Oh! uncle, this sweetens the bitterness of parting. Is not this the greatest gift you could possibly give me?'

Charles had broken in upon the old cooper's remarks before he quite understood their drift; he put his arms round his uncle's neck, and let fall tears of gratitude on the vine-grower's sunburned cheeks; Eugénie clasped her cousin's hand in one of hers, and her father's in the other, and held them tightly. Only the notary smiled to himself; he alone understood the worthy man, and he could not help admiring his astute cunning. The four Saumurois and a little group of onlookers hung about the diligence till the last moment; and looked after it until it disappeared across the bridge, and the sound of the wheels grew faint and distant.

'A good riddance!' said the cooper.

Luckily, no one but M. Cruchot heard this ejaculation; Eugénie and her mother had walked along the quay to a point of view whence they could still see the diligence, and stood there waving their handkerchiefs and watching Charles's answering signal till he was out of sight; then Eugénie turned.

'Oh, mother, mother, if I had God's power for one moment!' she said.

To save further interruption to the course of the story, it is necessary to glance a little ahead, and give a brief account of the course of events in Paris, of Grandet's calculations, and the action taken by his worthy lieutenant the banker in the matter of Guillaume Grandet's affairs. A month after des Grassins had gone, Grandet received a certificate for a hundred thousand livres per annum of *rentes*, purchased at eighty francs. No information was ever forthcoming as to how and when the actual coin had been paid, or the receipt taken, which in due course had been exchanged for the certificate. The inventory and statement of his affairs which the miser left at his death threw no light upon the mystery, and Cruchot fancied that in some way or other Nanon must have been the unconscious instrument employed; for about that time the faithful serving-maid was away from home for four or five days, ostensibly to see after matters at Froidfond, as if its worthy owner were likely to forget anything there that required looking after! As for Guillaume Grandet's creditors, everything had happened as the cooper had intended and foreseen.

At the Bank of France (as everybody knows) they keep accurate lists of all the great fortunes in Paris or in the departments. The names of des Grassins and of Félix Grandet of Saumur were duly to be found inscribed therein; indeed, they shone conspicuous there as well-known names in the business world, as men who were not only financially sound, but owners of broad acres unencumbered by mortgages. And now it was said that des Grassins of Saumur had come to Paris with intent to call a meeting of the creditors of the firm of Guillaume Grandet; the shade of the wine merchant was to be spared the disgrace of protested bills. The seals were broken in the presence of the creditors, and the family notary proceeded to make out an inventory in due form.

Before very long, in fact, des Grassins called a meeting of the creditors, who with one voice appointed the banker of Saumur as trustee conjointly with François Keller, the head of a large business house, and one of the principal creditors, empowering them to take such measures as they thought fit, in order to save the family name (and the bills) from being dishonoured. The fact that des Grassins was acting as his agent produced a hopeful tone in the meeting, and things went smoothly from the first; the banker did not find a single dissentient voice. No one thought of passing his bill to his profit and loss account, and each one said to himself:

'Grandet of Saumur is going to pay!'

Six months went by. The Parisian merchants had withdrawn the bills from circulation, and had consigned them to the depths of their portfolios. The cooper had gained his first point. Nine months after the first meeting the two trustees paid the creditors a dividend of forty-seven per cent. This sum had been raised by the sale of the late Guillaume Grandet's property, goods, chattels, and general effects; the most scrupulous integrity characterized these proceedings; indeed, the whole affair was conducted with the most conscientious honesty, and the delighted creditors fell to admiring Grandet's wonderful, indubitable, and high-minded probity. When these praises had duly circulated for a sufficient length of time, the creditors began to ask themselves when the remainder of their money would be forthcoming, and bethought them of collectively writing a letter to Grandet.

'Here we are!' was the old cooper's comment, as he flung the letter in the fire. 'Patience, patience, my dear friends.'

By way of a reply to the propositions contained in the letter, Grandet of Saumur required them to deposit with a notary all the bills and claims against the estate of his deceased brother, accompanying each with receipts for the payments already made. The accounts were to be audited, and the exact condition of affairs was to be ascertained. Innumerable difficulties were cleared away by this notion of the deposit.

A creditor, generally speaking, is a sort of maniac; there is no saying what a creditor will do. One day he is in a hurry to bring the thing to an end, the next he is all for fire and sword, a little later and he is sweetness and benignity itself. Today, very probably, his wife is in a good humour, his youngest hope has just cut a tooth, everything is going on comfortably at home, he has no mind to abate his claims one jot; but tomorrow comes, and it rains, and he cannot go out; he feels low in his mind, and agrees hastily to anything and everything that is likely to settle the affair; the next morning brings counsel; he requires a guarantee, and by the end of the month he talks about an execution, the inhuman, bloodthirsty wretch! The creditor is not unlike that common or house sparrow on whose tail small children are encouraged to try to put a grain of salt – a pleasing simile which the creditor may twist to his own uses, and apply to his bills, from which he fondly hopes to derive some benefit at last. Grandet had observed these atmospheric variations among creditors; and his forecasts in the present case were correct, his brother's creditors were behaving in every respect exactly as he wished. Some waxed wroth, and flatly declined to have anything to do with the deposit, or to give up the vouchers.

'Good!' said Grandet; 'that is all right!' He rubbed

his hands as he read the letters which des Grassins wrote to him on the subject.

Yet others refused to consent to the aforesaid deposit unless their position was clearly defined in the first place; it was to be made without prejudice, and they reserved the right to declare the estate bankrupt should they deem it advisable. This opened a fresh correspondence, and occasioned a further delay, after which Grandet finally agreed to all the conditions, and as a consequence the more tractable creditors brought the recalcitrant to hear reason, and the deposit was made, not, however, without some grumbling.

'That old fellow is laughing in his sleeve at you and at us too,' said they to des Grassins.

Twenty-three months after Guillaume Grandet's death, many of the merchants had forgotten all about their claims in the course of events in a business life in Paris, or they only thought of them to say to themselves:

'It begins to look as though the forty-seven per cent is about all I shall get out of that business.'

The cooper had reckoned on the aid of Time, who, so he was wont to say, is a good fellow. By the end of the third year, des Grassins wrote to Grandet saying that he had induced most of the creditors to give up their bills, in consideration of ten per cent on the outstanding two million four hundred thousand francs. Grandet replied that there yet remained the notary and the stockbroker, whose failures had been the death of his brother; *they* were still alive. They might be solvent again by this time, and proceedings ought to be taken against them; something might be recovered in this way which would still further reduce the sum total of the deficit.

When the fourth year drew to a close the deficit had been duly brought down to the sum of twelve hundred thousand francs; the limit appeared to have been reached. Six months were further spent in parleyings between the trustees and the creditors, and between Grandet and the trustees. In short, strong pressure being brought to bear upon Grandet of Saumur, he announced, somewhere about the ninth month of the same year, that his nephew, who had made a fortune in the East Indies, had signified his intention of settling in full all claims on his father's estate; and that meantime he could not take it upon himself to act, nor to defraud the creditors by winding up the affair before he had consulted his nephew; he added that he had written to him, and was now awaiting an answer.

The middle of the fifth year had been reached, and still the creditors were held in check by the magic words 'in full', let fall judiciously from time to time by the sublime cooper, who was laughing at them in his sleeve; 'those PARISIANS,' he would say to himself, with a mild oath, and a cunning smile would steal across his features.

In fact, a martyrdom unknown to the calendars of commerce was in store for the creditors. When next they appear in the course of this story, they will be found in exactly the same position that they were in now when Grandet had done with them. Consols went up to a hundred and fifteen, old Grandet sold out, and received from Paris about two million four hundred thousand francs in gold, which went into his wooden kegs to keep company with the six hundred thousand francs of interest which his investment had brought in.

Des Grassins stayed on in Paris, and for the following reasons. In the first place, he had been appointed a deputy; and in the second, he, the father of a family, bored by the exceeding dullness of existence in Saumur, was smitten with the charms of Mlle Florine, one of the prettiest actresses of the Théâtre de Madame, and there was a recrudescence of the quartermaster in the banker. It is useless to discuss his conduct; at Saumur it was pronounced to be profoundly immoral. It was very lucky for his wife that she had brains enough to carry on the concern at Saumur in her own name, and could extricate the remains of her fortune, which had suffered not a little from M. des Grassins's extravagance and folly. But the quasi-widow was in a false position, and the Cruchotins did all that in them lay to make matters worse; she had to give up all hope of a match between her son and Eugénie Grandet, and married her daughter very badly. Adolphe des Grassins went to join his father in Paris, and there acquired, so it was said, an unenviable reputation. The triumph of the Cruchotins was complete.

'Your husband has taken leave of his senses,' Grandet took occasion to remark as he accommodated Mme des Grassins with a loan (on good security). 'I am very sorry for you; you are a nice little woman.'

'Ah!' sighed the poor lady, 'who could have believed that day when he set out for Paris to see after that business of yours that he was hurrying to his own ruin?'

'Heaven is my witness, madame, that to the very last I did all I could to prevent him, and Monsieur le Président was dying to go; but we know now why your husband was so set upon it.'

Clearly, therefore, Grandet lay under no obligation to des Grassins.

In every situation a woman is bound to suffer in many ways that a man does not, and to feel her troubles more acutely than he can; for a man's vigour and energy is constantly brought into play; he acts and thinks, comes and goes, busies himself in the present, and looks to the future for consolation. This was what Charles was doing. But a woman cannot help herself – hers is a passive part; she is left face to face with her trouble, and has nothing to divert her mind from it; she sounds the depths of the abyss of sorrow, and its dark places are filled with her prayers and tears. So it was with Eugénie. She was beginning to understand that the web of a woman's life will always be woven of love and sorrow and hope and fear and self-sacrifice; hers was to be a woman's lot in all things without a woman's consolations and her moments of happiness (to make use of Bossuet's wonderful illustration) were to be like the scattered nails driven into the wall, when all collected together they scarcely filled the hollow of the hand. Troubles seldom keep us waiting for them, and for Eugénie they were gathering thick and fast.

The day after Charles had gone, the Grandet household fell back into the old ways of life; there was no difference for anyone but Eugénie – for her the house had grown very empty all on a sudden. Charles's room should remain just as he had left it; Mme Grandet and Nanon lent themselves to this whim of hers, willingly maintained the *status quo*, and said nothing to her father.

'Who knows?' Eugénie said. 'He may come back to us sooner than we think.'

'Ah! I wish I could see him here again,' replied Nanon. 'I was getting on with him very well! He was very nice, and an excellent gentleman; and he was pretty-like, his hair curled over his head just like a girl's.'

Eugénie gazed at Nanon.

'Holy Virgin! mademoiselle, with such eyes, you are like to lose your soul. You shouldn't look at people in that way.'

From that day Mlle Grandet's beauty took a new character. The grave thoughts of love that slowly enveloped her soul, the dignity of a woman who is beloved, gave to her face the sort of radiance that early painters expressed by the aureole. Before her cousin came into her life, Eugénie might have been compared to the Virgin as yet unconscious of her destiny; and now that he had passed out of it, she seemed like the Virgin Mother; she, too, bore love in her heart. Spanish art has depicted these two Marys, so different each from each – Christianity, with its many symbols, knows no more glorious types than these.

The day after Charles had left them, Eugénie went to mass (as she had resolved to do daily), and on her way back bought a map of the world from the only bookseller in the town. This she pinned to the wall beside her glass, so that she might follow the course of her cousin's voyage to the Indies; and night and morning might be beside him for a little while on that far-off vessel, and see him and ask all the endless questions she longed to ask.

'Are you well? Are you not sad? Am I in your thoughts when you see the star that you told me about? You made me see how beautiful it was.'

In the morning she used to sit like one in a dream under the great walnut tree, on the old grey, lichen-covered, worm-eaten bench where they had talked so kindly and so foolishly, where they had built such fair castles in the air in which to live. She thought of the future as she watched the little strip of sky shut in by the high walls on every side, then her eyes wandered over the old buttressed wall and the roof – Charles's room lay beneath it. In short, this solitary persistent love mingling with all her thoughts became the substance, or, as our forefathers would have said, the 'stuff' of her life.

If Grandet's self-styled friends came in of an evening, she would seem to be in high spirits, but the liveliness was only assumed; she used to talk about Charles with her mother and Nanon the whole morning through, and Nanon – who was of the opinion that without faltering in her duty to her master she might yet feel for her young mistress's troubles – Nanon spoke on this wise:

'If I had had a sweetheart, I would have . . . I would have gone with him to hell. I would have . . . well, then, I would just have laid down my life for him, but . . . no such chance! I shall die without knowing what it is to live. Would you believe it, mam'selle, there is that old Cornoiller, who is a good man all the same, dangling about after my savings, just like the others who come here paying court to you and sniffing after the master's money. I see through it; I may be as big as a haystack, but I am as sharp as a needle yet. Well! and yet do you know, mam'selle, it may not be love, but I rather like it.'

In this way two months went by. The secret that bound the three women so closely together had brought a new interest into the household life hitherto so monotonous. For them Charles still dwelt in the house, and came and went beneath the old grey rafters of the parlour. Every morning and evening Eugénie opened the dressing-case and looked at her aunt's portrait. Her mother, suddenly coming into her room one Sunday morning, found her absorbed in tracing out a likeness to Charles in the lady of the miniature, and Mme Grandet learned for the first time a terrible secret, how Eugénie had parted with her treasures and had taken the case in exchange.

'You have let him have it all!' cried the terrified mother. 'What will you say to your father on New Year's Day when he asks to see your gold?'

Eugénie's eyes were set in a fixed stare; the horror of this thought so filled the women that half the morning went by, and they were distressed to find themselves too late for high mass, and were only in time for the military mass. The year 1819 was almost over; there were only three more days left. In three days a terrible drama would begin, a drama undignified by poison, dagger, or bloodshed, but fate dealt scarcely more cruelly with the princely house of Atreus than with the actors in this bourgeois tragedy.

'What is to become of us?' said Mme Grandet, laying down her knitting on her knee.

Poor mother! all the events of the past two months had sadly hindered the knitting, the woollen cuffs for winter wear were not finished yet, a homely and apparently insignificant fact which was to work trouble enough for her. For want of warm cuffs she caught a chill after a violent perspiration brought on by one of her husband's fearful outbursts of rage.

'My poor child, I have been thinking that if you had only told me about this, we should have had time to write to Monsieur des Grassins in Paris. He might have managed to send us some gold pieces like those of yours; and although Grandet knows the look of them so well, still perhaps –'

'But where could we have found so much money?'

'I would have raised it on my property. Besides, Monsieur des Grassins would have befriended us –'

'There is not time enough now,' faltered Eugénie in a smothered voice. 'Tomorrow morning we shall have to go to his room to wish him a happy New Year, shall we not?'

'Oh, Eugénie! why not go and see the Cruchots about it?'

'No, no, that would be putting ourselves in their power; I should be entirely in their hands then. Besides, I have made up my mind. I have acted quite rightly, and I repent of nothing; God will protect me. May His holy will be done! Ah! if you had read that letter, mother, you would have thought of nothing but him.'

*

The next morning, 1st January 1820, the mother and daughter were in an agony of distress that they could not hide; sheer terror suggested the simple expedient of omitting the solemn visit to Grandet's room. The bitter weather served as an excuse; the winter of 1819–20 was the coldest that had been known for years, and snow lay deep on the roofs.

Mme Grandet called to her husband as soon as she heard him stirring, 'Grandet, just let Nanon light a bit of fire in here for me, the air is so sharp that I am shivering under the bedclothes, and at my time of life I must take care of myself. And then,' she went on after a little pause, 'Eugénie shall come in here to dress. The poor girl may do herself a mischief if she dresses in her own room in such cold. We will come downstairs into the sitting-room and wish you a happy New Year there by the fire.'

'Tut, tut, tut, what a tongue! What a way to begin the year, Madame Grandet! You have never said so much in your life before. You have not had a sop of bread in wine, I suppose?'

There was a moment's pause. Doubtless his wife's proposal suited his notions, for he said, 'Very well, I will do as you wish, Madame Grandet. You really are a good sort of woman, it would be a pity for you to expire before you are due, though, as a rule, the La Bertellières make old bones, don't they, hey?' he cried, after a pause. 'Well, their money has fallen in at last; I forgive them,' and he coughed.

'You are in spirits this morning,' said the poor wife.

'I always am in spirits.

> 'Hey! hey! cooper gay,
> Mend your tub and take your pay.'

He had quite finished dressing, and came into his wife's room. 'Yes, nom d'un petit bonhomme! it is a mighty hard frost, all the same. We shall have a good breakfast today, wife. Des Grassins has sent me a *pâté de foie gras*, truffled! I am going round to the coach office to see after it. He should have sent a double napoleon for Eugénie along with it,' said the cooper, coming closer, and lowering his voice. 'I have no gold, I certainly had a few old coins still left, I may tell you that in confidence, but I had to let them go in the course of business,' and by way of celebrating the first day of the year he kissed his wife on the forehead.

'Eugénie,' cried the kind mother, as soon as Grandet had gone, 'I don't know which side of the bed your father got out on, but he is in a good humour this morning.

'Pshaw! we shall pull through.'

'What can have come over the master?' cried Nanon as she came into the room to light the fire. 'First of all, he says, "Good morning, great stupid, a happy New Year! Go upstairs and light a fire in my wife's room; she is feeling cold." I thought I must be off my head when I saw him holding out his hand with a six-franc piece in it that hadn't been clipped a bit! There! madame, only look at it! Oh! he is a worthy man, all the same – he is a good man, he is. There are some as get harder-hearted the older they grow; but he turns sweeter, like your cordial that improves with keeping. He is a very good and a very excellent man. . .'

Grandet's speculation had been completely successful; this was the cause of his high spirits. M. des Grassins – after deducting various amounts which the cooper owed him, partly for discounting Dutch bills to the amount of a hundred and fifty thousand francs, and partly for advances of money for the purchase of a hundred thousand livres' worth of consols – M. des Grassins was sending him, by diligence, thirty thousand francs in crowns, the remainder (after the aforesaid deductions had been made) of the cooper's half-yearly dividends, and informed Grandet that consols were steadily rising. They stood at eighty-nine at the present moment, and well-known capitalists were buying for the next account at the end of January at ninety-two. In two months Grandet had made twelve per cent on his capital; he had straightened his accounts; and henceforward he would receive fifty thousand francs every half-year, clear of taxes or any outgoing expenses. In short, he had grasped the theory of consols (a class of investment of which the provincial mind is exceedingly shy), and looking ahead, he beheld himself the master of six millions of francs in five years' time – six millions, which would go on accumulating with scarcely any trouble on his part – six millions of francs! And there was the value of his landed property to add to this; he saw himself in a fair way to build up a colossal fortune. The six francs given to Nanon were perhaps in reality the payment for an immense service which the girl had unwittingly done her master.

'Oho! what can Goodman Grandet be after? He is running as if there were a fire somewhere,' the shop-keepers said to each other as they took down their shutters that New Year's morning.

A little later when they saw him coming back from the quay followed by a porter from the coach office, who was wheeling a barrow piled up with little bags full of something:

'Ah!' said they, 'water always makes for the river, the old boy was hurrying after his crowns.'

'They flow in on him from Paris, and Froidfond, and Holland,' said one.

'He will buy Saumur before he has done,' cried another.

'He does not care a rap for the cold; he is always looking after his business,' said a woman to her husband.

'Hi! M. Grandet! if you have more of that than you know what to do with, I can help you to get rid of some of it,' said his next-door neighbour, a cloth merchant.

'Eh! they are only coppers,' said the vine-grower.

'Silver, he means,' said the porter in a low voice.

'Keep a still tongue in your head, if you want me to bear you in mind,' said the goodman as he opened the door.

'Oh! the old fox, I thought he was deaf,' said the porter to himself, 'but it looks as though he can hear well enough in cold weather.'

'Here is a franc for a New Year's gift, and keep quiet about this. Off with you! Nanon will bring back the barrow. Nanon!' cried Grandet, 'are the womenfolk gone to mass?'

'Yes, sir.'

'Come, look sharp and lend a hand here, then,' he cried, and loaded her with the bags. In another minute the crowns were safely transferred to his room, where he locked himself in.

'Thump on the wall when breakfast is ready,' he called through the door, 'and take the wheelbarrow back to the coach office.'

It was ten o'clock before the family breakfasted.

'Your father will not ask to see your gold now,' said Mme Grandet as they came back from mass; 'and if he does, you can shiver and say it is too cold to go upstairs for it. We shall have time to make up the money again before your birthday. . .'

Grandet came down the stairs with his head full of schemes for transforming the five-franc pieces just received from Paris into gold coin, which should be neither clipped nor light weight. He thought of his admirably timed investment in Government stock, and made up his mind that he would continue to put his money into consols until they rose to a hundred francs.

Such meditations as these boded ill for Eugénie. As soon as he came in the two women wished him a prosperous New Year, each in her own way; Mme Grandet was grave and ceremonious, but his daughter put her arms round his neck and kissed him. 'Aha! child,' he said, kissing her on both cheeks, 'I am thinking and working for you, you see! . . . I want you to be happy and if you are to be happy, you must have money; for you won't get anything without it. Look! here is a brand-new napoleon, I sent to Paris on purpose for it. Nom d'un petit bonhomme! there is not a speck of gold in the house, except yours, you are the one who has the gold. Let me see your gold, little girl.'

'Bah! it is too cold, let us have breakfast,' Eugénie answered.

'Well, then, after breakfast we will have a look at it, eh? It will be good for our digestions. That great des Grassins sent us this, all the same,' he went on, 'so get your breakfasts, children, for it costs us nothing. Des Grassins is going on nicely; I am pleased with him; the old fish is doing Charles a service, and all free gratis. Really, he is managing poor dear Grandet's affairs very cleverly. Ououh! ououh!' he cried, with his mouth full, 'this is good! Eat away, wife; there is enough here to last us for two days at least.'

'I am not hungry. I am very poorly, you know that very well.'

'Oh! Ah! but you have a sound constitution; you are a La Bertellière, and you can put away a great deal without any fear of damaging yourself. You may be a trifle sallow, but I have a liking for yellow myself.'

The prisoner shrinking from a public and ignominious death could not well await his doom with a more sickening dread than Mme Grandet and Eugénie felt as they foresaw the end of breakfast and the inevitable sequel. The more boisterously the cooper talked and ate, the lower sank their spirits; but to the girl, in this crisis, a certain support was not lacking, love was strong within her. 'I would die a thousand deaths,' she thought, 'for him, for him!'

She looked at her mother, and courage and defiance shone in her eyes.

By eleven o'clock they had finished breakfast. 'Clear everything away,' Grandet told Nanon, 'but leave us the table. We can look over your little treasure more comfortably so,' he said with his eyes on Eugénie. '*Little*, said I? 'Tis not so small, though, upon my word. Your coins altogether are actually worth five thousand nine hundred and fifty-nine francs, then with forty more this morning, that makes six thousand francs all but one. Well, I will give you another franc to make up the sum, because, you see, little girl – Well, now, why are you listening to us? Just take yourself off, Nanon, and set about your work!'

Nanon vanished.

'Listen, Eugénie, you must let me have your gold. You will not refuse to let your papa have it? Eh, little daughter?'

Neither of the women spoke.

'I myself have no gold left. I had some once, but I have none now. I will give you six thousand francs in silver for it, and you shall invest it; I will show you how. There is really no need to think of a *dozen*. When you are married (which will be before very long) I will find a husband for you who will give you the handsomest *dozen* that has ever been heard of hereabouts. There is a splendid opportunity just now; you can invest your six thousand francs in Government stock, and every six months, when dividends are due, you will have about two hundred francs coming in, all clear of taxes, and no repairs to pay for, and no frosts nor hail nor bad seasons, none of all the tiresome drawbacks you have to lay your

account with if you put your money into land. You don't
like to part with your gold, eh? Is that it, little girl? Never
mind, let me have it all the same. I will look out for gold
coins for you, ducats from Holland, and genovines and
Portuguese moidores and rupees, the Mogul's rupees;
and what with the coins I shall give you on your birthday
and so forth, you will have half your little hoard again in
three years' time, beside the six thousand francs in the
funds. What do you say, little girl? Look up, child!
There! there! bring it here, my pet. You owe me a good
kiss for telling you business secrets and mysteries of the
life and death of five-franc pieces. Five-franc pieces!
Yes, indeed, the coins live and gad about just like men
do; they go and come and sweat and multiply.'

Eugénie rose and made a few steps towards the door;
then she turned abruptly, looked her father full in the
face, and said:

'All *my* gold is gone; I have none left.'

'All your gold is gone!' echoed Grandet, starting up,
as a horse might rear when the cannon thunders not ten
paces from him.

'Yes, it is all gone.'

'Eugénie! you are dreaming!'

'No.'

'By my father's pruning-hook!' Whenever the cooper
swore in this fashion, the floors and ceilings trembled.

'Lord have mercy!' cried Nanon; 'how white the
mistress is!'

'Grandet! you will kill me with your angry fits,' said
the poor wife.

'Tut, tut, tut; none of your family ever die. Now,
Eugénie! what have you done with your money?' he
burst out as he turned upon her.

The girl was on her knees beside Mme Grandet.

'Look, sir,' she said, 'my mother is very ill . . . do not
kill her.'

Grandet was alarmed; his wife's dark, sallow complexion had grown so white.

'Nanon, come and help me up to bed,' she said in a feeble voice. 'This is killing me...'

Nanon gave an arm to her mistress, and Eugénie supported her on the other side; but it was only with the greatest difficulty that they reached her room, for the poor mother's strength completely failed her, and she stumbled at every step. Grandet was left alone in the parlour. After a while, however, he came part of the way upstairs, and called out:

'Eugénie! Come down again as soon as your mother is in bed.'

'Yes, father.'

In no long time she returned to him, after comforting her mother as best she could.

'Now, my daughter,' Grandet addressed her, 'you will tell me where your money is.'

'If I am not perfectly free to do as I like with your presents, father, please take them back again,' said Eugénie coldly. She went to the chimney-piece for the napoleon, and gave it to her father.

Grandet pounced upon it, and slipped it into his waistcoat pocket.

'I will never give you anything again, I know,' he said, biting his thumb at her. 'You look down on your father, do you? You have no confidence in him? Do you know what a father is? If he is not everything to you, he is nothing. *Now*; where is your gold?'

'I do respect you and love you, father, in spite of your anger; but I would very humbly point out to you that I am twenty-two years old. You have told me that I am of age often enough for me to know it. I have done as I liked with my money, and rest assured that it is in good hands –'

'Whose?'

'That is an inviolable secret,' she said. 'Have you not your secrets?'

'Am I not the head of my family? May I not be allowed to have my own business affairs?'

'This is my own affair.'

'It must be something very unsatisfactory, Mademoiselle Grandet, if you cannot tell your own father about it.'

'It is perfectly satisfactory, and I cannot tell my father about it.'

'Tell me, at any rate, when you parted with your gold.'

Eugénie shook her head.

'You still had it on your birthday, hadn't you? Eh?'

But if greed had made her father crafty, love had taught Eugénie to be wary; she shook her head again.

'Did anyone ever hear of such obstinacy, or of such a robbery?' cried Grandet, in a voice which gradually rose till it rang through the house. 'What! *here*, in my house, in my own house, someone has taken your gold! Taken all the gold that there was in the place! And I am not to know who it was? Gold is a precious thing. The best of girls go wrong and throw themselves away one way or another; that happens among great folk, and even among decent citizens; but think of throwing gold away! For you gave it to somebody, I suppose, eh?'

Eugénie gave no sign.

'Did anyone ever see such a daughter! Can you be a child of mine? If you have parted with your money, you must have a receipt for it –'

'Was I free to do as I wished with it – yes or no? Was it mine?'

'Why, you are a child.'

'I am of age.'

At first Grandet was struck dumb by his daughter daring to argue with him, and in this way! He turned pale, stamped, swore, and finding words at last, he shouted:

'Accursed serpent! Miserable girl! Oh! you know well that I love you, and you take advantage of it! You ungrateful child! She would rob and murder her own father! Pardieu! you would have thrown all we have at the feet of that vagabond with the morocco boots. By my father's pruning-hook, I cannot disinherit you, but, nom d'un tonneau, I can curse you; you and your cousin and your children. Nothing good can come out of this; do you hear? If it was to Charles that – But, no, that is impossible. What if that miserable puppy should have robbed me?'

He glared at his daughter, who was still silent and unmoved.

'She does not stir! She does not flinch! She is more of a Grandet than I am. You did not give your gold away for nothing, anyhow. Come, now; tell me about it.'

Eugénie looked up at her father; her satirical glance exasperated him.

'Eugénie, this is my house; so long as you are under your father's roof you must do as your father bids you. The priests command you to obey me.'

Eugénie bent her head again.

'You are wounding all my tenderest feelings,' he went on. 'Get out of my sight until you are ready to obey me. Go to your room and stay there until I give you leave to come out of it. Nanon will bring you bread and water. Do you hear what I say? Go!'

Eugénie burst into tears, and fled away to her mother. Grandet took several turns in his garden without heeding the snow or the cold; then, suspecting that his daughter would be in his wife's room, and delighted with the idea of catching them in flagrant disobedience to orders, he climbed the stairs as stealthily as a cat, and suddenly appeared in Mme Grandet's room. He was right; she was stroking Eugénie's hair, and the girl lay with her face hidden in her mother's breast.

'Poor child! Never mind, your father will relent.'

'She no longer has a father!' said the cooper. 'Is it really possible, Madame Grandet, that we have brought such a disobedient daughter into the world? A pretty bringing up; and pious, too, above all things! Well! how is it you are not in your room? Come, off to prison with you; to prison, miss.'

'Do you mean to take my daughter away from me, sir?' said Mme Grandet, as she raised a flushed face and bright, feverish eyes.

'If you want to keep her, take her along with you, and the house will be rid of you both at once. . . . Tonnerre! Where is the gold? What has become of the gold?'

Eugénie rose to her feet, looked proudly at her father, and went into her room; the goodman turned the key in the door.

'Nanon!' he shouted, 'you can rake out the fire in the parlour'; then he came back and sat down in an easy-chair that stood between the fire and his wife's bedside, saying as he did so, 'Of course she gave her gold to that miserable seducer, Charles, who only cared for our money.'

Mme Grandet's love for her daughter gave her courage in the face of this danger; to all appearance she was deaf, dumb, and blind to all that was implied by this speech. She turned on her bed so as to avoid the angry glitter of her husband's eyes.

'I knew nothing about all this,' she said. 'Your anger makes me so ill, that if my forebodings come true I shall only leave this room when they carry me out feet fore-most. I think you might have spared me this scene, sir. I, at all events, have never caused you any vexation. Your daughter loves you, and I am sure she is as inno-cent as a new-born babe; so do not make her miserable, and take back your word. This cold is terribly sharp; it might make her seriously ill.'

'I shall neither see her nor speak to her. She shall stop in her room on bread and water until she has done as her father bids her. What the devil! the head of a family ought to know when gold goes out of his house, and where it goes. She had the only rupees that there are in France, for aught I know; then there were geno-vines besides, and Dutch ducats –'

'Eugénie is our only child, and even if she had flung them into the water –'

'Into the water!' shouted the worthy cooper. '*Into the water!* Madame Grandet, you are raving! When I say a thing I mean it, as you know. If you want to have peace in the house, get her to confess to you, and worm this secret out of her. Women understand each other, and are cleverer at this sort of thing than we are. Whatever she may have done, I certainly shall not eat her. Is she afraid of me? If she had covered her cousin with gold from head to foot, he is safe on the high seas by this time, hein! We cannot run after him –'

'Really, sir –' his wife began.

But Mme Grandet's nature had developed during her daughter's trouble; she felt more keenly, and per-haps her thoughts moved more quickly, or it may be that excitement and the strain upon her overwrought nerves had sharpened her mental faculties. She saw the wen on her husband's face twitch ominously as she began to speak, and changed her purpose without changing her voice.

'Really, sir, have I any more authority over her than you have? She has never said a word about it to me. She takes after you.'

'Goodness! your tongue is hung in the middle this morning! Tut, tut, tut; you are going to fly in my face, I suppose? Perhaps you and she are both in it.'

He glared at his wife.

'Really, Monsieur Grandet, if you want to kill me, you have only to keep on as you are doing. I tell you, sir, and if it were to cost me my life, I would say it again – you are too hard on your daughter; she is a great deal more sensible than you are. The money belonged to her; she could only have made a good use of it, and our good works ought to be known to God alone. Sir, I implore you, take Eugénie back into favour. It will lessen the effect of the shock your anger gave me, and perhaps will save my life! My daughter, sir; give me back my daughter!'

'I am off,' he said. 'It is unbearable here in my house, when a mother and daughter talk and argue as if – Brooough! Pouah! You have given me bitter New Year's gifts, Eugénie!' he called. 'Yes, yes, cry away! You shall repent it, do you hear? What is the good of taking the sacrament six times a quarter if you give your father's gold away on the sly to an idle rascal who will break your heart when you have nothing else left to give him? You will find out what he is, that Charles of yours, with his morocco boots and his stand-off airs. He can have no heart and no conscience either, when he dares to carry off a poor girl's money without the consent of her parents.'

As soon as the street door was shut, Eugénie stole out of her room and came to her mother's bedside.

'You were very brave for your daughter's sake,' she said.

'You see where crooked ways lead us, child! . . . You have made me tell a lie.'

'Oh, mother, I will pray to God to let all the punishment fall on me.'

'Is it true?' asked Nanon, coming upstairs in dismay, 'that mademoiselle here is to be put on bread and water for the rest of her life?'

'What does it matter, Nanon?' asked Eugénie calmly.

'Why, before I would eat *kitchen* while the daughter of the house is eating dry bread, I would – No, no, it won't do.'

'Don't say a word about it, Nanon,' Eugénie warned her.

'It would stick in my throat; but you shall see.'

Grandet dined alone, for the first time in twenty-four years.

'So you are a widower, sir,' said Nanon. 'It is a very dismal thing to be a widower when you have a wife and daughter in the house.'

'I did not speak to you, did I? Keep a still tongue in your head, or you will have to go. What have you in that saucepan that I can hear boiling away on the stove?'

'Some dripping that I am melting down –'

'There will be some people here this evening; light the fire.'

The Cruchots and their friends, Mme des Grassins and her son, all came in about eight o'clock, and to their amazement saw neither Mme Grandet nor her daughter.

'My wife is not very well today, and Eugénie is upstairs with her,' replied the old cooper, without a trace of perturbation on his face.

After an hour spent, in more or less trivial talk, Mme des Grassins, who had gone upstairs to see Mme Grandet, came down again to the dining-room, and was met with a general inquiry of, 'How is Madame Grandet?'

'She is very far from well,' the lady said gravely. 'Her health seems to me to be in a very precarious state. At her time of life you ought to take great care of her, Papa Grandet.'

'We shall see,' said the vine-grower abstractedly, and the whole party took leave of him. As soon as the Cruchots were out in the street and the door was shut behind them, Mme des Grassins turned to them and said, 'Something has happened among the Grandets. The mother is very ill; she herself has no idea how ill she is, and the girl's eyes are red, as if she had been crying for a long while. Are they wanting to marry her against her will?'

That night, when the cooper had gone to bed, Nanon, in list slippers, stole up to Eugénie's room, and displayed a raised pie, which she had managed to bake in a saucepan.

'Here, mademoiselle,' said the kind soul, 'Cornoiller brought a hare for me. You eat so little that the pie will last you for quite a week, and there is no fear of its spoiling in this frost. You shall not live on dry bread, at any rate; it is not at all good for you.'

'Poor Nanon!' said Eugénie, as she pressed the maid's hand.

'I have made it very dainty and nice, and *he* never found out about it. I paid for the lard and the bayleaves out of my six francs; I can surely do as I like with my own money,' and the old servant fled, thinking that she heard Grandet stirring.

Several months went by. The cooper went to see his wife at various times in the day, and never mentioned his daughter's name – never saw her, nor made the slightest allusion to her. Mme Grandet's health grew worse and worse; she had not once left her room since that terrible January morning. But nothing shook the old cooper's determination; he was hard, cold, and unyielding as a block of granite. He came and went, his manner of life was in no wise altered; but he did not stammer now, and he talked less; perhaps, too, in matters of business, people found him harder than before, but errors crept into his book-keeping.

Something had certainly happened in the Grandet family, both Cruchotins and Grassinistes were agreed on that head; and 'What can be the matter with the Grandets?' became a stock question which people asked each other at every social gathering in Saumur.

Eugénie went regularly to church, escorted by Nanon. If Mme des Grassins spoke to her in the porch as she came out, the girl would answer evasively, and the lady's curiosity remained ungratified. But after two months spent in this fashion it was almost impossible to hide the real state of affairs from Mme des Grassins or from the Cruchots; a time came when all pretexts were exhausted, and Eugénie's constant absence still demanded an explanation. A little later, though no one could say how or when the secret leaked out, it became common property, and the whole town knew that ever since New Year's Day Mlle Grandet had been locked up in her room by her father's orders, and that there she lived on bread and water in solitary confinement, and without a fire. Nanon, it was reported, cooked dainties for her, and brought food secretly to her room at night. Further particulars were known. It was even said that only when Grandet was out of the house could the young girl nurse her mother, or indeed see her at all.

People blamed Grandet severely. He was regarded as an outlaw, as it were, by the whole town; all his hardness, his bad faith was remembered against him, and every one shunned him. They whispered and pointed at him as he went by; and as his daughter passed along the crooked street on her way to mass or to vespers, with Nanon at her side, people would hurry to their windows and look curiously at the wealthy heiress's face – a face so sad and so divinely sweet.

The town gossip reached her ears as slowly as it reached her father's. Her imprisonment and her father's displeasure was as nothing to her; had she not her map

of the world? And from her window could she not see
the little bench, the old wall, and the garden walks?
Was not the sweetness of those past kisses still upon her
lips? So, sustained by love and by the consciousness of
her innocence in the sight of God, she could patiently
endure her solitary life and her father's anger; but there
was another sorrow, so deep and so overwhelming that
Eugénie could not find a refuge from it. The gentle, patient mother was gradually passing away; it seemed as if
the beauty of her soul shone out more and more brightly in those dark days as she drew nearer to the tomb.
Eugénie often bitterly blamed herself for this illness,
telling herself that she had been the innocent cause of
the painful malady that was slowly consuming her
mother's life; and, in spite of all her mother said to comfort her, this remorseful feeling made her cling more
closely to the love she was to lose so soon. Every morning, as soon as her father had left the house, she went to
sit at her mother's bedside. Nanon used to bring her
breakfast to her there. But for poor Eugénie in her sadness, this suffering was almost more than she could
bear; she looked at her mother's face, and then at
Nanon, with tears in her eyes, and was dumb; she did
not dare to speak of her cousin now. It was always Mme
Grandet who began to talk of him; it was she who was
forced to say, 'Where is *he*? Why does *he* not write?'

Neither mother nor daughter had any idea of the distance.

'Let us think of him without talking about him,
mother,' Eugénie would answer. 'You are suffering; you
come before everyone'; and when she said 'everyone',
Eugénie meant '*him*'.

'I have no wish to live any longer, children,' Mme
Grandet used to say. 'God in His protecting care has led
me to look forward joyfully to death as the end of my
sorrows.'

Everything that she said was full of Christian piety. For the first few months of the year her husband breakfasted in her room, and always, as he walked restlessly about, he heard the same words from her, uttered with angelic gentleness, but with firmness; the near approach of death had given her the courage which she had lacked all her life.

'Thank you, sir, for the interest which you take in my health,' she said in response to the merest formality of an inquiry; 'but if you really wish to sweeten the bitterness of my last moments, and to alleviate my sufferings, forgive our daughter, and act like a Christian, a husband and father.'

At these words Grandet would come and sit down by the bed, much as a man who is threatened by a shower betakes himself resignedly to the nearest sheltering archway. He would say nothing, and his wife might say what she liked. To the most pathetic, loving, and fervent prayers, he would reply, 'My poor wife, you are looking a bit pale today.'

His daughter seemed to have passed entirely out of his mind; the mention of her name brought no change over his stony face and hard-set mouth. He always gave the same vague answers to her pleadings, couched in almost the same words, and did not heed his wife's white face, nor the tears that flowed down her cheeks.

'May God forgive you, as I do, sir,' she said. 'You will have need of mercy some day.'

Since his wife's illness had begun he had not ventured to make use of his formidable 'Tut, tut, tut', but his tyranny was not relaxed one whit by his wife's angelic gentleness.

Her plain face was growing almost beautiful now as a beautiful nature showed itself more and more, and her soul grew absolute. It seemed as if the spirit of prayer had purified and refined the homely features – as if they were lit up by some inner light. Which of us has not known such faces as this, and seen their final trans-figuration – the triumph of a soul that has dwelt for so long among pure and lofty thoughts that they set their seal unmistakably upon the roughest lineaments at last? The sight of this transformation wrought by the physical suffering which stripped the soul of the rags of humanity that hid it, had a certain effect, however feeble, upon that man of bronze – the old cooper. A stubborn habit of silence had succeeded to his old contemptuous ways; a wish to keep up his dignity as a father of a family was apparently the motive for this course.

The faithful Nanon no sooner showed herself in the market-place than people began to rail at her master and to make jokes at his expense; but however loudly public opinion condemned old Grandet, the maid-servant, jealous for the honour of the family, stoutly defended him.

'Well, now,' she would say to those who spoke ill of her master, 'don't we all grow harder as we grow older? And would you have him different from other people? Just hold your lying tongues. Mademoiselle lives like a queen. She is all by herself, no doubt, but she likes it; and my master and mistress have their very good reasons for what they do.'

At last, one evening towards the end of spring, Mme Grandet, feeling that this trouble, even more than her illness, was shortening her days, and that any further attempt on her part to obtain forgiveness for Eugénie was hopeless, confided her troubles to the Cruchots.

'To put a girl of twenty-three on a diet of bread and water! . . .' cried the Président de Bonfons, 'and without just and sufficient cause! Why, that constitutes legal cruelty; she might lodge a complaint; *inasmuch as* –'

'Come, nephew,' said the notary, 'that is enough of

your law-court jargon. Be easy, madame; I will bring this imprisonment to an end tomorrow.'

Eugénie heard, and came out of her room.

'Gentlemen,' she said, impelled by a certain pride, 'do nothing in this matter, I beg of you. My father is master in his own house, and so long as I live under his roof I ought to obey him. No one has any right to criticize his conduct; he is answerable to God, and to God alone. If you have any friendly feeling for me, I entreat you to say nothing whatever about this. If you expose my father to censure, you would lower us all in the eyes of the world. I am very thankful to you, gentlemen, for the interest you have taken in me, and you will oblige me still further if you will put a stop to the gossip that is going on in the town. I only heard of it by accident.'

'She is right,' said Mme Grandet.

'Mademoiselle, the best possible way to stop people's talk would be to set you at liberty,' said the old notary respectfully; he was struck with the beauty which solitude and love and sadness had brought into Eugénie's face.

'Well, Eugénie, leave it in Monsieur Cruchot's hands, as he seems to think success is certain. He knows your father, and he knows, too, how to put the matter before him. You and your father must be reconciled at all costs, if you want me to be happy during the little time I have yet to live.'

The next morning Grandet went out to take a certain number of turns round the little garden, a habit that he had fallen into during Eugénie's incarceration. He chose to take the air while Eugénie was dressing; and when he had reached the great walnut tree, he stood behind it for a few moments and looked at her window. He watched her as she brushed her long hair, and there was a sharp struggle, doubtless, between his natural stubborn will and a longing to take his daughter in his arms and kiss her.

He would often go to sit on the little worm-eaten bench where Charles and Eugénie had vowed to love each other for ever; and she, his daughter, also watched her father furtively, or looked into her glass and saw him reflected there, and the garden and the bench. If he rose and began to walk again, she went to sit in the window. It was pleasant to her to be there. She studied the bit of old wall, the delicate sprays of wild flowers that grew in its crevices, the maidenhair fern, the morning glories, and a little plant with thick leaves and white or yellow flowers, a sort of stonecrop that grows everywhere among the vines at Saumur and Tours.

Old M. Cruchot came early on a bright June morning and found the vine-grower sitting on the little bench with his back against the wall, absorbed in watching his daughter.

'What can I do for you, M. Cruchot?' he asked, as he became aware of the notary's presence.

'I have come about a matter of business.'

'Aha! Have you some gold to exchange for crowns?'

'No, no. It is not a question of money this time, but of your daughter Eugénie. Everybody is talking about you and her.'

'What business is it of theirs? A man's house is his castle.'

'Just so; and a man can kill himself if he has a mind, or he can do worse, he can throw his money out of the windows.'

'What?'

'Eh! but your wife is very ill, my friend. You ought even to call in Monsieur Bergerin, her life is in danger. If she were to die for want of proper care, you would hear of it, I am sure.'

'Tut, tut, tut! you know what is the matter with her, and when once one of these doctors sets foot in your house, they will come five or six times a day.'

'After all, Grandet, you will do as you think best. We are old friends; there is no one in all Saumur who has your interests more at heart than I, so it was only my duty to let you know this. Whatever happens, you are of age, and you understand your own business, so there it is. Besides, that was not what I came to speak about. There is something else more serious for you, perhaps; for, after all, you do not wish to kill your wife, she is too useful to you. Just think what your position would be if anything happened to Madame Grandet; you would have your daughter to face. You would have to give an account to Eugénie of her mother's share of your joint estate; and if she chose, your daughter might demand her mother's fortune, for she, and not you, will succeed to it; and in that case, you might have to sell Froidfond.'

Cruchot's words were like a bolt from the blue; for much as the worthy cooper knew about business, he knew very little law. The idea of a forced sale had never occured to him.

'So I should strongly recommend you to treat her kindly,' the notary concluded.

'But do you know what she has done, Cruchot?'

'No. What was it?' asked the notary; he felt curious to know the reason of the quarrel, and a confidence from old Grandet was an interesting novelty.

'She has given away her gold.'

'Oh, well, it belonged to her, didn't it?'

'That is what they all say!' said the goodman, letting his arms fall with a tragic gesture.

'And for a trifle like that you would shut yourself out from all hope of any concessions which you will want her to make if her mother dies?'

'Ah! do you call six thousand francs in gold a trifle?'

'Eh, my old friend! have you any idea what it will cost you to have your property valued and divided if Eugénie should compel you to do so?'

'What would it cost?'

'Two, three, or even four hundred thousand francs. How could you know what it is worth unless you put it up to public auction? While if you come to an understanding –'

'By my father's pruning-hook!' cried the vine-grower, sinking back and turning quite pale. 'We will see about this, Cruchot.'

After a moment of agony or of dumb bewilderment, the worthy man spoke, with his eyes fixed on his neighbour's face. 'Life is very hard!' he said. 'It is full of troubles. Cruchot,' he went on earnestly, 'you are incapable of deceiving me; give me your word of honour that this ditty of yours has a solid foundation. Let me look at the Code; I want to see the Code!'

'My poor friend,' said the notary, 'I ought to understand my own profession.'

'Then it is really true? I shall be plundered, cheated, robbed, and murdered by my own daughter!'

'She is her mother's heiress.'

'Then what is the good of having children? Oh! my wife, I love my wife; luckily she has a sound constitution; she is a La Bertellière.'

'She has not a month to live.'

The cooper struck his forehead, took a few paces, and then came back again.

'What is to be done?' he demanded of Cruchot, with a tragic expression on his face.

'Well, perhaps Eugénie might simply give up her claims to her mother's property. You do not mean to disinherit her, do you? But do not treat her harshly if you want her to make a concession of that kind. I am speaking against my own interests, my friend. How do I make a living but by drawing up inventories and conveyances and deeds of arrangement and by winding up estates?'

'We shall see, we shall see. Let us say no more about this now, Cruchot. You have wrung my very soul. Have you taken any gold lately?'

'No; but I have some old louis, nine or ten perhaps, which you can have. Look here, my good friend, make it up with Eugénie; all Saumur is pointing a finger at you.'

'The rogues!'

'Well, consols have risen to ninety-nine, so you should be satisfied for once in your life.'

'To ninety-nine, Cruchot?'

'Yes.'

'Hey! hey! ninety-nine!' the old man said, as he went with the notary to the street door. He felt too much agitated by what he had just heard to stay quietly at home; so he went up to his wife's room.

'Come, mother, you may spend the day with your daughter, I am going to Froidfond. Be good, both of you, while I am away. This is our wedding day, dear wife. Stay! here are ten crowns for you, for the Corpus Christi shrine; you have wanted to have one for long enough. Take a holiday! have some fun, keep up your spirits and get well. Vive la joie!'

He threw down ten crowns of six francs each upon the bed, took her face in his hands, and kissed her on the forehead.

'You are feeling better, dear wife, are you not?'

'But how can you think of receiving the God of forgiveness into your house, when you have shut your heart against your daughter?' she said, with deep feeling in her voice.

'Tut, tut, tut!' said the father soothingly; 'we will see about that.'

'Merciful heaven! Eugénie!' called the mother, her face flushed with joy; 'Eugénie, come and give your father a kiss, you are forgiven!' But her worthy father had vanished. He fled with all his might in the direction of his vineyards, where he set himself to the task of constructing his new world out of this chaos of strange ideas.

Grandet had just entered upon his seventy-sixth year. Avarice had gained a stronger hold upon him during the past two years of his life; indeed, all lasting passions grow with man's growth; and it had come to pass with him, as with all men whose lives are ruled by one master-idea, that he clung with all the force of his imagination to the symbol which represented that idea for him. Gold – to have gold, that he might see and touch it, had become with him a perfect monomania. His disposition to tyrannize had also grown with his love of money, and it seemed to him to be *monstrous* that he should be called upon to give up the management of the least portion of his property on the death of his wife. Was he to render an account of her fortune, and to have an inventory drawn up of everything he possessed – personality and real estate – and put it all up to auction?

'That would be stark ruin,' he said aloud to himself, as he stood among his vines and examined their stems.

He made up his mind at last, and came back to Saumur at dinner-time fully determined on his course. He would humour Eugénie, and coax and cajole her so that he might die royally, keeping the control of his millions in his hands until his latest sigh. It happened that he let himself in with his master key; he crept noiselessly as a wolf up the stairs to his wife's room, which he entered just as Eugénie was setting the dressing-case, in all its golden glory, upon her mother's bed. The two women had stolen a pleasure in Grandet's absence; they were looking at the portraits and tracing out Charles's features in his mother's likeness.

'It is just his forehead and his mouth!' Eugénie was saying, as the vine-grower opened the door.

Mme Grandet saw how her husband's eyes darted upon the gold. 'God, have pity upon us!' she cried.

The vine-grower seized upon the dressing-case as a tiger might spring upon a sleeping child.

'What may this be?' he said, carrying off the treasure to the window, where he ensconced himself with it. 'Gold! solid gold!' he cried, 'and plenty of it too; there is a couple of pounds' weight here. Aha! so this was what Charles gave you in exchange for your pretty gold pieces! Why did you not tell me? It was a good stroke of business, little girl. You are your father's own daughter, I see.' (Eugénie trembled from head to foot.) 'This belongs to Charles, doesn't it?' the goodman went on.

'Yes, father; it is not mine. That case is a sacred trust.'

'Tut, tut, tut! he has gone off with your money; you ought to make good the loss of your little treasure.'

'Oh, father! . . .'

The old man had taken out his pocket-knife, with a view to wrenching away a plate of the precious metal, and for the moment had been obliged to lay the case on a chair beside him. Eugénie sprang forward to secure her treasure; but the cooper, who had kept an eye upon his daughter as well as upon the casket, put out his arm to prevent this, and thrust her back so roughly that she fell on to the bed.

'Sir! sir!' cried the mother, rising and sitting upright.

Grandet had drawn out his knife, and was about to insert the blade beneath the plate.

'Father!' cried Eugénie, going down on her knees and dragging herself nearer to him as she knelt; 'father, in the name of all the saints, and the Holy Virgin, for the sake of Christ who died on the cross, for your own soul's salvation, father, if you have any regard for my life, do not touch it! The case is not yours, and it is not mine. It belongs to an unhappy kinsman, who gave it into my keeping, and I ought to give it back to him untouched.'

'What do you look at it for if it is a deposit? Looking at it is worse than touching it.'

'Do not pull it to pieces, father! You will bring dishonour upon me. Father! do you hear me?'

'For pity's sake, sir!' entreated the mother.

'Father!'

The shrill cry rang through the house and brought the frightened Nanon upstairs. Eugénie caught up a knife that lay within her reach.

'Well?' said Grandet calmly, with a cold smile on his lips.

'Sir! you are killing me!' said the mother.

'Father, if you cut away a single scrap of gold, I shall stab myself with this knife. It is your doing that my mother is dying, and now my death will also be laid at your door. It shall be wound for wound.'

Grandet held his knife suspended above the case, looked at his daughter, and hesitated.

'Would you really do it, Eugénie?' he asked.

'Yes, sir!' said the mother.

'She would do as she says,' cried Nanon. 'Do be sensible, sir, for once in your life.'

The cooper wavered for a moment, looking first at the gold, and then at his daughter.

Mme Grandet fainted.

'There, sir! you see, the mistress is dying,' cried Nanon.

'There, there, child! do not let us fall out about a box. Just take it back!' cried the cooper hastily, throwing the case on to the bed. 'And, Nanon, go for Monsieur Bergerin. Come, come, mother!' he said, and he kissed his wife's hand; 'never mind, there, there! we

have made it up, haven't we, little girl? No more dry
bread; you shall eat whatever you like... Ah! she is
opening her eyes. Well, now, little mother, dear little
mother, don't take on so! Look! I am going to kiss
Eugénie! She loves her cousin, does she? She shall
marry him if she likes; she shall keep his little case for
him. But you must live for a long while yet, my poor
wife! Come! turn your head a little. Listen! you shall
have the finest altar at for Corpus Christi that has ever
been seen in Saumur.'

'Oh, mon Dieu! how can you treat your wife and
daughter in this way!' moaned Mme Grandet.

'I will never do so again, never again!' cried the
cooper. 'You shall see, my poor wife.'

He went to his strong-room and returned with a
handful of louis d'or, which he scattered on the cover-
let.

'There, Eugénie! there, wife! those are for you,' he
said, fingering the gold coins as they lay. 'Come! cheer
up, and get well, you shall want for nothing, neither you
nor Eugénie. There are a hundred louis for her. You will
not give them away, will you, eh, Eugénie?'

Mme Grandet and her daughter gazed at each other
in amazement.

'Take back the money, father; we want nothing,
nothing but your love.'

'Oh, well, just as you like,' he said, as he pocketed
the louis, 'let us live together like good friends. Let us
all go down to the dining-room and have dinner, and
play lotto every evening, and put our two sous into the
pool, and be as merry as the maids. Eh, my wife?'

'Alas! how I wish that I could, if you would like it,'
said the dying woman, 'but I am not strong enough to
get up.'

'Poor mother!' said the cooper, 'you do not know
how much I love you; and you too, child!'

He drew his daughter to him and embraced her with fervour.

'Oh, how pleasant it is to kiss one's daughter after a squabble, my little girl! There, mother, do you see? We are quite at one again now. Just go and lock that away,' he said to Eugénie, as he pointed to the case. 'There, there! don't be frightened; I will never say another word to you about it.'

M. Bergerin, who was regarded as the cleverest doctor in Saumur, came before very long. He told Grandet plainly after the interview that the patient was very seriously ill; that any excitement might be fatal to her; that with a light diet, perfect tranquillity, and the most constant care, her life might possibly be prolonged until the end of the autumn.

'Will it be an expensive illness?' asked the worthy householder. 'Will she want a lot of physic?'

'Not much physic, but very careful nursing,' answered the doctor, who could not help smiling.

'After all, Monsieur Bergerin, you are a man of honour,' said Grandet uneasily. 'I can depend upon you, can I not? Come and see my wife whenever and as often as you think it really necessary. Preserve her life. My good wife – I am very fond of her, you see, though I may not show it; it is all shut up inside me, and I am one that takes things terribly to heart; I am in trouble too. It all began with my brother's death; I am spending, oh! heaps of money in Paris for him – the very eyes out of my head in fact – and it seems as if there were no end to it. Good day, sir. If you can save my wife, save her, even if it takes a hundred, or two hundred, francs.'

In spite of Grandet's fervent wishes that his wife might be restored to health, for this question of the inheritance was like a foretaste of death for him; in spite of his readiness to fulfil the least wishes of the astonished mother and daughter in every possible way;

in spite of Eugénie's tenderest and most devoted care, it was evident that Mme Grandet's life was rapidly drawing to a close. Day by day she grew weaker, and, as often happens at her time of life, she had no strength to resist the disease that was wasting her away. She seemed to have no more vitality than the autumn leaves; and as the sunlight shining through the leaves turns them to gold, so she seemed to be transformed by the light of heaven. Her death was a fitting close to her life, a death wholly Christian; is not that saying that it was sublime? Her love for her daughter, her meek virtues, her angelic patience, had never shone more brightly than in that month of October 1822, when she passed away. All through her illness she had never uttered the slightest complaint, and her spotless soul left earth for heaven with but one regret – for the daughter whose sweet companionship had been the solace of her dreary life, and for whom her dying eyes foresaw troubles and sorrows manifold. She trembled at the thought of this lamb, spotless as she herself was, left alone in the world among selfish beings who sought to despoil her of her fleece, her treasure.

'There is no happiness save in heaven,' she said just before she died; 'you will know that one day, my child.'

On the morrow after her mother's death, it seemed to Eugénie that she had yet one more reason for clinging fondly to the old house where she had been born, and where she had found life so hard of late – it became for her the place where her mother had died. She could not see the old chair set on little blocks of wood, the place by the window where her mother used to sit, without shedding tears. Her father showed her such tenderness, and took such care of her, that she began to think that she had never understood his nature; he used to come to her room and take her down to breakfast on his arm, and sit looking at her for whole hours with something almost like kindness in his eyes, with the same brooding look that he gave his gold. Indeed, the old cooper almost trembled before his daughter, and was altogether so unlike himself, that Nanon and the Cruchotins wondered at these signs of weakness, and set it down to his advanced age; they began to fear that the old man's mind was giving way. But when the day came on which the family began to wear their mourning, M. Cruchot, who alone was in his client's confidence, was invited to dinner, and these mysteries were explained. Grandet waited till the table had been cleared, and the doors carefully shut.

Then he began. 'My dear child, you are your mother's heiress, and there are some little matters of business that we must settle between us. Is not that so, eh, Cruchot?'

'Yes.'

'Is it really pressing; must it be settled today, father?'

'Yes, yes, little girl. I could not endure this suspense any longer, and I am sure that you would not make things hard for me.'

'Oh, father! –'

'Well, then, everything must be decided tonight.'

'Then what do you want me to do?'

'Why, little girl, it is not for me to tell you. You tell her, Cruchot.'

'Mademoiselle, your father wants neither to divide nor to sell his property, nor to pay a heavy succession duty upon the ready money he may happen to have just now. So if these complications are to be avoided, there must be no inventory made out, and all the property must remain undivided for the present –'

'Cruchot, are you quite sure of what you are saying that you talk in this way before a child?'

'Let me say what I have to say, Grandet.'

'Yes, yes, my friend. Neither you nor my daughter would plunder me. You would not plunder me, would you, little girl?'

'But what am I to do, Monsieur Cruchot?' asked Eugénie, losing patience.

'Well,' said the notary, 'you must sign this deed, by which you renounce your claims to your mother's property; the property would be secured to you, but your father would have the use of it for his life, and there would be no need to make a division now.'

'I understand nothing of all this that you are saying,' Eugénie answered; 'give me the deed, and show me where I am to sign my name.'

Grandet looked from the document to his daughter, and again from his daughter to the document. His agitation was so great that he actually wiped several drops of perspiration from his forehead.

'I would much rather you simply waived all claim to your poor dear mother's property, little girl,' he broke in, 'instead of signing that deed. It will cost a lot to register it. I would rather you renounced your claims and trusted to me for the future. I would allow you a good round sum, say a hundred francs every month. You could pay for masses then, you see; you could have masses said for anyone that . . . Eh? A hundred francs (in livres) every month?'

'I will do just as you like, father.'

'Mademoiselle,' said the notary, 'it is my duty to point out to you that you are robbing yourself without guarantee –'

'Eh! mon Dieu!' she answered. 'What does that matter to me?'

'Do be quiet, Cruchot. So it is settled, quite settled!' cried Grandet, taking his daughter's hand and striking his own into it. 'You will not go back from your word, Eugénie? You are a good girl, hein!'

'Oh, father! –'

In his joy he embraced his daughter, almost suffocating her as he did so.

'There, child! you have given fresh life to your father; but you are only giving him what he gave you, so we are quits. This is how business ought to be conducted, and life is a business transaction. Bless you! You are a good girl, and one that really loves her old father. You can do as you like now. Then good-bye till tomorrow, Cruchot,' he added to the horrified notary. 'You will see that the deed of renunciation is properly drawn up for the clerk of the court.'

By noon next day the declaration was drawn up, and Eugénie herself signed away all her right to her heritage. Yet a year slipped by, and the cooper had not kept his promise, and Eugénie had not received a sou of the monthly income which was to have been hers; when Eugénie spoke to him about it, half laughingly, he could not help blushing; he hurried up to his room, and when he came down again he handed her about a third of the jewellery which he had purchased of his nephew.

'There, child!' he said, with a certain sarcastic ring in his voice; 'will you take these for your twelve hundred francs?'

'Oh, father, really? Will you really give them to me?'

'You shall have as much next year again,' said he, flinging it into her lap; 'and so, before very long, you will have all his trinkets,' he added, rubbing his hands. He had made a very good bargain, thanks to his daughter's sentiment about the jewellery, and was in high good humour.

Yet, although the old man was still hale and vigorous, he began to see that he must take his daughter into his confidence, and that she must learn to manage his concerns. So with this end in view he required her to be present while he gave out the daily stores, and for two years he made her receive the portion of the rent which was paid in kind. Gradually she came to know the names of the vineyards and farms; he took her with him when he visited his tenants. By the end of the third year he considered the initiation was complete; and, in truth, she had fallen into his ways unquestioningly, till it had become a matter of habit with her to do as her father had done before her. He had no further doubts, gave over the keys of the store-room into her keeping, and installed her as mistress of the house.

Five years went by in this way, and no event disturbed their monotonous existence. Eugénie and her father lived a life of methodical routine with the same regularity of movement that characterized the old clock; doing the same things at the same hour day after day, year after year. Everyone knew that there had been a profound sorrow in Mlle Grandet's life; every circle in Saumur had its theories of this secret trouble, and its suspicions as to the state of the heiress's heart, but she never let fall a word that could enlighten anyone on either point.

She saw no one but the three Cruchots and a few of their friends, who had gradually been admitted as visitors to the house. Under their instruction she had mastered the game of whist, and they dropped in nearly every evening for a rubber. In the year 1827 her father began to feel the infirmities of age, and was obliged to take her still further into his confidence; she learned the full extent of his landed possessions, and was recommended in all cases of difficulty to refer to the notary Cruchot, whose integrity could be depended upon. Grandet had reached the age of eighty-two, and towards the end of the year had a paralytic seizure, from which he never rallied. M. Bergerin gave him up, and Eugénie realized that very shortly she would be quite alone in the world; the thought drew her more closely to her father; she clung to this last link of affection that bound her to another soul. Love was all the world for her, as it is for all women who love; and Charles had gone out of her world. She nursed her father with sublime devotion; the old man's intellect had grown feeble, but the greed of gold had become an instinct which survived his faculties.

Grandet died as he had lived. Every morning during that slow death he had himself wheeled across his room to a place beside the fire, whence he could keep the door of his cabinet in view; on the other side of the door, no doubt, lay his hoarded treasures of gold. He sat there, passive and motionless; but if anyone entered the room, he would glance uneasily at the new-comer, and then at the door with its sheathing of iron plates. He would ask the meaning of every sound, however faint, and, to the notary's amazement, the old man heard the dog bark in the yard at the back of the house. He roused from this apparent stupor at the proper hour on the days for receiving his rents and dues, for settling accounts with his vine-dressers, and giving receipts. Then he shifted his arm-chair round on its castors, until he faced the door of his cabinet, and his daughter was called upon to open it, and to put away the little bags of money in neat piles, one upon the other. He would watch her until it was all over and the door was locked again; and as soon as she had returned the precious key to him, he would turn round noiselessly and take up his old position, putting the key in his waistcoat pocket, where he felt for it from time to time.

His old friend the notary felt sure that it was only a question of time, and that Eugénie must of necessity marry his nephew the magistrate, unless, indeed, Charles Grandet returned; so he redoubled his attentions. He came every day to take Grandet's instructions, went at his bidding to Froidfond, to farm and meadow and vineyard; sold vintages, and exchanged all moneys received for gold, which was secretly sent to join the piles of bags stored up in the cabinet.

Then death came up close at last, and the vine-grower's strong frame wrestled with the Destroyer. Even in those days he would sit as usual by the fire, facing the door of his cabinet. He used to drag off the blankets that they wrapped round him, and try to fold them, and say to Nanon, 'Lock that up; lock that up, or they will rob me.'

So long as he could open his eyes, where the last sparks of life seemed to linger, they used to turn at once to the door of the room where all his treasures lay, and he would say to his daughter, in tones that seemed to thrill with a panic of fear:

'*Are they there still?*'

'Yes, father.'

'Keep watch over the gold! . . . Let me see the gold.'

Then Eugénie used to spread out the louis on a table before him, and he would sit for whole hours with his eyes fixed on the louis in an unseeing stare, like that of a child who begins to see for the first time; and sometimes a weak infantine smile, painful to see, would steal across his features.

'That warms me!' he muttered more than once, and his face expressed a perfect content.

When the curé came to administer the sacrament, all the life seemed to have died out of the miser's eyes, but they lit up for the first time for many hours at the sight of the silver crucifix, the candlesticks, and holy-water vessel, all of silver; he fixed his gaze on the precious metal, and the wen twitched for the last time.

As the priest held the gilded crucifix above him that the image of Christ might be laid to his lips, he made a frightful effort to clutch it – a last effort which cost him his life. He called to Eugénie, whom he could not see, though she was kneeling beside him, bathing in tears the hand that was growing cold already. 'Give me your blessing, father,' she entreated. 'Be very careful!' the last words came from him; 'one day you will render an account to me of everything here below.' Which utterance clearly shows that a miser should adopt Christianity as his religion.

So Eugénie Grandet was alone in the world, and her house was left to her desolate. There was no one but Nanon with whom she could talk over her troubles; she could look into no other eyes and find a response in them; big Nanon was the only human being who loved her for herself. For Eugénie, Nanon was a providence; she was no longer a servant, she was a humble friend.

M. Cruchot informed Eugénie that she had three hundred thousand livres a year, derived from landed property in and around Saumur, besides six millions in the three per cents (invested when the funds were at sixty francs, whereas they now stood at seventy-seven), and in ready money two millions in gold and a hundred thousand francs in silver, without counting any arrears that were due. Altogether her property amounted to about seventeen million francs.

'Where can my cousin be?' she said to herself.

On the day when M. Cruchot laid these facts before his new client, together with the information that the estate was now clear and free from all outstanding liabilities, Eugénie and Nanon sat on either side of the hearth, in the parlour, now so empty and so full of memories; everything recalled past days, from her mother's chair set on its wooden blocks, to the glass tumbler out of which her cousin once drank.

'Nanon, we are alone, you and I.'

'Yes, mam'selle; if I only knew where he was, the

charming young gentleman, I would set off on foot to find him.'

'The sea lies between us,' said Eugénie.

While the poor lonely heiress, with her faithful old servant for company, was shedding tears in the cold, dark house, which was all the world she knew, men talked from Orleans to Nantes of nothing but Mlle Grandet and her seventeen millions. One of her first acts was to settle a pension of twelve hundred francs on Nanon, who, possessing already an income of six hundred francs of her own, at once became a great match. In less than a month she exchanged her condition of spinster for that of wife, at the instance and through the persuasion of Antoine Cornoiller, who was promoted to the position of bailiff and keeper to Mlle Grandet. Mme Cornoiller had an immense advantage over her contemporaries; her large features had stood the test of time better than those of many a comelier woman. She might be fifty-nine years of age, but she did not look more than forty; thanks to an almost monastic regimen, she possessed rude health and a high colour, time seemed to have no effect on her, and perhaps she had never looked so well in her life as she did on her wedding day. She had the compensating qualities of her style of ugliness; she was tall, stout, and strong; her face wore an indestructible expression of good humour, and Cornoiller's lot seemed an enviable one to many beholders.

'Fast colour,' said the draper.

'She might have a family yet,' said the drysalter; 'she is as well preserved as if she had been kept in brine, asking your pardon.'

'She is rich; that fellow Cornoiller has done a good day's work,' said another neighbour.

When Nanon left the old house and went down the crooked street on her way to the parish church, she met with nothing but congratulations and good wishes. Nanon was very popular with her neighbours. Eugénie gave her three dozen spoons and forks as a wedding present. Cornoiller, quite overcome with such munificence, spoke of his mistress with tears in his eyes; he would have let himself be cut in pieces for her. Mme Cornoiller became Eugénie's confidential servant; she was not only married, and had a husband of her own, her dignity was yet further increased, her happiness was doubled. *She* had at last a store-room and a bunch of keys; *she* too gave out provisions just as her late master used to do. Then she had two subordinates – a cook and a waiting-woman, who took charge of the house linen and made Mlle Grandet's dresses. As for Cornoiller, he combined the functions of forester and steward. It is needless to say that the cook and waiting-woman of Nanon's choosing were real domestic *treasures*. The tenants scarcely noticed the death of their late landlord; they were thoroughly broken in to a severe discipline, and M. and Mme Cornoiller's reign was no whit less rigorous than the old regime.

Eugénie was a woman of thirty, and as yet had known none of the happiness of life. All through her joyless, monotonous childhood she had had but one companion, the broken-spirited mother, whose sensitive nature had found little but suffering in a hard life. That mother had joyfully taken leave of existence, pitying the daughter who must still live on in the world. Eugénie would never lose the sense of her loss, but little of the bitterness of self-reproach mingled with her memories of her mother.

Love, her first and only love, had been a fresh source of suffering for Eugénie. For a few brief days she had seen her lover; she had given her heart to him between two stolen kisses; then he had left her, and had set the lands and seas of the world between them. Her father had cursed her for this love; it had nearly cost her her mother's life; it had brought her pain and sorrow and a few faint hopes. She had striven towards her happiness till her own forces had failed her, and another had not come to her aid.

Our souls live by giving and receiving; we have need of another soul; whatever it gives us we make our own, and give back again in overflowing measure. This is as vitally necessary for our inner life as breathing is for our corporeal existence. Without that wonderful physical process we perish; the heart suffers from lack of air, and ceases to beat. Eugénie was beginning to suffer.

She found no solace in her wealth; it could do nothing for her; her love, her religion, her faith in the future made up all her life. Love was teaching her what eternity meant. Her own heart and the Gospel each spoke to her of a life to come; life was everlasting, and love no less eternal. Night and day she dwelt with these two infinite thoughts, perhaps for her they were but one. She withdrew more and more into herself; she loved, and believed that she was loved.

For seven years her passion had wholly engrossed her.

Her treasures were not those millions left to her by her father, the money that went on accumulating year after year; but the two portraits which hung above her bed, Charles's leather case, the jewels which she had bought back from her father, and which were now proudly set forth on a layer of cotton-wool inside the drawer in the old chest, and her aunt's thimble which Mme Grandet had used; every day Eugénie took up a piece of embroidery, a sort of Penelope's web, which she had only begun that she might wear the golden thimble, endeared to her by so many memories.

It seemed hardly probable that Mlle Grandet would marry while she still wore mourning. Her sincere piety was well known. So the Cruchot family, counselled by the astute old abbé, was fain to be content with surrounding the heiress with the most affectionate attentions. Her dining-room was filled every evening with the warmest and most devoted Cruchotins, who endeavoured to surpass each other in singing the praises of the mistress of the house in every key. She had her physician in ordinary, her grand almoner, her chamberlain, her mistress of the robes, her prime minister, and last, but by no means least, her chancellor – a chancellor whose aim it was to keep her informed of everything. If the heiress had expressed any wish for a train-bearer, they would have found one for her. She was a queen in fact, and never was queen so adroitly flattered. A great soul never stoops to flattery; it is the resource of little natures, who succeed in making themselves smaller still, that they may the better creep into the hearts of those about whom they circle. Flattery, by its very nature, implies an interested motive. So the people who filled Mlle Grandet's sitting-room every evening (they addressed her and spoke of her among themselves as Mlle de Froidfond now) heaped their praises upon their hostess in a manner truly marvellous. This chorus of praise embarrassed Eugénie at first; but however gross the flattery might be, she became accustomed to hear her beauty extolled, and if some new-comer had considered her to be plain, she certainly would have winced more under the criticism than she might have done eight years ago. She came at last to welcome their homage, which in her secret heart she laid at the feet of her idol. So also, by degrees, she accepted the position, and allowed herself to be treated as a queen, and saw her little court full every evening.

M. le Président de Bonfons was the hero of the circle; they lauded his talents, his personal appearance, his learning, his amiability; he was an inexhaustible subject of admiring comment. Such a one would call attention to the fact that in seven years the magistrate had largely increased his fortune; Bonfons had at least ten thousand francs a year; and his property, like the lands of all the Cruchots in fact, lay within the compass of the heiress's vast estates.

'Do you know, mademoiselle,' another courtier would remark, 'that the Cruchots have forty thousand livres a year among them!'

'And they are putting money by,' said Mlle de Gribeaucourt, an old and trusty Cruchotine. 'Quite lately a gentleman came from Paris on purpose to offer Monsieur Cruchot two hundred thousand francs for his professional connection. If he could gain an appointment as justice of the peace, he ought to take the offer.'

'He means to succeed Monsieur de Bonfons as president, and is taking steps to that end,' said Mme d'Orsonval, 'for Monsieur le Président will be a councillor, and then a president of a court; he is so gifted that he is sure to succeed.'

'Yes,' said another, 'he is a very remarkable man. Do you not think so, mademoiselle?'

'Monsieur le Président' had striven to act up to the part he wanted to play. He was forty years old, his countenance was dark and ill-favoured, he had, moreover, the wizened look which is frequently seen in men of his profession; but he affected the airs of youth, sported a malacca cane, refrained from taking snuff in Mlle Grandet's house, and went thither arrayed in a white cravat and a shirt with huge frills, which gave him a quaint family resemblance to a turkey-gobbler. He called the fair heiress 'our dear Eugénie', and spoke as if he were an intimate friend of the family. In fact, but for the number of those assembled, and the substitution of whist for lotto, and the absence of M. and Mme Grandet, the scene was scarcely changed; it might almost have been that first evening on which this story began.

The pack was still in pursuit of Eugénie's millions; it was a more numerous pack now; they gave tongue together, and hunted down their prey more systematically.

If Charles had come back from the far-off Indies, he would have found the same motives at work and almost the same people. Mme des Grassins, for whom Eugénie had nothing but kindness and pity, still remained to vex the Cruchots. Eugénie's face still shone out against the dark background, and Charles (though invisible) reigned there supreme as in other days.

Yet some advance had been made. Eugénie's birthday bouquet was never forgotten by the magistrate. Indeed, it had become an institution; every evening he brought the heiress a huge and wonderful bouquet. Mme Cornoiller ostentatiously placed these offerings in a vase, and promptly flung them into a corner of the yard as soon as the visitors had departed.

In the early spring Mme des Grassins made a move, and sought to trouble the felicity of the Cruchotins by talking to Eugénie of the Marquis de Froidfond, whose ruined fortunes might be retrieved if the heiress would return his estate to him by a marriage contract. Mme des Grassins lauded the marquis and his title to the skies; and, taking Eugénie's quiet smile for consent, she went about saying that M. le Président Cruchot's marriage was not such a settled thing as *some* people imagined.

'Monsieur de Froidfond may be fifty years old,' she said, 'but he looks no older than Monsieur Cruchot; he is a widower, and has a family, it is true; but he is a marquis, he will be a peer of France one of these days, it is not such a bad match as times go. I know of my own certain knowledge that when old Grandet added his own property to the Froidfond estate he meant to graft his family into the Froidfonds. He often told me as much. Oh! he was a shrewd old man, was Grandet.'

'Ah, Nanon,' Eugénie said one evening, as she went to bed, 'why has he not once written to me in seven years?' . . .

While these events were taking place in Saumur, Charles was making his fortune in the East. His first venture was very successful. He had promptly realized the sum of six thousand dollars. Crossing the line had cured him of many early prejudices; he soon saw very clearly that the best and quickest way of making money was the same in the tropics as in Europe – by buying and selling men. He made a descent on the African coasts and bargained for negroes and other goods in demand in various markets. He threw himself heart and soul into his business, and thought of nothing else. He set one clear aim before him, to reappear in Paris, and to dazzle the world there with his wealth, to attain a position even higher than the one from which he had fallen.

By dint of rubbing shoulders with many men, travelling in many lands, coming in contact with various customs and religions, his code had been relaxed, and he had grown sceptical. His notions of right and wrong became less rigid when he found that what was looked upon as a crime in one country was held up to admiration in another. He saw that everyone was working for himself, that disinterestedness was rarely to be met with, and grew selfish and suspicious; the hereditary failings of the Grandets came out in him – the hardness, the shiftiness, and the greed of gain. He sold Chinese coolies, negro slaves, swallow-nests, children, artists, anything and everything that brought in money. He became a moneylender on a large scale. Long practice in cheating the customs authorities had made him unscrupulous in other ways. He would make the voyage to St Thomas, buy booty of the pirates there for a low price, and sell the merchandise in the dearest market.

During his first voyage Eugénie's pure and noble face had been with him, like the image of the Virgin which Spanish sailors set on the prows of their vessels; he had attributed his first success to a kind of magical efficacy possessed by her prayers and vows; but as time went on, the women of other countries, negresses, mulattoes, white skins, and yellow skins, orgies and adventures in many lands, completely effaced all recollection of his cousin, of Saumur, of the old house, of the bench, and of the kiss that he had snatched in the passage. He remembered nothing but the little garden shut in by its crumbling walls where he had learned the fate that lay in store for him; but he rejected all connection with the family. His uncle was an old fox who had filched his jewels. Eugénie had no place in his heart, he never gave her a thought; but she occupied a page in his ledger as a creditor for six thousand francs.

Such conduct and such ideas explained Charles Grandet's silence. In the East Indies, at St Thomas, on the coast of Africa, at Lisbon, in the United States, Charles Grandet the adventurer was known as Carl Sepherd, a pseudonym which he assumed so as not to compromise his real name. Carl Sepherd could be indefatigable, brazen, and greedy of gain; could conduct himself, in short, like a man who resolves to make a fortune *quibuscumque viis*, and makes haste to have done with villainy as soon as possible, in order to live respected for the rest of his days.

With such methods his career of prosperity was rapid and brilliant, and in 1827 he returned to Bordeaux on board the *Marie Caroline*, a fine brig belonging to a Royalist firm. He had nineteen hundred thousand francs with him in gold dust, carefully secreted in three strong casks; he hoped to sell it to the Paris mint, and to make eight per cent on the transaction. There was also on board the brig a gentleman-in-ordinary to His

Majesty Charles X, a M. d'Aubrion, a worthy old man
who had been rash enough to marry a woman of fashion
whose money came from estates in the West India
Islands. Mme d'Aubrion's reckless extravagance had
obliged him to go out to the Indies to sell her property.
M. and Mme d'Aubrion, of the house of d'Aubrion de
Buch, which had lost its *captal* or chieftain just before
the Revolution, were now in straitened circumstances.
They had a bare twenty thousand francs of income and
a daughter, a very plain girl, whom her mother made up
her mind to marry without a dowry; for life in Paris
is expensive, and, as has been seen, their means were
reduced. It was an enterprise the success of which
might have seemed somewhat problematical to a man
of the world, in spite of the cleverness with which a
woman of fashion is generally credited. Perhaps even
Mme d'Aubrion herself, when she looked at her
daughter, was almost ready to despair of getting rid of
her to anyone, even to the most besotted worshipper of
rank and titles.

Mlle d'Aubrion was a tall, spare damsel, somewhat
like her namesake the insect; she had a disdainful
mouth, overshadowed by a long nose, thick at the tip,
sallow in its normal condition, but very red after a meal,
an organic change which was all the more unpleasant by
reason of contrast with a pallid, insipid countenance.
From some points of view she was all that a worldly
mother, who was thirty-eight years of age, and had still
some pretensions of beauty, could desire. But by way of
compensating advantages, the Marquise d'Aubrion's
distinguished air had been inherited by her daughter,
and that young lady had been submitted to a Spartan
regimen, which for the time being subdued the offending hue in her feature to a reasonable flesh-tint. Her
mother had taught her how to dress herself. Under the
same instructor she had acquired a charming manner,

and had learned to assume that pensive expression which interests a man and leads him to imagine that here, surely, is the angel for whom he has hitherto sought in vain. She was carefully drilled in a certain manœuvre with her foot – to let it peep forth from beneath her petticoat, and so call attention to its small size – whenever her nose became unseasonably red; indeed, the mother had made the very best of her daughter. By means of large sleeves, stiff skirts, puffs, padding, and high-pressure corsets she had produced a highly curious and interesting result, a specimen of femininity which ought to have been put into a museum for the edification of mothers generally.

Charles became very intimate with Mme d'Aubrion; the lady had her own reasons for encouraging him. People said that during the time on board she left no stone unturned to secure such a prize for a son-in-law. It is certain that when they landed at Bordeaux in June 1827 Charles stayed in the same hotel with M., Mme, and Mlle d'Aubrion, and they all travelled together to Paris. The Hôtel d'Aubrion was hampered with mortgages, and Charles was intended to come to the rescue. The mother had gone so far as to say that it would give her great pleasure to establish a son-in-law on the ground floor. She did not share M. d'Aubrion's aristocratic prejudices, and promised Charles Grandet to obtain letters patent from that easy-tempered monarch, Charles X, which should authorize him, Grandet, to bear the name and assume the arms of the d'Aubrions, and (by purchasing the entail) to succeed to the property of Aubrion, which was worth about thirty-six thousand livres a year, to say nothing of the titles of Captal de Buch and Marquis d'Aubrion. They could be very useful to each other in short; and what with this arrangement of a joint establishment, and one or two posts about the court, the Hôtel d'Aubrion might count upon an income of a hundred thousand francs and more.

'And when a man has a hundred thousand francs a year, a name, a family, and a position at court – for I shall procure an appointment for you as gentleman of the bedchamber – the rest is easy. You can be anything you choose' (so she instructed Charles), 'Master of Requests in the Council of State, Prefect, Secretary to an Embassy, the Ambassador himself if you like. Charles X is much attached to d'Aubrion; they have known each other from childhood.'

She fairly turned his head with these ambitious schemes, and during the voyage Charles began to cherish the hopes and ideas which had been so cleverly insinuated in the form of tender confidences. He never doubted but that his uncle had paid his father's creditors; he saw himself suddenly launched into the society of the Faubourg Saint-Germain, at that time the goal of social ambition; and beneath the shadow of Mlle Mathilde's purple nose, he was shortly to appear as the Comte d'Aubrion, very much as the Dreux shone forth transformed into Brézés. He was dazzled by the apparent prosperity of the restored dynasty, which had seemed to be tottering to its fall when he left France; his head was full of wild ambitious dreams, which began on the voyage, and did not leave him in Paris. He resolved to strain every nerve to reach those pinnacles of glory which his egotistical would-be mother-in-law had pointed out to him. His cousin was only a dim speck in the remote past; she had no place in this brilliant future, no part in his dreams, but he went to see Annette. That experienced woman of the world gave counsel to her old friend; he must by no means let slip such an opportunity for an alliance; she promised to aid him in all his schemes of advancement. In her heart she was delighted to see Charles thus secured to such a plain and uninteresting girl. He had grown very attractive during his stay in the Indies; his complexion had grown darker, he had gained in manliness and self-possession; he spoke in the firm, decided tones of a man who is used to command and to success. Ever since Charles Grandet had discovered that there was a definite part for him to play in Paris, he was himself at once.

Des Grassins, hearing of his return, his approaching marriage, and his large fortune, came to see him, and spoke of the three hundred thousand francs still owing to his father's creditors. He found Charles closeted with a goldsmith, from whom he had ordered jewels for Mlle d'Aubrion's *corbeille*, and who was submitting designs. Charles himself had brought magnificent diamonds from the Indies; but the cost of setting them, together with the silver plate and jewellery of the new establishment, amounted to more than two hundred thousand francs. He did not recognize des Grassins at first, and treated him with the cool insolence of a young man of fashion who is conscious that he has killed four men in as many duels in the Indies. As M. des Grassins had already called three or four times, Charles vouchsafed to hear him, but it was with bare politeness, and he did not pay the slightest attention to what the banker said.

'My father's debts are not mine,' he said coolly. 'I am obliged to you, sir, for the trouble you have been good enough to take, but I am none the better for it that I can see. I have not scraped together a couple of millions, earned with the sweat of my brow, to fling it to my father's creditors.'

'But suppose that your father were to be declared bankrupt in a few days' time?'

'In a few days' time I shall be the Comte d'Aubrion, sir; so you can see that it is a matter of entire indifference to me. Besides, you know even better than I do that when a man has a hundred thousand livres a year,

his father never has been a bankrupt,' and he politely
edged the deputy des Grassins to the door.

In the early days of the month of August, in that same
year, Eugénie was sitting on the little bench in the garden where her cousin had sworn eternal love, and
where she often took breakfast in summer mornings.
The poor girl was almost happy for a few brief moments; she went over all the great and little events of
her love before those catastrophes that followed. The
morning was fresh and bright, and the garden was full
of sunlight; her eyes wandered over the wall with its
moss and flowers; it was full of cracks now, and all but in
ruins, but no one was allowed to touch it, though Cornoiller was always prophesying to his wife that the
whole thing would come down and crush somebody or
other one of these days. The postman knocked at the
door, and gave a letter into the hands of Mme Cornoiller, who hurried into the garden, crying, 'Mademoiselle!
A letter! Is it *the* letter?' she added, as she handed it to
her mistress.

The words rang through Eugénie's heart as the
spoken sounds rang from the ramparts and the old garden wall.

'Paris! . . . It is his writing! Then he has come back.'

Eugénie's face grew white; for several seconds she
kept the seal unbroken, for her heart beat so fast that
she could neither move nor see. Big Nanon stood and
waited with both hands on her hips; joy seemed to puff
like smoke from every wrinkle in her brown face.

'Do read it, mademoiselle!'

'Oh! why does he come back by way of Paris, Nanon,
when he went by way of Saumur?'

'Read it; the letter will tell you why.'

Eugénie's fingers trembled as she opened the en-
velope; a cheque on the firm of 'MM. des Grassins et

Corret, Saumur' fell out of it and fluttered down.
Nanon picked it up.

'MY DEAR COUSIN . . .'

('I am not "Eugénie" now,' she thought, and her
heart stood still.) 'You . . .'

'He used to say *thou*!' She folded her arms and
dreaded to read any further; great tears gathered in her
eyes.

'What is it? Is he dead?' asked Nanon.

'If he were, he could not write,' said Eugénie, and
she read the letter through. It ran as follows:

MY DEAR COUSIN,

You will, I am sure, hear with pleasure of the success
of my enterprise. You brought me luck; I have come
back to France a wealthy man, as my uncle advised. I
have just heard of his death, together with that of my
aunt, from M. des Grassins. Our parents must die in the
course of nature, and we ourselves must follow them. I
hope that by this time you are consoled for your loss;
time cures all trouble, as I know by experience. Yes, my
dear cousin, the day of illusions is gone by for me. I am
sorry, but it cannot be helped. I have knocked about the
world so much, and seen so much, that I have been led
to reflect on life. I was a child when I went away; I have
come back a man, and I have many things to think
about now which I did not even dream of then. You are
free, my cousin, and I too am free still; there is apparently nothing to hinder the realization of our youthful
hopes, but I am too straightforward to hide my present
situation from you. I have not for a moment forgotten
that I am bound to you; through all my wanderings I
have always remembered the little wooden bench –

Eugénie started up as if she were sitting on burning coals, and sat down on one of the broken stone steps in the yard.

– the little wooden bench where we vowed to love each other for ever; the passage, the grey parlour, my attic room, the night when in your thoughtfulness and tact you made my future easier to me. Yes, these memories have been my support; I have said in my heart that you were always thinking of me when I thought of you at the hour we had agreed upon. Did you not look out into the darkness at nine o'clock? Yes, I am sure you did. I would not prove false to so sacred a friendship; I cannot deal insincerely with you.

A marriage has been proposed to me, which is in every way satisfactory to my mind. Love in a marriage is romantic nonsense. Experience has clearly shown me that in marrying we must obey social laws and conform to conventional ideas. There is some difference of age between you and me, which would perhaps be more likely to affect your future than mine, and there are other differences of which I need not speak; your bringing up, your ways of life, and your tastes have not fitted you for Parisian life, nor would they harmonize with the future which I have marked out for myself. For instance, it is a part of my plan to maintain a great household, and to see a good deal of society; and you, I am sure, from my recollections of you, would prefer a quiet, domestic life and home-keeping ways. No, I will be open with you; I will abide by your decision; but I must first, however, lay all the facts of the case before you, that you may the better judge.

I possess at the time of writing an income of eighty thousand livres. With this fortune I am able to marry into the d'Aubrion family; I should take their name on my marriage with their only daughter, a girl of nineteen, and secure at the same time a very brilliant position in society, and the post of gentleman of the bedchamber. I will assure you at once, my dear cousin, that I have not the slightest affection for Mlle d'Aubrion, but by this marriage I shall secure for my children a social rank which will be of inestimable value in the future. Monarchical principles are daily gaining ground. A few years hence my son, the Marquis d'Aubrion, would have an entailed estate and a yearly rental of forty thousand livres; with such advantages there would be no position to which he might not aspire. We ought to live for our children.

You see, my cousin, how candidly I am laying the state of my heart, my hopes, and my fortunes before you. Perhaps after seven years of separation you may yourself have forgotten our childish love affair, but I have never forgotten your goodness or my promise. A less conscientious, a less upright man, with a heart less youthful than mine, might scarcely feel himself bound by it; but for me a promise, however lightly given, is sacred. When I tell you plainly that my marriage is solely a marriage of suitability, and that I have not forgotten the love of our youthful days, am I not putting myself entirely into your hands, and making you the arbitress of my fate? Is it not implied that if I must renounce my social ambitions, I shall willingly content myself with the simple and pure happiness which is always called up by the thought of you. . .

'Tra-la-la-tan-ta-ti!' sang Charles Grandet to the air of *Non più andrai*, as he signed himself,

Your devoted cousin,

CHARLES.

'By Jove! that is acting handsomely,' he said to himself. He looked about him for the cheque, slipped it in, and added a postscript.

PS. – I enclose a cheque on MM. des Grassins for eight thousand francs, payable in gold to your order, comprising the capital and interest of the sum you were so kind as to advance me. I am expecting a case from Bordeaux which contains a few things which you must allow me to send you as a token of my unceasing gratitude. You can send my dressing-case by the diligence to the Hôtel d'Aubrion, rue Hillerin-Bertin.

'By the diligence!' cried Eugénie, 'when I would have given my life for it a thousand times!'

Terrible and complete shipwreck of hope; the vessel had gone down, there was not a spar, not a plank in the vast ocean. There are women who when their lover forsakes them will drag him from a rival's arms and murder her, and fly for refuge to the ends of the earth, to the scaffold, or the grave. There is a certain grandeur in this, no doubt; there is something so sublime in the passion of indignation which prompts the crime, that man's justice is awed into silence; but there are other women who suffer and bow their heads. They go on their way, submissive and broken-hearted, weeping and forgiving, praying till their last sigh for him whom they never forget. And this no less is love, love such as the angels know, love that bears itself proudly in anguish, that lives by the secret pain of which it dies at last. This was to be Eugénie's love now that she had read that horrible letter.

She raised her eyes to the sky and thought of her mother's prophetic words, uttered in the moment of clear vision that is sometimes given to dying eyes; and as she thought of her mother's life and death, it seemed to her that she was looking out over her own future. There was nothing left to her now but to live prayerfully till the day of her deliverance should come and the soul spread its wings for heaven.

'My mother was right,' she said, weeping. 'Suffer – and die.'

She went slowly from the garden into the house, avoiding the passage; but when she came into the old grey parlour, it was full of memories of her cousin. On the chimney-piece there stood a certain china saucer, which she used every morning, and the old Sèvres sugar basin.

It was to be a memorable and eventful day for Eugénie. Nanon announced the curé of the parish church. He was related to the Cruchots, and therefore in the interests of the Président de Bonfons. For some days past the abbé had urged the curé to speak seriously to Mlle Grandet about the duty of marriage from a religious point of view for a woman in her position. Eugénie, seeing her pastor, fancied that he had come for the thousand francs which she gave him every month for the poor of his parish, and sent Nanon for the money; but the curate began with a smile, 'Today, mademoiselle, I have come to take counsel with you about a poor girl in whom all Saumur takes an interest, and who, through lack of charity to herself, is not living as a Christian should.'

'Mon Dieu! Monsieur le Curé, just now I can think of nobody but myself. I am very miserable, my only refuge is in the Church; her heart is large enough to hold all human sorrows, her love so inexhaustible that we need never fear to drain it dry.'

'Well, mademoiselle, when we speak of this girl, we shall speak of you. Listen! If you would fain work out your salvation, there are but two ways open to you; you must either leave the world, or live in the world and submit to its laws – you must choose between the earthly and the heavenly vocation.'

'Ah! your voice speaks to me when I need to hear a voice. Yes, God has sent you to me. I will bid the world farewell, and live for God alone, in silence and seclusion.'

'But, my daughter, you should think long and prayerfully before taking so strong a measure. Marriage is life, the veil and the convent is death.'

'Yes, death. Ah! if death would only come quickly, Monsieur le Curé,' she said, with dreadful eagerness.

'Death? But you have great obligations to fulfil towards society, mademoiselle. There is your family of poor, to whom you give clothes and firing in winter and work in summer. Your great fortune is a loan, of which you must give account one day. You have always looked on it as a sacred trust. It would be selfish to bury yourself in a convent, and you ought not to live alone in the world. In the first place, how can you endure the burden of your vast fortune alone? You might lose it. You will be involved in endless litigation; you will find yourself in difficulties from which you will not be able to extricate yourself. Take your pastor's word, a husband is useful; you ought not to lose what God has given into your charge. I speak to you as to a cherished lamb of my flock. You love God too sincerely to find hindrances to your salvation in the world; you are one of its fairest ornaments, and should remain in it as an example of holiness.'

At this point Mme des Grassins was announced. The banker's wife was smarting under a grievous disappointment, and thirsted for revenge.

'Mademoiselle –' she began. 'Oh! Monsieur le Curé is here. . . I will say no more then. I came to speak about some matters of business, but I see you are deep in something else.'

'Madame,' said the curé, 'I leave the field to you.'

'Oh, Monsieur le Curé, pray come back again; I stand in great need of your help just now.'

'Yes, indeed, my poor child!' said Mme des Grassins.

'What do you mean?' asked Eugénie and the curé both together.

'Do you suppose that I haven't heard that your cousin has come back, and is going to marry Mademoiselle d'Aubrion? A woman doesn't go about with her wits in her pocket.'

Eugénie was silent, there was a red flush on her face, but she made up her mind at once that henceforward no one should learn anything from her, and looked as impenetrable as her father used to do.

'Well, madame,' she said, with a tinge of bitterness in her tones, 'it seems that I, at any rate, carry my wits in my pocket, for I am quite at a loss to understand you. Speak out and explain yourself; you can speak freely before Monsieur le Curé, he is my director, as you know.'

'Well, then, mademoiselle, see for yourself what des Grassins says. Here is the letter.'

Eugénie read:

My dear Wife,

Charles Grandet has returned from the Indies, and has been in Paris this last month –

'A month!' said Eugénie to herself, and her hand fell to her side. After a moment she went on reading:

I had to dance attendance on him, and called twice before the future Comte d'Aubrion would condescend to see me. All Paris is talking about his marriage, and the banns are published –

'And he wrote to me after that?' Eugénie said to herself. She did not round off the sentence as a Parisienne would have done, with 'Wretch that he is!' but her scorn was not one whit the less because it was unexpressed.

– but it will be a good while yet before he marries; it is not likely that the Marquis d'Aubrion will give his daughter to the son of a bankrupt wine merchant. I called and told him of all the trouble we had been at, his uncle and I, in the matter of his father's failure, and of our clever dodges that had kept the creditors quiet so far. The insolent puppy had the effrontery to say to me – to *me*, who for five years have toiled day and night in his interest and to save his credit – that *his father's affairs were not his*! A solicitor would have wanted thirty or forty thousand francs of him in fees at the rate of one per cent on the total of the debt! But, patience! There is something that he does owe, however, and that the law shall make him pay, that is to say, twelve hundred thousand francs to his father's creditors, and I shall declare his father bankrupt. I mixed myself up in this affair on the word of that old crocodile of a Grandet, and I have given promises in the name of the family. M. le Comte d'Aubrion may not care for his honour, but I care a good deal for mine! So I shall just explain my position to the creditors. Still, I have too much respect for Mlle Eugénie (with whom, in happier days, we hoped to be more closely connected) to take any steps before you have spoken to her –

There Eugénie paused, and quietly returned the letter.

'I am obliged to you,' she said to Mme des Grassins. '*We shall see. . .*'

'Your voice was exactly like your father's just then,' exclaimed Mme des Grassins.

'Madame,' put in Nanon, producing Charles's cheque, 'you have eight thousand francs to pay us.'

'True. Be so good as to come with me, Madame Cornoiller.'

'Monsieur le Curé,' said Eugénie, with a noble composure that came of the thought which prompted her, 'would it be a sin to remain in a state of virginity after marriage?'

'It is a case of conscience which I cannot solve. If you care to know what the celebrated Sanchez says in his great work, *De Matrimonio*, I could inform you tomorrow.'

The curé took leave. Mlle Grandet went up to her father's room and spent the day there by herself; she would not even come down to dinner, though Nanon begged and scolded. She appeared in the evening at the hour when the usual company began to arrive. The grey parlour in the Grandets' house had never been so well filled as it was that night. Every soul in the town knew by that time of Charles's return, and of his faithlessness and ingratitude; but their inquisitive curiosity was not to be gratified. Eugénie was a little late, but no one saw any traces of the cruel agitation through which she had passed; she could smile benignly in reply to the compassionate looks and words which some of the group thought fit to bestow on her; she bore her pain behind a mask of politeness.

About nine o'clock the card-players drew away from the tables, paid their losses, and criticized the game and the various points that had been made. Just as there was a general move in the direction of the door, an unexpected development took place; the news of it rang through Saumur and four prefectures round about for days after.

'Please stay, Monsieur le Président.'

There was not a person in the room who did not thrill with excitement at the words; M. de Bonfons, who was about to take his cane, turned quite white, and sat down again.

'The president takes the millions,' said Mlle de Gribeaucourt.

'It is quite clear that Président de Bonfons is going to marry Mademoiselle Grandet,' cried Mme d'Orsonval.

'The best trick of the game!' commented the abbé.

'A very pretty *slam*,' said the notary.

Everyone said his say and cut his joke, everyone thought of the heiress mounted upon her millions as if she were on a pedestal. Here was the catastrophe of the drama, begun nine years ago, taking place under their eyes. To tell the president in the face of all Saumur to 'stay' was as good as announcing at once that she meant to take the magistrate for her husband. Social conventionalities are rigidly observed in little country towns, and such an infraction as this was looked upon as a binding promise.

'Monsieur le Président,' Eugénie began in an unsteady voice, as soon as they were alone, 'I know what you care about in me. Swear to leave me free till the end of my life, to claim none of the rights which marriage will give you over me, and my hand is yours. Oh!' she said, seeing him about to fall on his knees, 'I have not finished yet. I must tell you frankly that there are memories in my heart which can never be effaced; that friendship is all that I can give my husband; I wish neither to affront him nor to be disloyal to my own heart. But you shall only have my hand and fortune at the price of an immense service which I want you to do me.'

'Anything, I will do anything,' said the president.

'Here are fifteen hundred thousand francs, Monsieur le Président,' she said, drawing from her bodice a certificate for a hundred shares in the Bank of France; 'will you set out for Paris? You must not even wait till the morning, but go at once, tonight. You must go straight to Monsieur des Grassins, ask him for a list of my uncle's creditors, call them together, and discharge all outstanding claims upon Guillaume Grandet's estate. Let the creditors have capital and interest at five per cent from the day the debts were contracted to the present time; and see that in every case a receipt in full is given, and that it is made out in proper form. You are a magistrate, you are the only person whom I feel that I can trust in such a case. You are a gentleman and a man of honour: you have given me your word, and, protected by your name, I will make the perilous voyage of life. We shall know how to make allowances for each other, for we have been acquainted for so long that it is almost as if we were related, and I am sure you would not wish to make me unhappy.'

The president fell on his knees at the feet of the rich heiress in a paroxysm of joy.

'I will be your slave!' he said.

'When all the receipts are in your possession, sir,' she went on, looking quietly at him, 'you must take them, together with the bills, to my cousin Grandet, and give them to him with this letter. When you come back, I will keep my word.'

The president understood the state of affairs perfectly well. 'She is accepting me out of pique,' he thought, and he hastened to do Mlle Grandet's bidding with all possible speed, for fear some chance might bring about a reconciliation between the lovers.

As soon as M. de Bonfons left her, Eugénie sank into her chair and burst into tears. All was over, and *this* was the end.

The president travelled post to Paris and reached his journey's end on the following evening. The next morning he went to des Grassins, and arranged for a meeting of the creditors in the office of the notary with whom the bills had been deposited. Every man of them appeared, every man of them was punctual to a moment – one should give even creditors their dues.

M. de Bonfons, in Mlle Grandet's name, paid down the money in full, both capital and interest. They were paid interest! It was an amazing portent, a nine days' wonder in the business world of Paris. After the whole affair had been wound up, and when, by Eugénie's desire, des Grassins had received fifty thousand francs for his services, the president betook himself to the Hôtel d'Aubrion, and was lucky enough to find Charles at home, and in disgrace with his future father-in-law. The old marquis had just informed that gentleman that until Guillaume Grandet's creditors were satisfied, a marriage with his daughter was not to be thought of.

To Charles, thus despondent, the president delivered the following letter:

DEAR COUSIN,

M. le Président de Bonfons has undertaken to hand you a discharge of all claims against my uncle's estate, and to deliver it in person, together with this letter, so that I may know that it is safely in your hands. I heard rumours of bankruptcy, and it occurred to me that difficulties might possibly arise as a consequence in the matter of your marriage with Mlle d'Aubrion. Yes, cousin, you are quite right about my tastes and manners; I have lived, as you say, so entirely out of the world, that I know nothing of its ways or its calculations, and my companionship could never make up to you for the loss of the pleasures that you look to find in society. I hope that you will be happy according to the social conventions to which you have sacrificed our early love. The only thing in my power to give you to complete your happiness is your father's good name. Farewell; you will always find a faithful friend in your cousin,

EUGÉNIE.

In spite of himself an exclamation broke from the man of social ambitions when his eyes fell on the discharge and receipts. The president smiled.

'We can each announce our marriage,' said he.

'Oh! you are to marry Eugénie, are you? Well, I am glad to hear it; she is a kind-hearted girl. Why!' struck with a sudden luminous idea, 'she must be rich?'

'Four days ago she had about nineteen millions,' the president said, with a malicious twinkle in his eyes, 'today she has only seventeen.'

Charles was dumbfounded; he stared at the president.

'Seventeen mil –'

'Seventeen millions. Yes, sir; when we are married, Mademoiselle Grandet and I shall muster seven hundred and fifty thousand livres a year between us.'

'My dear cousin,' said Charles, with some return of assurance, 'we shall be able to push each other's fortunes.'

'Certainly,' said the president. 'There is something else here,' he added, 'a little case that I was to give only into your hands,' and he set down a box containing the dressing-case upon the table.

The door opened, and in came Mme la Marquise d'Aubrion; the great lady seemed to be unaware of Cruchot's existence. 'Look here, dear,' she said, 'never mind what that absurd Monsieur d'Aubrion has been saying to you; the Duchesse de Chaulieu has quite turned his head. I repeat it, there is nothing to prevent your marriage –'

'Nothing, madame,' answered Charles. 'The three millions which my father owed were paid yesterday.'

'In money?' she asked.

'In full, capital and interest; I mean to rehabilitate his memory.'

'What nonsense!' cried his mother-in-law. 'Who is this person?' she asked in Charles's ear, as she saw Cruchot for the first time.

'My man of business,' he answered in a low voice. The marquise gave M. de Bonfons a disdainful bow, and left the room.

'We are beginning to push each other's fortunes already,' said the president dryly, as he took up his hat. 'Good day, cousin.'

'The old cockatoo from Saumur is laughing at me; I have a great mind to make him swallow six inches of cold steel,' thought Charles.

But the president had departed.

Three days later M. de Bonfons was back in Saumur again, and announced his marriage with Eugénie. After about six months he received his appointment as Councillor to the Court-Royal at Angers, and they went thither. But before Eugénie left Saumur she melted down the trinkets that had long been so sacred and so dear a trust, and gave them, together with the eight thousand francs which her cousin had returned to her, to make a reredos for the altar in the parish church whither she had gone so often to pray to God for him. Henceforward her life was spent partly at Angers, partly at Saumur. Her husband's devotion to the Government at a political crisis was rewarded; he was made President of the Chamber, and finally First President. Then he awaited a general election with impatience; he had visions of a place in the Government; he had dreams of a peerage; and then, and then . . .

'Then he would call cousins with the king, I suppose?' said Nanon, big Nanon, Mme Cornoiller, wife of a burgess of Saumur, when her mistress told her of these lofty ambitions and high destinies.

Yet, after all, none of these ambitious dreams were to be realized, and the name of M. de Bonfons (he had finally dropped the patronymic Cruchot) was to undergo no further transformation. He died only eight days after his appointment as deputy of Saumur. God, who sees all hearts, and who never strikes without cause, punished him, doubtless, for his presumptuous schemes, and for the lawyer's cunning with which, *accurante Cruchot*, he had drafted his own marriage contract; in which husband and wife, *in case there was no issue of the marriage, bequeathed to each other all their property, both real estate and personalty, without exception or reservation, dispensing even with the formality of an inventory, provided that the omission of the said inventory should not injure their heirs and assigns, it being understood that this deed of gift, etc.*, a clause which may throw some light on the profound respect which the president constantly showed for his wife's desire to live apart. Women cited M. le Premier Président as one of the most delicately considerate of men, and pitied him, and often went so far as to blame Eugénie for clinging to her passion and her sorrow; mingling, according to their wont, cruel insinuations with their criticisms of the president's wife.

'If Madame de Bonfons lives apart from her husband, she must be in very bad health, poor thing. Is she likely to recover? What can be the matter with her? Is it cancer or gastritis, or what is it? Why does she not go to Paris and see some specialist? She has looked very sallow for a long time past. How can she not wish to have a child? They say she is very fond of her husband; why not give him an heir in his position? Do you know, it is really dreadful! If it is only some notion which she has taken into her head, it is unpardonable. Poor president!'

There is a certain keen insight and quick apprehensiveness that is the gift of a lonely and meditative life – and loneliness, and sorrow, and the discipline of the last few years had given Eugénie this clairvoyance of the narrow lot. She knew within herself that the president was anxious for her death that he might be the sole possessor of the colossal fortune, now still further increased by the deaths of the abbé and the notary, whom providence had lately seen fit to promote from works to rewards. The poor solitary woman understood and pitied the president. Unworthy hopes and selfish calculations were his strongest motives for respecting Eugénie's hopeless passion. To give life to a child would be death to the egotistical dreams and ambitions that the president hugged within himself; was it for all these things that his career was cut short, while she must remain in her prison house, and the coveted gold for which she cared so little was to be heaped upon her? It was she who was to live, with the thought of heaven always before her, and holy thoughts for her companions, to give help and comfort secretly to those who were in distress. Mme de Bonfons was left a widow three years after her marriage, with an income of eight hundred thousand livres.

She is beautiful still, with the beauty of a woman who is nearly forty years of age. Her face is very pale and quiet now, and there is a tinge of sadness in the low tones of her voice. She has simple manners, all the dignity of one who has passed through great sorrows, and the saintliness of a soul unspotted by the world; and, no less, the rigidness of an old maid, the little penurious ways and narrow ideas of a dull country town.

Although she has eight hundred thousand livres a year, she lives just as she used to do in the days of stinted allowances of fuel and food while she was still Eugénie Grandet; the fire is never lighted in the parlour before or after the dates fixed by her father, all the regulations in force in the days of her girlhood are still adhered to. She dresses as her mother did. That cold, sunless, dreary house, always overshadowed by the dark ramparts, is like her own life.

She looks carefully after her affairs; her wealth accumulates from year to year; perhaps she might even be called parsimonious, if it were not for the noble use she makes of her fortune. Various pious and charitable institutions, almshouses, and orphan asylums, a richly endowed public library, and donations to various churches in Saumur, are a sufficient answer to the charge of avarice which some few people have brought against her.

They sometimes speak of her in joke as *mademoiselle*, but, in fact, people stand somewhat in awe of Mme de Bonfons. It was as if she, whose heart went out so readily to others, was always to be the victim of their interested calculations, and to be cut off from them by a barrier of distrust; as if for all warmth and brightness in her life she was to find only the pale glitter of metal.

'No one loves me but you,' she would sometimes say to Nanon.

Yet her hands are always ready to bind the wounds that other eyes do not see, in any house; and her way to heaven is one long succession of kindness and good deeds. The real greatness of her soul has risen above the cramping influences of her early life. And this is the life history of a woman who dwells in the world, yet is not of it, a woman so grandly fitted to be a wife and mother, but who has neither husband nor children nor kindred.

Of late the good folk of Saumur have begun to talk of a second marriage for her. Rumour is busy with her name and that of the Marquis de Froidfond; indeed, his family have begun to surround the rich widow, just as the Cruchots once flocked about Eugénie Grandet. Nanon and Cornoiller, so it is said, are in the interest of the marquis, but nothing could be more false; for big Nanon and Cornoiller have neither of them wit enough to understand the corruptions of the world.